Journey into the Shimmering

Where Truth and Mercy Meet

THOMAS JUDE FREITAG

Copyright © 2025 Thomas Jude Freitag
Published by Skinny Brown Dog Media
Atlanta, GA /Punta del Este, Uruguay

All rights reserved. No part of this book may be reproduced in any form or by any electronic or mechanical means, including information storage and retrieval systems, without permission in writing from the publisher, except by a reviewer who may quote brief passages in a review.

All Scripture quotations, unless otherwise indicated, are taken from the Holy Bible, New International Version®, NIV®. Copyright © 2011 by Biblica, Inc.™ Used by permission of Zondervan. All rights reserved worldwide. www.zondervan.com. The "NIV" and "New International Version" are trademarks registered in the United States Patent and Trademark Office by Biblica, Inc.™

Scripture quotations taken from the Holy Bible marked NASB®, New American Standard Bible®. Copyright © 1995 by The Lockman Foundation. Used by permission. All rights reserved. lockman.org.

Photo: Huimin Kim

Cover illustration: Gro Rykkelid. www.heart-language.com. Certain sections of this book were inspired by the heart pictures created by Gro Rykkelid. Her work has been integral to the development of this narrative.

Distributed by Skinny Brown Dog Media
SkinnyBrownDogMedia.com
Email: Info@SkinnyBrownDogMedia.com

Journey into the Shimmering
Where Truth And Mercy Meet
Thomas Jude Freitag

Library of Congress Cataloging-in-Publication Data
ISBN (eBook): 978-1-965235-52-2
ISBN (digital cloth™ cover): 978-1-965235-50-8
ISBN (case laminate): 978-1-965235-51-5
ISBN (perfect bound) 978-1-965235-49-2

CONTENTS

Dedication vii
Author's Note ix

Part One: A Holy Mess 1
    1. The Storm.. 3
    2. The Worms 12
    3. The Cleanup Operation.. 24

Part Two: And So It Begins 33
    4. Entering the Shimmering 35
    5. The Trysting Place 39
    6. Galaxies and Guideposts.. 49
    7. Heart Truths 62

Part Three: Going Deep 67
    8. The Playground of Shame 69
    9. The Church Bazaar of Rejection 80
    10. The Bridge of Trust 89
    11. The Dunes of Control.. 94
    12. The Tempests of Injustice 106

Part Four: Going Deeper Still 117
13. International Night 119
14. The Forest of Temptation 128
15. 'The Temple Of My Heart' 131
16. Sharers of the Road Less Traveled 136
17. The Altar of Darkness 143

Part Five: Pilgrims' Progress 165
18. Simon 167
19. Émile 191
20. Anastazja 205
21. Renata 218
22. Kenneth 230

Part Six: Via Dolorosa 237
23. Ascent To The Descent 239
24. Crossroad 244
25. The Baseball Fields of Abandonment 250
26. Streams of Healing Love 260

Part Seven: Coming Home 275
27. The Place of Praise 277
28. Joy in the Journey 285
29. The Heartbeat of God 292
30. Abiding in the Shimmering 296

Acknowledgements 311

Graciousness and truth have met together;
Righteousness and peace have kissed each other.
Truth sprouts from the earth,
And righteousness looks down from heaven.
Indeed, the Lord will give what is good,
And our land will yield its produce.
Righteousness will go before Him
And will make His footsteps into a way.

Psalm 85:10–13 NASB

DEDICATION

To my wife, Lene
And our children Benjamin, Katrine, and Elisabeth

AUTHOR'S NOTE

This is a work of fiction. Sort of.

Some of my life experiences are woven into the narrative; not all of the stories in the narrative are my own. Those who know me well know the stories that are mine, and those that are not. Most characters are fictitious. Since some of the stories are my own, some of the characters have elements of people that I know or have known. Only a handful of people are mentioned specifically by name. They will know themselves when they read it.

I touch on themes often considered taboo, both within church circles and without. You will be provoked. You will think, "I'm not as bad as so-and-so in the story, so I must be doing alright!" I warn you: we are all the same at the foot of the cross of Jesus.

About Jesus: In the book I present him as a very real Jesus—whether in the flesh or in a vision or dream—as if he lives today. He does live today, in fact. Jesus lives both in time and out of time. He appeared to the two men walking the road to Emmaus. He appeared to Peter by the sea. He appeared, startlingly, to a group of his followers gathered in an upper room who were convinced that he was lying cold in a tomb. All of these events were before his ascension into heaven, of course, though he clearly revealed himself to Saul on the road to Damascus and to the apostle John on the island of Patmos. Could Jesus appear to someone today if he wanted to? Does he? Being God, he can probably do whatever he wants to do. Can Jesus reveal himself in a dream, or a vision? We hear stories of Jesus revealing himself in such a way to people all over the world.

While I have been careful to base the narrative and principles presented in the book on Scripture, much of what Jesus is given to say will not be found in red-letter editions of the Bible. As John wrote, "Jesus did many other things as well. If every one of them were written down, I suppose that even the whole world would not have room for the books that would be written," (John 21:25). The gospel writers recorded events that were essential in presenting Jesus' life and teaching, and didn't bother filling up their accounts with such statements as "Andrew, can you pass me the salt, please?"

My hope is that you will allow yourself to enter into the story, live the story, make the story your own. Allow Jesus to lead you, by his Spirit, deeper into your own heart, so that you may draw deeper into his heart of love for you.

As you read this book, you may be confronted with things in your life that you can't do anything with on your own. You cannot fix yourself, at least not without the power, grace and love of Jesus. Jesus often recruits the help of others in this process—one of the prime purposes of his church—so find someone to talk and pray with, a friend you can trust, someone from church. If you don't have a church or a gathering of believers, ask Jesus to guide you to one. Jesus knows your need but often meets those needs through his people.

As you read this book, my prayer for you is this:

> "For this reason I kneel before the Father, from whom his whole family in heaven and on earth derives its name. I pray that out of his glorious riches he may strengthen you with power through his Spirit in your inner being, so that Christ may dwell in your hearts through faith. And I pray that you, being rooted and established in love, may have power, together with all

AUTHOR'S NOTE

the saints, to grasp how wide and long and high and deep is the love of Christ, and to know this love that surpasses knowledge—that you may be filled to the measure of all the fulness of God. Now to him who is able to do immeasurably more than all we ask or imagine, according to his power that is at work within you, to him be glory in the church and in Christ Jesus throughout all generations, for ever and ever! Amen."

Ephesians 3:14-21

One more thing: the narrative is written in first person present tense, a literary style termed 'stream of consciousness'. You will be viewing events as they happen, through the eyes and brain and heart of Kenny, the main character. The pace will seem intense at first, but you will soon adapt as you ease yourself into the story and make it your own.

Thomas Jude Freitag
Kristiansand, Norway
April 2025

PART ONE

A Holy Mess

1

THE STORM

GOOD GOD IN HEAVEN HELP ME!

Oh, the pressure on my chest! I can't breathe! I can't move my limbs!

"Jane! It's my heart! Help me!"

What's going on? My body is convulsing! Do they have me on a defibrillator? Oh God, I think I'm about to die!

"I can't… breathe… help me, Jane!"

"Kenny!" Jane's voice calls to me, from far off in the distance.

"Jane! I'm not ready! Please take my hand!" I shout as I descend through a tunnel of blinding light. "I'm too young for this! I'm in the prime of life, for crying out loud!"

"Daddy!"

The sound of a child's voice is pulling me back from the brink of eternity.

Jane's voice, muffled: "Kenny, do you hear me? Get up! The kids need you!"

I KNOW my kids need me! Oh God, I can't die now!"

"Daddy! Daddy," the desperate voice of my child reverberates on the strings of my heart.

"Oh God, I'll do anything you want, but please, *spare my life*!"

Jane's voice rings more clearly now, "Kenny, do you always have to be so dramatic? Just get yourself out of bed!"

"What the—?"

"Come, Daddy! I'm hungry!"

"Kyle, what are you doing, jumping on me like that? Gawd, I thought I was having a heart attack! And get that flashlight out of my face!"

"It's Monday," Jane continues, matter-of-factly. She's not speaking from within a tunnel, but from under her covers. "You take care of the kids *every* Monday. I have a double shift at the hospital *every* Monday."

"I know, I know. Just give me a chance to wake up, wouldja? Sheesh. Look at me, sweating like a pig. I thought I was laying on a gurney on my way to the ER!" My heart's still pounding, sweat soaking the sheets beneath me.

Jane again. "With the junk you eat, I wouldn't be surprised if you do have a coronary."

"Do you always have to be so dieticiany with me?"

"That is not a word," she says, like a dietician.

"Well, it is now!"

"Daddy, I'll go make my own breakfast."

"Wait! Kyle! Let Daddy help you. And where are you going with my duvet?"

Just a few more seconds of sleep is all I ask for, just a few precious moments to clear my head. I guess that's what I get, trying to finish that level of *The Quest of Articand* until three a.m. But I'm duvet-less and curled up in a ball to reserve body heat.

Look at her… Jane. Her hair, so thick and straight and dark, never fails to amaze me. Her body is so slender and long. Lithe. That's a good word. *She breathes wistfully, her lithe body rises and falls beneath the blue satin sheets.* Not that our sheets are blue. Or satin. Just feel the roughness of this cotton.

THE STORM

A wadded-up tissue falls from her hand onto her pillow, a remnant from last night's battle. It'll take me days to get over what happened between us last night.

But I need her. I'm feeling a bit insecure about the meeting this morning. That father-in-law-slash-boss of mine has been putting pressure on me to make this new business deal. Besides, I'm getting chilled without my duvet. All I need is a little cuddle. If I scooch over to her side, touch her shoulder ever so lightly, cross the Maginot Line...

Her body stiffens; she turns farther away from me. And all I needed was for her to make me feel a bit less unsure of myself. Ah, well. It's time to get up, anyway.

Morning after morning, my feet hit this very same spot on the floor. I love this original 1950s oak wood. How many men before me have started their day by landing their bare feet on this floor? I bet they only had 'Leave It to Beaver' kinds of problems. 'Dear, Beaver was late delivering newspapers this morning.' 'I'll talk to him about it, June, when I'm done smoking my pipe.' Look at that. I did it again, I only managed to clip the nails on one foot but not on the other. Some family emergency always seems to disrupt me one way or another. I bet Ward Cleaver never went to work without all of his toenails clipped.

What time is it? Stupid phone is dead, again. This thing's so old they barely have updates for it anymore, but there's never enough money to buy me a new one. I get up the same time every morning with or without an alarm, but it would've been nice to check the stats, find out how the Cardinals did. I had to miss the opening game of the season last night, because of our brawl.

C'mon Kenny, stop with the procrastinating and get up.

Those clouds, churning in the west. Will they bring rain? An ice storm? Hail? Tornado? All of the above? St. Louis in April, anything can happen.

Look at her medals, hanging over her mirror. She's got more medals than jewelry, much to her mother's chagrin. Her newest medal, gleaming silver, from the St. Louis half-marathon last weekend. It still bothers her that she came in second. Maybe we can use her prize money to buy me a new phone.

I better hit the shower.

There it is, sitting on my nightstand, Dad's old baseball, basted with oil from his hands. Hup! Dang. I dropped it. I better dive for it. *And he made the play! The crowds go wild!* Not as easy getting up off the floor as it used to be.

"Remember to give Julia her meds." Now *that* woke me up.

"As if I'd forget."

"You forgot yesterday."

Sheesh.

What was that?! A metal bowl, falling to the floor, in the kitchen. Kyle. I better get down there before he turns the kitchen upside-down.

"You need to get down there and help Elmer."

"His name is *Kyle*." Ouch. That was a well-shot bullet on her part. *Elmer*, like the school glue. "Things aren't *so* bad between us, are they? And do you always have to tell me what to do at the exact moment I'm about to do it? It's totally demotivating!"

No answer.

"Hello? Aren't you going to say something?"

No answer.

I'll take a quick look in the mirror, check the status of the Battle of the Bulge. Could be worse. She's a complete thorn in the flesh, always harping on what I shove in my mouth. I guess it's better than her becoming a thorn in my ever-expanding flesh. But I got things under control. Now, *there's* a good angle, when I turn my torso, suck in my gut just so. Wow, what a bicep! I'll give it a little kiss. Here's one for the adulating crowds.

The black-and-white print of my dad, in his baseball uniform, slender, handsome. Why do I torment myself with it, keeping it there, jammed in the mirror frame? He was sixteen there, for crying out loud! I wish I'd gotten his dark hair and not all of this red stuff. I need a haircut. Keeping it short helps with the frizz, at least. But there's always that bald spot. Ah, well, you can't choose your genes. Or your parents-in-law.

"Go deal with the twins," Jane commands from under her duvet.

There's a ruckus down the hall.

"Gosh, what's going on now?" Uh-oh, here they come.

"Kenneth! Tell her I *neeeeed* to wear her hoodie today!" It's Jessie. "Because there never seems to be enough money in this house to buy me one, too!"

Her constant dig on finances hits me at my core. And she never calls me 'Dad' anymore. I don't know what to do about this.

"But it's my hoodie!" weeps Julia, hugging her pillow. If it wasn't for them still liking to wear matching pajamas, you'd never know they're identical twins.

"Why must she always borrow my clothes? Why?" weeps Julia as if performing in a school play. Her braces protrude from her thin lips. She turns and weeps down the hallway.

"Jessica! Don't upset your sister like that," whispers Jane.

"But Mom! I let her borrow my headphones!"

There goes Jessie, stomping down the hallway to continue her badgering.

Uh-oh. Jane's hoisted herself up on her elbows. I better brace myself.

"You never stick up for Julia!" Her eyes are all puffy.

"And you never stop smothering her to death!"

A bad choice of words on my part.

I hate it when Jane cries, it makes me feel lousy. I wish we could erase last night and start over.

What do I do? Do I stay here with Jane, or help the girls negotiate? And Kyle's downstairs making his own breakfast!

Yesterday, at Sunday service, Pastor called 'family' a 'holy mess.' This family has a whole lot more mess than holy, is all I have to say.

"Give me some help down here, wouldja? I mean, please, Lord," I plead under my breath.

Rats. I missed the ball. There it goes, bouncing down the steps.

"I don't care because I'm wearing it, anyway!" It's Jessie again. I better get in there before they break out into a major cat fight. (Mental note: lightbulb needs replacing in the hallway).

Jess is frizzing her red hair with a metal pick, Jewels is meticulously weaving her red hair into a triple braid. How did I get such lovely daughters? Seeing them always takes my breath away. But their constant bickering wears on me. And what's the story with Jessie wearing all that makeup? I never know what to do with her. But I *do* know what to do with the hoodie: rip it out of Jessie's hands, fling it over to Jewels. There, that's done. The look on their faces! Ha! It's suddenly, blissfully quiet. I'm rather pleased with myself!

They're already quibbling over jeans.

NOW I've got to get downstairs to Kyle.

Jane's still crying. Will talking with her help or make things worse? She's sitting up in bed now. She's got my old Mizzou T-shirt tugged over her knees. The faded maroon compliments her complexion, the yellow trim does not.

"You know what your problem is? You never open up to me. You never share anything with me!" She almost yells this through her sobs.

There it is: The shot that assassinated Prince Ferdinand. Close the door, so the kids can't hear.

"Whaddya mean? I talk to you all the time!" I yell-whisper.

"But not about what's important. Not the stuff that's going on inside you. And when you finally do open up, you explode and say things you don't mean."

"Like you shagging my best friend, things like that?"

Her mouth opens. She looks shocked. She bursts into tears.

"But I'm not doing anything like that with Mitt!"

"Then why do you spend so much time with him, then?!"

"I'm spending time with Annie, too! I need someone to talk with!"

THE STORM

I'm tired of her lame excuses. I better get downstairs. Wait. One more volley.

"And why do you let your daughter dress up like a whore?"

"Julia? She doesn't—"

"You've got *two* daughters, may I remind you!" I'll slam the door for good measure.

Now I really need to get downstairs.

My head is heavy, I need a Diet Coke. Why's the TV on? And where did my baseball end up?

No Diet Coke. "And why didn't you go shopping like you said you would?" I shout at her up the steps. "And who turned on the TV before school? Heads are going to roll, is all I have to say!" The noise is driving me crazy! And I can't find my baseball!

What's that? Purple milk? All over the floor?!

"Kyle! Where *are you*?"

I see him, his legs at least, dangling happily beneath the breakfast table. How on earth did he climb up and get that box of Frosted Fruit Loops? I was keeping that for a special treat!

"Kyle! Look at me! Did you dump the entire box of cereal into that mixing bowl? And with so much milk? Don't you look so pleased with yourself, I told you to wait for Daddy to help you! You've had enough, I'm taking the bowl from you. I'm putting it here until I get back so don't you touch it! And stop with the screaming!"

The TV. It's still blaring.

"What's going on in here? Everyone knows the TV isn't supposed to be on before—*Kevin*? Why are you curled up on the sofa like that? And why are you still in your pajamas? What's going on, buddy? Aren't you feeling well? Where are your glasses—there they are, you dropped them on the floor." Is he sucking his thumb? He hasn't sucked his thumb in years. Is he going to—

"Kevin—wait! Let me run and get you a bucket! No no no no no no—not on the *carpet*!!

"Now, look what you made Kevin do!" scolds Julia from behind me. She is clinging to her respirator, looking a bit gray.

"Julia Caroline, don't you talk to your father like that! But you've got to regulate your breathing!"

"Mom!" cries Julia.

"Jewels, please, honey, come back here—don't bother your mother with this!" I'm already in enough hot water with your mother.

How did things get so out of whack this morning?

I've *got* to turn off the TV. But I can never find the stupid remote control!

Kevin moans. Great, just great. He's sick again and I still haven't fetched him a bucket. But what on earth is Kyle up to?

"Kyle—do you have that bowl again?! How did you get it down—oh, whatever. Just come here and give it back to me, you're spilling milk all over the floor! Okay, that's it. I'm throwing out the cereal." Cripes. He's driving me up a wall.

I open the front door, look this way and that, and throw the soggy cereal into the flower bed. I feel like I'm being watched. I shouldn't be too surprised, with me standing in my underwear. I'd better get inside.

What's that noise coming from the garage? Oh no. Is Keenan playing his drums before school?! The neighbors are going to have a conniption fit! I've got to get in there and stop him!

"Kyle, let go of my leg, I've got to get to the garage! Fine by me, your jammies are going to sop up all that milk you spilled on the floor—" What's Jane saying?

"Kenny! Can you please stop for a minute?"

"But somebody's got to get in there and stop Keenan!" I tell her, and dash through the kitchen to the door into the garage. Whoa—I almost slipped on the spilled milk!

"KEENAN!" Stop with the drums! NOW!"

Keenan stops with the drums.

"And why on earth did you stay out so late again last night?"

Keenan removes his headphones and looks at me. "I was late last night? You have no idea how late you are this morning." He replaces his earphones and resumes his banging.

I'm confused by his statement of lateness.

There's the doorbell. *The neighbors.*

Jane grabs me by the arm. "Kenny! My father called *my* phone because you're not answering *yours*, because your meeting started twenty minutes ago! And why on earth did you buy that awful cereal for Kyle? You know it spikes his blood sugar and...."

How can I be late? I can't be late for the meeting. I must've overslept. I never oversleep. Stupid cell phone!

I'm the stupid one, gaming until three in the morning.

I'm standing here in my boxers. And I haven't even shaved yet.

"WHY DIDN'T ANYONE TELL ME WE WERE RUNNING LATE THIS MORNING?!" I yell at everybody.

"I didn't want to make you upset," Julia bursts into sobs.

I see Keenan, leaning against the door into the garage, twirling his drumsticks. He's wearing that smirk of his.

"Jessica, stop!" shouts Jane.

"Jess? Ow! What the—what'd you slap me across the face for?!"

"That's for calling me a whore!" spits Jessica through streams of tears.

2

THE WORMS

I've *got* to get to work!

I don't need a neighbor lecturing me right now. "Who do you think you're talking to, you old fart! Get off my lawn!"

"Julia! What're you standing there for? You're supposed to be in the van already!"

"I was struggling with my respirator!"

"Just get in the van!" I speed my truck in reverse.

Dang. How did I end up in the neighbor's flowerbed? Here she comes, shouting at the top of her lungs. I don't have time for this!

"What? You want me to roll down my window? But it's starting to rain! And I gotta get to work!… Sorry about your flower bed, I'll get it fixed… Lady, I'm running late! And I said I was sorry!… *What* did you say?… Go ahead, call the cops for all I care!… Yeah, well, your dog poops all over my yard! Maybe I'll call the cops on *you*!"

It's pouring down like crazy now! I can barely see out of my windshield!

The traffic's terrible, as usual. I'm running late! Every second feels like an eternity! I've *got* to cut through traffic.

"Move it, people!"

There's an open space in that lane... I'll squeeze between those two cars, work my way into the fast lane... now, *gun it Kenny!*

"Stop with your horn, you stupid moron!"

Dang. I forgot about my 'Jesus Is My Copilot' bumper sticker. Either live it or remove it, for crying out loud.

I better apologize to the father-in-law.

"Yes, Dad. I mean Karl, sorry... Sorry for being late... I know, it won't happen again, I promise... Is the new client still here? Okay, great... No, I didn't bring an extra shirt—I'll see what I can do. I'll only be a second, Dad—I mean Karl."

Look at this mess. I can barely open my eye. Jessie must've had a ring on. Or brass knuckles. Man, it hurts. The extra sports coat in my office should cover most of these blood stains. Oh no—why does *she* have to show up now?

"Yeah, hi, Tiffany. Nice to see you, too... Now I *know* you're flattering me... Yeah, 'the rugged look' and all... You're not looking too bad yourself... No, I can't talk now, I gotta get into that meeting... Don't give me those Bambi eyes of yours... Come here, let me give you a hug... There, feel better now? Wait, let go, my phone's ringing—"

What is it now?

"Hello? Yes, this is Keenan's father... What did you say? Did something happen to him?... Did he say that?... He's pretty upset?... No, I can't come and pick him up, I'm in the middle of a meeting... Can't you call his mother?... What? He just stormed out the front doors?!... Well, do your job and go get him, then! What are we paying that private school of yours for!"

What my parents-in-law are paying for, that is.

"I did my best, alright, Karl?... Well, if it's not good enough for you, you know where to shove it... Yeah, you heard me... Go ahead and tell Jane, for all I care!... And you're un-invited to Kyle's birthday party, just to let you know. Just leave his gift at the door... Sayonara, jackass."

Ha! Grabbed this bottle of Scotch right off Karl's desk! He bought it to celebrate the new client. Which he won't be needing, since we lost the contract. Or I lost the contract.
    I shouldn't have called him a jackass. Stupid stupid *stupid* stupid stupid.

    Dark waters.
    Dark thoughts.
    Dark wants.
    I feel like dirt.
    There's Tiffany.

Whew. I escaped from the storage room just in the nick of time. My palms are sweating. I better leave the premises before she finds me again.
    Maybe I should just drive home—Jane hasn't left for work yet, and I could get Kyle to daycare. But what am I going to say to her? 'Hi, honey, I find myself unexpectedly free from the drudgeries of employment'?
    I can't sit here in the parking lot with the engine running all day. There's Karl, his dour self, looking down at me from his window. He always looks down on me. He probably wants his bottle of scotch back. Fat chance. I think he's coming! I better hit the road.

But where do I go? I could drive to Laumeier Park, maybe, and walk off some steam. But in all this rain? I used to spend a lot of time there, with Jesus. It was my secret hiding place with him. That was ages ago. He probably doesn't want anything to do with me now.

Hm. I think I'll drive into the city, cruise around my old stomping ground.

Look at this mess! Because nobody knows how to drive in a little rain in this town! Typical I-270 traffic. Six lanes of white lights, six lanes of red lights, everybody's going nowhere fast.

Just like me.

Dead-end career.

Dead-end life.

What *on earth* is going on in me today? Everybody knows how to push my buttons, that's what's going on in me today! And they're pushing them all the time! Of course I'm going to lose it.

Can't they stop with the doom and gloom on the radio already? It's enough to make a guy depressed. The skyrocketing prices are going to make it even harder to put food on the table—especially if Karl won't take me back. Oh God, what have I *done*?

What, *another* virus is about to hit?

Climate change this, climate change that, it's all they talk about anymore. Climate change might actually bring some stability to St. Louis weather! It can't get much worse than this.

A Christian station. 'Oh, how he loves me, Oh how he loves me so…' I seriously doubt that.

'St. Louis Country'. That's better. 'Your Cheatin' Heart.' How appropriate.

I hate it when I choke up like this. Things are starting to pile up, I guess.

Should I drive up Elm and just go home?

I'm not ready to go home.

I'll head over to Ted Drewes, get myself a frozen custard. Tiramisu-flavored this time.

Man, look at River Des Peres. It's so swollen from all this rain that it's almost up to the bottom of the bridge! Just like when I was in high school, during those dark days. How easy it would've been back then, to drive the car into those dark, churning waters, if it hadn't been for Jesus.

Where's Jesus now? He's probably given up on me. I wouldn't blame him if he has.

What a loser. Look at me, waiting in line for a frozen custard with all of these school kids. Who's that guy looking at me? Is that the bum Jessie's been hanging out with? "Heh you! Yeah, I'm talking to you, pal! Just stay away from my daughter, or I'll turn you into a eunuch. Yeah, you heard me!" That put some fear of Kenny into him! "Yeh, hi, I'd like a large tiramisu please… What? You can't serve me? Why not?… For what, disturbing the peace?!… C'mon—I haven't scared away any customers!… Oh. I guess you have a point there."

I forgot I look like Rocky Balboa, with my eye swollen the way it is. Not to mention the blood on my shirt.

St. Louis Hills. My old stomping ground. I love this neighborhood. Not quite the full experience without a tiramisu frozen custard.

If streets could talk, all the cruising we did around here, the old gang … Look at all these big, beautiful trees, bursting in the palate of spring, and tulips everywhere. All of these lovely brick homes, solid, stable. Jeez, there's still a bunch of Saint Pat's Day decorations up.

Heh, there's my old friend Mary's house! The house with the turret! Mary always believed in me.

I'll swing by and see the old homestead.

There it is. Strange, how it looks, the same house but with a different soul. Too bad we had to sell the place. Mom and Dad are both gone now. Wish they could've met my kids, and the kids them—Mom was able to hold Keenan as a baby, at least, before she passed.

What a mess, crying like this.

THE WORMS

There's the old high school, good ol' Bishop DuBourg. Me, voted MVP, Homecoming King, Most Likely To Succeed. If they could see me now, Mr. Loser. But this is where I first met Jesus. Though we're barely on speaking terms these days.

Maybe I'll drive to Wilmore Park, park next to the river, watch the waters swirl by. I'll stop at Schnucks first, get some Diet Coke, since she didn't, and a gallon or two of milk, after Kyle's escapade this morning. And a sixpack of Budweiser for the park, for old-time's sake.

Why did I have to make that remark to the checkout girl, about her green hair? It made her cry. I could have just bagged my groceries, paid her, thanked her and made my way back to my truck, quiet and adult-like, reputation intact. But no. At least I got my Diet Coke. And my Bud. My buddy.

Gosh. The river has risen even higher. Which means that the park could flood any time now. I'll be here just long enough to throw down a couple of beers.

Gawd, look at all those worms coming up out of the ground. Disgusting.

My outbursts, my tantrums, my sulking, my whining when I don't get my way, my lusts— they're a lot like these worms. They move in the dark, beneath my surface. I can't seem to control them. And when they're out, they're out, for everyone to see. Like how everybody stared at me at the check-out just now. I'm ashamed of myself. I tried to cover it up with a little joke, my dashing smile. Absolutely ridiculous. I'm an adult, for crying out loud! I should know better—especially since I've followed Jesus all these years!

The things that happened in this park! Good times. The parties. My first making-out. And my second. And my third….

It's getting dark now. And lonely.

I just don't know where all this stuff comes from. My worms.

I better head home. Not that anyone would miss me if I disappeared into these swirling waters.

But I try to be strong, do my best. I just wish someone could be strong for me, sometimes.

It's raining again, I better get back to the truck.

I just don't want to go home yet. I don't know what Jane's going to say to me. Or throw at me.

You spend half your life waiting at red lights in this town. I don't know why I didn't turn left out of the park, drive straight up Jamieson to Chippewa and left over the bridge toward home, but here I am, stuck at this eternal red light. Maybe I can cut through Walgreen's parking lot. It used to be Red Bird Lanes—now, that was the place to be!—which has been bulldozed to the ground. Just like me. Dang, there's a cop. Better behave myself and wait for the light to turn green, like the good boy everybody thinks I am.

"Stupid moron!" Why's she talking on her phone? The light's turned green, for crying out loud! I'll give her a good dose of my horn. That woke her up, the way she jumped! It feels good to blow off some steam now and then, when do I get the chance to do that?

Come on, do I have to wait for the light again?!

But everybody's got their secrets. I've got mine, that idiot's got hers. Things I've done that I'm not proud of. Maybe some things that've been done to me. Wouldn't they be surprised, at the Wednesday night Bible study group, if I went deep, spilled my guts all over the place. Just see how they'd react to that!

Man, look at the river now. And if River Des Peres is like this, the Mississippi is about to burst, too. I hope the levees hold.

There's Syberg's, the old watering hole. Like Cheers, where everybody knows your name. I'll swing by there, say hello to the old gang, wait out the storm until it passes. If it ever passes.

"It was good to see you too, man! Just like the old days! I guess I'll head home, face the music. Face the music?! She'll be like the MIZZOU marching band playing right in my face!…Yeah, you know how it is… Thanks, you too, man. Maybe I'll see you at the class reunion at DuBourg? … Yeah, they're all a bunch of geezers now, but no, not us! … Thanks! You're holding up pretty good yourself. And do you want me to tell you another lie before I go? Ha! … Yeah, say hello to the missus."—who was my first kiss at Wilmore Park sophomore year. And my second… and my third… I got quality in Jane, for sure. His wife ended up with *that* loser, poor girl.

At least the rain's beginning to let up a bit. But it's getting late—and where'd I park my truck? I probably should've refrained from that last pint. There she is! My faithful steed.

Should I head north along the river up to Watson Road, and then west toward home? That section of the road could already be flooded—yep, Gravois is bumper to bumper heading into the city. That leaves me no choice but to drive into Affton to Rock Hill and then north up Elm. But the road under the train viaduct is probably flooded, too. Yep, traffic's already backed up going west. That means taking MacKenzie up to Watson, or Gravois to Weber, straight over to Laclede Station, then make that dog-leg turn and connect to Rock Hill. I'm starting to feel trapped in all this traffic, and I *hate* feeling trapped. But if I take Weber, I can swing by Mitt's house, to see if Jane's parked the minivan in front of his house—no, Kenny, what are you thinking?! Get a grip, it's Mitt you're talking about here!

But why is she over there so often?

Golden Oldies. Take me back. 'Unchained Melody.' The Righteous Brothers! Mom and Dad used to slow dance to this in the living room…

> *Oh, my love*
> *My darling*
> *I've hungered for your touch*

A long, lonely time...

Oh, Janie! I miss you, babe. What's happened to us?

*And time goes by so slowly
And time can do so much
Are you still mine?*

Don't leave me! I need you, Janie!

*I need your love
I need your love
God speed your love to me.*

This part always chokes me up...

*Lonely rivers flow to the sea, to the sea
To the open arms of the sea...
Yes, lonely rivers sigh, 'Wait for me, wait for me
I'll be coming home, wait for me.'*

Janie! I'll be coming home!
I'm almost home!
There's my home!

"Janie! Babe!"
"Where have you been?" she demands.
"What? What's going on? Mitt's SUV. What's *he* doing here?"
"Answer me! Where have you been?"
"I was just—"
"Have you been drinking again?"
"I just stopped by Syberg's—"
"You forgot to pick up Kyle from daycare! I had to take off work to go get him!"
"Oh gosh, is it that late? Sorry, babe—"

"Don't you call me 'babe'! My father called me about what you did. And Westminster called about Keenan—they said you were rude and then hung up on them! He's home now— he's really upset about how you treated him this morning."

"How I treated *him*? He's the one that disobeyed *me*!"

"Well, you need to give him a reason to respect you enough to listen to you. And it was a good thing I'd taken off work already, because you didn't bother to pick up the kids from Westminster, either…."

I see him through the front door. Mitt. He's in the kitchen, holding Kevin.

"Kenny! Answer me!" Jane yells.

"Not now!" I've got to get into the kitchen!

"Mitt! What are you doing here? Kevin, come here, buddy. Let Daddy take you."

"Kenny! Uh, you probably shouldn't be here," says Mitt.

"Kevin, it's okay, Daddy's here now."

"It's okay, Kev, Uncle Mitt's got you." Mitt won't let go of Keven!

"Give me my son!" I grab Keven.

"He's a bit afraid of you right now. He told me."

"We'll see about that. Jane, could you have a word with your boyfriend? He isn't being very cooperative at the moment."

"Kids! Everybody! Get in the van, NOW." It's Jane. Kyle's screaming.

"Jane! What's going on? Come here for a moment—"

"Don't touch me."

"Janie, honey—"

What's Mitt babbling on about?

"Kenny, it's just that you kind of went off the deep end this morning. They were afraid to come home, so I came here, to be like a buffer. I mean, to make sure you're okay—"

"What did you say?" I'm fuming.

"Listen to me. They were afraid to come home today, after what happened this morning."

"What business is that of yours?"

"I mean, Annie and me, we were thinking, since it's Easter vacation, we thought we'd take Jane and the kids—"
"You're taking my family from me?"
"No! We're just going to the house on the lake. To let them defuse a bit. Rest."
"You. My 'best friend.' I turn my back on you for one second, and look what you get up to, stealing my family from underneath my nose!"
"What? No, buddy, listen. Jane's been coming over to our house now and then, to talk, think things through—"
"So, you *have* been shagging my wife! I knew it!"
"What?! Huh? Kenny, no! It's nothing like that!"
"Why you lousy S.O.B.—"
"Kenny, Get off him!" It's Jane.
I fling around to face her. "I just *knew* you'd take his side!"
"Kenny, brother, just stop," says the traitor.
"Hit me!" I tell him, "Just hit me like a man!"
"Oh, Daddy, what are you doing?" Julia cries.
"Julia, get out of the kitchen NOW!" I command.
"Kenny, brother, please. Stop," Mitt pleads. "Get away from me. Get off me, Kenny. Get *off me!*"
"Get away from my Dad!" It's Jessie. Jess is *defending me?*
"Jess! Babe, take it easy with him!" She just pushed him against the fridge!
What was that 'crack' sound?
"OW! My head!" Mitt moans.
"Heh, did you just push Jess? Get away from my daughter—"
"I didn't mean to, I slipped on something—"
The purple milk.
"Yeah, look at you, holding onto the fridge like a woos!"
"I—I can't breathe—" Mitt's wheezing.
"Mitt! You're *bleeding!*" screams Jane.
"You care more about him than you do me," I say to Jane.
"Mitt, hon, let me help you up," says Jane. "Keenan can drive you in your SUV. Keenan! Here are Mitt's keys!"

"Janie! Don't leave me!"

Keenan and Jane are carrying Mitt between them, out through the front door. Keenan looks at me over his shoulder.

"It was Mitt's fault!" I shout to Keenan in my defense.

What do I do?

"Janie, please stay," I yell out to her.

"Please, don't close the door on me!"

I don't know what to do.

I just don't know what to do.

3

THE CLEANUP OPERATION

"Kenneth. Kenny. Wake up."

A voice pierces through the fog.

"Wait, what?"

"Let me stop the bleeding," says the voice. My senses are blasted with the smell of disinfectant.

"Oh God, I feel sick," I groan.

"Here, let me help you up."

"I said I feel sick!"

"Okay. Grab my hand."

"I'm a failure. 'Mr. Most Likely To Fail.'"

"That's not true, Kenny. Get up on your feet."

"I'm wedged between the wall and the toilet?!"

"Yes. I've got you now."

"How did I get here?!"

"That's a very good question."

"I *hate* getting sick!" My head is pounding.

"No one particularly likes it. Just do it and get it over with. I'll hold you," he reassures.

"Did I pass out?"

"Yes, though it looks like you're finally waking up," he replies, his grip steadying me.

Who is this guy? He looks Middle Eastern. "You're part of the family that moved into the house down the street, right? Over there on the cul-de-sac?" His cologne, musky. I probably smell like Tiffany's perfume. 'Candy Hearts'.

"Now, where'd that bottle of Scotch go? 'Aged 25 years'! Do you want a swig?"

"No, thanks. Here, let me take that."

"Okay, okay, just one for the road."

"No, I don't think so."

"Heh, you've got no right!"

"Just put your head under the faucet, rinse out your mouth."

"You're *drowning* me!"

"'Down by the riverside, down by the riverside…' Here, take this towel and let's get you out of here. Just put your arm around my shoulder, we'll get you into the living room."

"Heh, why's the sun shining so brightly? I must've really slept. What time is it, anyway?"

"It's later than you think."

"Woah! We're going down for a landing!"

"It's okay—I've got you. Now, rest there, on the floor."

"You must've read my mind."

"Here's a pillow," he says, easing it under my head.

From this angle, I can see under the sofa. What the—no baseball? I can't find my baseball!

Look at me, crying in front of this stranger. And all because I lost my baseball? How pathetic.

But there is something familiar about him….

"Here. Wipe your nose with this." He hands me a Kleenex.

A framed family photo lay broken on the floor—and so does my grandmother's heirloom vase!

"Heh! You! Did *you* break those? You broke in and smashed up the place looking for money and jewelry, didn't you!" I can't get up from the floor to defend myself because my head's too heavy. I grab Kyle's light laser and threaten him with it.

"I'm not known to steal and destroy things, no," he says, matter-of-factly. "And you can put that 'weapon' down, if you like."

The guy's walking around my living room as if he owns the place, looking at the photos on the wall—our wedding, the kids in different ages, stages, and hairstyles—pictures that chart my life falling apart. He bends down to take a look at the broken vase.

"Do you remember that night? In the basement of your high school, down in the counselor's office? When you first met me. How many years has it been now?"

"Who? Wait. What?! What are you talking about? I don't remember you being at that prayer meeting!"

"We had wonderful times back then, you and me. Everything was fresh, and powerful, and new. But then—"

"But then what? How do you know about the 'but then' part? You're starting to freak me out here!"

"—But then you chose to go through all *this*, mostly in your own strength, and mostly without me," he motions to the family pictures on the wall.

"You mean like when Jane told me she was pregnant, turning my whole life upside down?"

He's offering me a hand. "No, thanks, I can get up on my own." I have to regain some semblance of dignity.

I stumble over to the picture wall—avoiding the broken glass on the floor—and touch the frames of the pictures with my fingers.

I'm feeling all sad and pensive all of a sudden.

"Sitting together in the dorm cafeteria, over her chicken salad and my lasagna, we always found it easy to talk. About the dreams we shared. Maybe we didn't *share* so many dreams—they touched at certain points—but we were both pretty much into Jesus back then. That's how we first met, at a worship night at Christian Fellowship. Things developed pretty quickly between us. Maybe a bit *too* quickly, if you know what I mean. I wanted to wait for marriage, and she did, too, but it just kind of happened. She ran varsity track for MIZZOU. I found her sitting on the bench, watching the others run, tears she rarely shed streaming down her face. She looked so vulnerable. I sat next to her, I didn't know what to do or say. And that's when she told me. We were just eighteen! I didn't know anything about being a dad, with my dad dying when I was young and all. I felt numb for days. Years, even."

I take a good look at him. "Why are you dressed-up like that? Are you on your way to a costume party or something?" A subtle smile crosses his face.

"Where was I? I don't know why I'm telling all this to a perfect stranger, but I stood up to the plate, you know? I took the fastball. We figured things out together, Jane and me. I put my English degree on hold for a while and got a job at her dad's construction firm. But everything came so fast, the wedding, the bills, the responsibilities, and I watched my dreams deflate as fast as the new life expanded her belly. Look at Keenan as a baby, all that dark hair! I never called him 'The Mistake' to his face, of course. I tried to make it up to him in a million different ways through the years—I mean, it wasn't *his* fault. But the distance between him and me—I just got so wrapped up in trying to survive, with the twins coming and Jewel's medical issues—Keenan got pushed to the side. I'm probably boring you with my sob story, but this one is Jess—her name's Jessica—and this one is Jewels—Julia. You'd never know they're identical twins in this picture, would you! With all that red hair, there's no denying that they're mine! Sorry, I guess that was a bit 'off color'!

"And here's our dear Kevin. Quirky, Quasar Kevin. All I have to do to make him tummy-giggle is to call him Charles Wallace. He's so smart he's been bumped up three grades and his teachers still barely comprehend what he's talking about. We had a long break between the twins and Kevin, so we had the chance to form ourselves around Julia's needs.

"But do you know what happened? We almost lost Julia. She and Jess were developing at different rates during the pregnancy, it took the doctors a while to discover her heart defect," I say, the memory still painful. "So I guess everybody—Keenan, Jessica, Kevin—*everybody* got pushed to the side so we could survive Julia, so Julia could survive.

"And what do you think it was like for me, watching Jane obtain her degree after the family situation stabilized somewhat? I got stuck counting nuts and bolts in her father's business! Jane's successes always remind me of how far I haven't come, what I haven't achieved in life."

I must be getting hungry because all I can think about is what might be in the fridge, but I want to finish my story.

"I wanted to leave her—you know, Jane, to forget it all. And she was pretty fed up with my mood swings. We contacted a lawyer, drew up the papers.

But then, Christ Jesus—sorry, you're probably Muslim, right? Jewish you said? I thought you all lived in Clayton, Ladue, places like that. Anyway, Jesus kind of let us know that we were taking the easy way out, so we put down our hatchets and tried again. It wasn't easy, no-siree. That's where Kyle came into the picture: he's the glue that sealed our marriage together. Sometimes we call him Elmer, like the school glue. We don't call him that to his face, of course. I just haven't had much left over for him. For any of them, truth be told.

But we made it work—at least for awhile. Things have been getting pretty tough lately. Things really blew up this morning, to say the least. Man, what a day it's been. Sorry, I uh, you're getting an earful."

The man has set himself on the sofa next to a pile of clean laundry.

It's quiet between us. I've run out of things to say.

He folds a red kid-size Cardinals T-shirt. He's pretty good at it. Jane would like this guy.

He looks up from the T-shirt and says, "You know, there's been something I've been trying to get your attention on, something you've been keeping from me for a very long time."

It's getting really uncomfortable in here.

"Because you keep avoiding what I've been wanting to talk with you about, I feel our times together have become shallow. And infrequent." He returns to his folding.

No. It can't be. Come on, Kenny, get a grip. It's the Scotch that's messing with your head.

"Gee, look at the time! Shouldn't you be on your way to your costume party? I don't want to hold you up—"

"Kenny, it's time to go."

"And I'm not stopping you!"

The man stands to his feet and walks toward me.

"Kenny, I know who you are—"

Oh my gosh.

"—and you know who I am—"

Oh my gosh oh my gosh oh my gosh oh my gosh.

"—and I'm calling you on a journey with me—"

Oh my gosh oh my gosh oh my gosh oh my gosh.

"—the journey of all journeys!"

No no no no no no no no.

"Journeying through the deepest caverns of your heart—"

This can't be happening, this simply cannot be happening.

"—you will arrive at the center of the universe, *where lies the very center of my heart.*"

I'm hyperventilating. I'm hyperventilating!

"Now, let's get you cleaned up, get you out of those clothes. Do you have any other shoes besides those wet penny loafers?"

I can't take this in!

"Wait here. I'll run upstairs and find some clean clothes for you."

Okay, he's gone. Oh my gosh, what do I do? Think, Kenny, *think*! I'll dash downstairs into the basement, he won't find me down there! Oh shoot, he's coming back already! Dive into the dining room, hide under the table!

"These should do for the time being, I found these khaki pants in one of your drawers—"

Oh God *please please please* don't let him find me! What's that light, shining through the window?

"—and this green Cardinals polo shirt—"

Something really strange is happening outside—

"—and I grabbed your baseball cap."

Am I having DTs? Is there a UFO landing outside my house?

"*Of course* it's not a UFO, you funny man!"

How'd he know what I was thinking? Wait, the air—it's starting to *shimmer*, like heat on a highway—

"Kenny? Where did you go?"

Don't breathe, Kenny, don't move a muscle! Maybe he won't see me under here. But what's happening to *him* now? From under here I can only see his legs, but they're starting to shimmer, too!

"There you are! What are you doing under the dining room table?!"

"I was just a, uh, looking for my baseball."

Is he getting under the table with me? Gosh, his face is radiating. I'm sitting crossed-legged under the dining room table, face-to-face with *him*! He keeps looking at me! His face, his *whole being* is shining! All this light is exposing all this old chewing gum stuck under the tabletop! And I'm feeling exposed, too. I've got to get out of here! But he keeps looking at me and I almost can't take it but I can't get away from him because I'm stuck under here and I think I'm going to be sick again—

"Kenny, you are about to discover who you truly are, in me, and who I truly am, in you—not who you *think* you are, or who you *think* I am—"

The sky, outside my dining room window: it's the wrong color! Or it's the right color but the wrong intensity at the wrong time of day—

"—and you will realize, with ever-expanding joy, how wide, how deep, and how high my love truly is, for you. Now, let's get out from under here, we've got a big day ahead of us!"

I have to think. I have to think! I mean, there's *no way* he'll want me once he finds out about my weaknesses, my lusts, my thousand-million failings, my sins. My worms!

"Here, give me that dirty shirt and put this one on. Hello, aren't you going to come out? You can't stay under there forever! And take off those dress pants while you're at it." He's leaning over, peaking underneath the table. His dark curls glow neon purple, and his shining arm reaches out toward me.

On his wrist, a big, nasty scar.

I look up at him and start to tremble.

"Yes, I made the way for you. I will be going with you, journeying with you toward the center of the universe, toward my heart of hearts."

"But-but-but do you really want me?"

He touches his scar. "What kind of question is that? *Of course* I really want you!"

What's happening *now*? Outside, through the window—my neighborhood is unraveling like everything else in my life: picked apart, fiber by fiber, peeled away like layers of dry skin, exposing my soft underlayers, revealing what is always there but not always seen—my hidden hopes, my pains, my woes. My neighborhood glows in this otherworldly light, shimmering with hope, of unrestrained beauty, of pure bliss. I can't handle this! It's too much! I can't take it in! I can't breathe! I can't move!

I panic. "Have I been turned into a pillar of salt? I feel like I've been turned into a pillar of salt!"

"Kenny, you haven't been turned into a pillar of salt, you funny man!"

"Are you sure?"

"Yes, of course! You're just 'freaking-out' a bit, as you say in these parts. Now, please, *take my hand!*"

I feel overwhelmed with his brilliance, his unrelenting beauty. My heart races, my legs tremble. I reach out and grab onto his hand.

"Into the Shimmering!" he declares like a buccaneer.

What does that even mean?! I'm holding on for dear life as he flings me out from underneath my dining room table and hurls me through the entryway and slings me out the front door and into all this brilliant otherness!

"But wait!" I scream. "Wait wait wait wait wait! I still haven't found my baseball!"

PART TWO

And So It Begins

4

ENTERING THE SHIMMERING

What on earth just happened?

    He's let go of my arm. He's got some grip, that's all I have to say. I'm surprised my shoulder hasn't been dislocated, the way he swung me through the air like a baseball bat. I mean, couldn't we have just *walked* out of my house like normal people do?

    Gosh, I can barely open my eyes, it's so bright. Light is bombarding me from all sides, not just from the sun blasting me from the sky. It's like I'm looking through a giant Polaroid filter that makes everything around me look hyper-real—or it's like someone's turned up a giant dimmer switch, making light not just bright but brilliant, and hazeless, and shimmering. Which makes me feel strange and discombobulated. And it isn't doing my hangover any good.

    We must have landed on my front lawn. He's lying next to me in the grass, breathing hard, joyful-like—but this can't be *my* front lawn, because I don't think I've ever seen my front lawn look this plush and green, with hardly a weed to be seen!

    He reaches out an arm and helps me up from the ground. His grin, his teeth are beaming, his dark curls gleaming in all this incredible light!

    Oh no! Have I died and gone to heaven? Maybe I really *did* have a coronary! That feeling I had in bed this morning—like I was lying on a gurney. Maybe it wasn't just Kyle jumping the living daylights out of me, but one of those premonitions people talk about. Jane's going to write on my tombstone 'I told you so'!

But if this is heaven, it sure looks a whole lot like my own front yard, which is pretty disappointing, to say the least.

But wait! Look at my house! It's stuck in some sort of giant bubble! Inside that bubble is a muggy St. Louis evening, while out here it's not like St. Louis at all! Out here everything dazzles in spectacular color, like I'm looking *through* a kaleidoscope but from *inside* a kaleidoscope. And the air is fresh and clean and clear, descending from those alpine mountains, over there in Illinois. Which doesn't make sense, because there's hardly a *hill* in Illinois!

What is going on around here?! There's nothing normal about this place—though looking through the open front door into my house, I can see that everything looks normal and in place—or *out* of place like normal; but out here—I don't *think* my house has been transported to a different place like in The Wizard of Oz; it's more like a different place has been transported *here*, or everything's been morphed into a different reality, or stacked like pancakes between layers of realities, I don't know; but my house still needs a coat of paint under the eaves, not to mention a new garage door we never seem to have money for; and the front door is still painted in that bizarre fuchsia color Jane insisted would be "inviting". My pickup truck is still there, thankfully.

But wait! Everything else is gone! My neighborhood is gone! And Webster Groves is gone! And the entire metropolitan area of St. Louis is gone! Maybe the whole state of Missouri is gone, too! Illinois might still be there for all I know, across the Mississippi, but if it is, it's buried under all those mountains!

Come on, Kenny, get out of your funk. Because where Webster Groves was, but isn't, is a valley that wasn't, but is—a valley laden with a meadow of undulating grass in more shades of green than a box of 64 crayons. And the meadow is embroidered with purple clover, and hemmed in yellow hollyhock. The entire scene is abuzz with life—with bumbling bumble bees and fluttering butterflies and blue jays serenading the sky with song! This just can't be happening to me!

And yet—if this were some sort of a doomsday world and I'm the only survivor because that's what it feels like, it's not at all like one of those apocalyptic zombie movies I probably shouldn't have watched, but have. This place is too beautiful, too pure, too kind to be the death of me, at least not yet, so things will probably work out okay; but I don't want to think about it because I don't know what's going to happen and something about this place is touching something deep in me and I'm feeling all emotional, and a bit lonely, too. But I guess I'm not really alone because *he's* with me, which is freaking me out, I'm freaked-out by being so close to *him* all of a sudden! But where did he go?

Oh, wait, there he is—he hasn't abandoned me like everybody else has, at least not yet. But what on earth is he doing, twirling around with his arms stretched out? Has he watched The Sound of Music one too many times? But it's more like all of this grandeur is swirling around *him*, and if he keeps twirling like that he's going suck the whole universe into himself! Which makes me want to turn around and run right straight back through that fuchsia-colored front door of mine, because I don't want to disappear into him with everything else. I mean, this is *Jesus* we're talking about here!

This is Jesus, like the Jesus in the Bible I've read about (in the parts of the Bible I've read), swirling there in his linen tunic and sandals. Which means that, oh gosh, was it *the Son of God* that pulled me out from behind the toilet—and not a neighbor on his way to a costume party? How embarrassing, how absolutely, utterly humiliating. He even changed my clothes, for Pete's sake! There it goes, my Irish blush, spreading from the top of my head to the tip of my toes just from *thinking* about the King of Kings seeing me in my underwear!

But why is he doing this for me? Why is he bothering with *me*? Doesn't he have more important things to deal with, like peace in the Middle East or something? Why is he bringing me here to this—what did he call it—this Shimmering place? I don't deserve any of this. I don't deserve him. Doesn't he know who I am?

He's stopped with the twirling, laughing heartily.

"My dear Kenny. It is *precisely* because I *do* know who you are—and who you are in me—that I am bringing you on this journey!" he says with a booming voice that echoes across the valley.

He's coming toward me. I'm scared witless. I'm not in a huggy mood—I hope he picks up on this.

5

THE TRYSTING PLACE

Whew. No hug. He only wanted to hand me a backpack. It's not a run-of-the-mill backpack; this one is beautifully hand-sewn, in honey-colored leather, the same color as my old baseball mitt. I never did find my baseball, which makes me blue; it makes me think of Dad, who gave it to me. It's got to be somewhere in my house! But I can't go look for it—my house is stuck in that weird bubble that I doubt I can pass through. Jesus is putting on a backpack that's pretty much like mine.

Let's see what's inside here… A toothbrush in a plastic travel case; travel-sized toothpaste, shower gel and shampoo; SPF 50 sunscreen (he obviously knows my skin type), extra boxer shorts, socks, a travel first aid kit, blister bandages, a water bottle, a travel flashlight, and my Cardinals baseball cap! No Diet Coke. Toilet paper? Why would I need that?—oh, whatever. Cute—a plastic container filled with trail mix, just like Mom would take in the car on our family trips. And a travel Bible. What's this? *The Pilgrim's Progress*, By John Bunyan? I read the CliffsNotes about it, for English class, but only because I had to and under extreme duress. And in this pocket is…*worms*?! Dozens of slimy worms slithering in the bottom of my backpack!

"Ee-gad! What are *those* doing in there?"

"You were wondering about where your 'worms' had come from, weren't you? You're about to find out. And find out how to deal with them," he says with a smile.

He nods in the direction of the path. Unsure of whether or not I will return from this journey, at least in one piece, I take one long, last look at my house, there, encased in St. Louis mugginess. Well, it's not my house *per se*; it's owned by the bank and purchased with a hefty loan from the parents-in-law that we'll never be able to pay back, at least not in this lifetime. A solid, 1950s okay-kind-of-house. The brick is holding up alright, though the gables need some maintenance. Good neighborhood, nothing to sneeze at really, though I do miss the house I grew up in, in the city, of course. This place isn't at all like Jane's parents' place on the other side of Webster Groves, or like her sister's behemoth out in West County. But you can't have everything. Since she and that A-list husband of hers have it all already. Sheesh.

What a day it's been, a miserable, lousy, stressful day. It's no wonder I'm feeling a bit heavy. I don't know what I'm feeling, really. Guilt? Shame? Excitement? I mean, who wouldn't want to go on an adventure like this at least once in their life? Mostly, I feel regret over how botched-up everything's gotten, there in my empty home. I'm not exactly thrilled that Jane and the kids, probably right this very minute, are on their way to Benedict Arnold's house on the lake, without me.

* * *

He's taking me down a stone path that hadn't led from my front porch before, which leads down a broad hill toward a big lake that hadn't been in Webster before, if Webster were still here, which it isn't. We're pretty much heading west, following Highway 66—Watson Road in these parts—which is buried under all of these trees. I love telling people we can see ol' Route 66 from our house! A bit of a stretch of the truth, but hey, life needs to be embellished now and then. Pretty soon we'll be walking right over the burial site of Crestwood Plaza, now sadly bull-dozed to the ground. Which is too bad because I could really use a Cinnabon or three right now.

Wow! Look at all these aspens—my favorite! And those mountains! I need to take some pictures, pucker-up my lips, stick out my hip, put it on Instagram—wouldn't the girls get a laugh! I'd probably end up embarrassing them to death. Where's my phone? I'm sure I put it in my pocket—

He's grinning at me. "You won't be needing that around here," he says.

I hope he doesn't mind me walking behind him, I need some personal space. Which gives me the opportunity to observe him without him knowing it. He's pretty average, really, average height, with no striking feature that makes him stand out—apart from the tunic and sandals, of course. But he's a bit perky, the way he walks on the balls of his feet, like he could spring into the air at any moment. The sun has colored his legs a darker shade than the skin protected by his tunic. A definite inverted shoulder-to-torso triangle can be seen beneath the linen cloth—the kind that is shaped, not by working out at a gym, but by *working*. There is something endearing about him, I must admit, something about his tangle of black curls, and big eyes, and half-grin—the scruffy beard does a poor job hiding those dimples of his. Despite the pockmarks scattered across his face—telltale signs of past battles with acne or illness—I can almost picture the young women of Nazareth, gathered at the well, sharing furtive glances, and whispered speculations, their voices hushed yet animated, as he darted a glance and a smile their way while walking past them. Did the girls make him blush like girls made me blush when I was young? What a funny thought! Okay, women still make me blush.

He's starting to get the better of me, truth be told. Which really freaks me out.

* * *

The stone path turned into an earthen trail a long way back, our footsteps tempered under the canopy of trees. It's real quiet here. Almost perfect.
A summer breeze flirts with the jaded leaves bejeweled with sunlight, revealing their demure undersides.
Where do these thoughts come from?
It's like I see words, scattered like leaves along a path; I pick them up, enjoy their uniqueness and beauty, arranging then rearranging them until, satisfied, I carefully paste them together into a sentence.
But I'm just this guy who counts nuts and bolts for his father-in-law for a living!
Come on, Kenny, you *know* you do more than that, working in sales now and all.
But what I've had to do to keep the family afloat has been as meaningful to me as counting nuts and bolts—not that there's anything wrong with people doing that sort of thing if that's what they want to do. It's just that there have been other things I've wanted to do, to be. But just look at me.
There is something about this valley…. When I look at it a certain way, it looks a lot like a giant baseball mitt, the way those mountains curve upward, as if they're the fingers of the mitt. And that giant rockface over there, far in the distance, that's where the thumb of the mitt would be. I don't know, I'm probably reading more into this than I should, but those rolling green hills over there, toward the west—that's where I'd put my hand in the mitt, if this valley were a mitt. And toward the south are miles and miles of aspens, with that dark line of pine trees hovering ominously in the background.
We've walked nearly the entire time in silence, which has been fine by me. Now and then he looks back at me and smiles, probably to let me know that he knows I'm here. His look is, what, penetrating? That's too strong of a word. Disarming, maybe. And

I'm not yet ready to be disarmed. So I find something along the path to turn my attention to each time he looks at me.

But haven't we walked long enough? I mean, my bones are feeling out of joint, my thumbs keep looking for my phone, I've already eaten up all the trail mix and my stomach is letting me know that it's in some serious need of attention!

Wait—what's that under those trees? A wooden bench!

Is that our destination?

Seeing this bench stirs something inside me, a longing for something, something more than even dinner.

Cradled within the sturdy arms of a wooden trellis, a cascade of wisteria blossoms dances in the breeze, their blues, whites, and purples meld into a living watercolor, mesmerizing me.

I should write that one down. The wisteria bush in our back yard was the pride and joy of the retired couple we bought the house from. I hope they never see what we did to it. But it's comforting to see these familiar blossoms hanging above the wooden bench. It lifts my spirits a bit.

He takes off his backpack, sets himself down on the bench, and gestures for me to do the same. Suddenly spending so much time with him feels foreign, strained. Like when I was a boy, when we visited relatives we hadn't seen in a long time, and how I felt lost and wanted to go home.

I want to go home now.

Then again, he *wants* to spend time with me; he *wants* me to spend time with him.

I sit down with a huff. Even if I did agree to this journey it doesn't mean I have to like it. I'll scoot myself as far away from him as possible, to make a point. Woah—I almost fell off the end of the bench! How embarrassing.

He settles in with an ease that suggests familiarity, a natural fit with these surroundings. From the corner of my eye I observe him as he perches a sandal-clad foot on the bench, places an arm on his knee, rests his chin on his arm, his deep breaths bring the world around us into a calm rhythm with himself.

I stretch my legs out in front of me, cross them at the ankle, trying to look cool. But I've folded my arms across my chest as tight as a straitjacket, I've got to hold myself together, there's something building inside me, an unease that could explode any minute. I'm not at all relaxed, not one bit.

He gazes toward the snowy mountains in the distance, then turns to me. I turn my head as far away from him as anatomically possible. I can't look at him. I'm already rubbing away tears that are falling from my eyes without my consent. I know my face is all red because that's what happens to me when I get emotional. A pure embarrassment.

"This is our trysting place, our secret meeting place, where my heart meets yours," I hear him say. His voice blends with the surrounding tranquility. He doesn't move closer because he must know I don't want him to; I want to do things on my own. Yet I also want him to come closer and I hope he senses my ambiguity. He leans over to me, places his hand on my arm.

His touch breaks the levee. The disaster of the day surges out of me like sand out of a leaky burlap sack. Which reminds me of that Halloween costume I made for Keenan, out of burlap. Keenan was supposed to look like a giant ham, like Scout in *To Kill a Mockingbird*, but he ended up looking exactly like a burlap sack. He cried the whole night. One of my million failures.

I wipe off these ridiculous tears with my sleeve, pull my baseball cap down to hide my face. What a mess. My body does what it can to bring homeostasis to my slobbery sobs.

"Hungry?" he asks. I glance at him quickly from underneath my baseball cap. He smiles, takes my hand, and I let him pull me up from the wooden bench.

He leads me behind a tall hedge of bushes, to a picnic table, and he motions for me to sit. He disappears into some overgrowth and returns with a lacquered tray holding two large bowls and a Chinese tea set. He sets the tray on the table before me.

Spicy Sichuan noodles? How did he know I've been hankering for them? Just what I need after, well, after all that's happened. I just hope they're as good as we get at The Peking Palace next to Happy Joe's. I murmur my thanks.

He hands me a pair of chopsticks and we entwine them within our fingers with familiar ease. He brings the brimming bowl close to his mouth. I've seen this done in movies before but have never tried it myself, so I join him in the shoveling and slurping. The world narrows to just the two of us and our culinary conquest. He breaks the silence with a complimentary burp to the chef, whoever it was, and I follow his lead. We laugh. It's a bit of an ice-breaker.

I steal a glance at him. I mean, this is a lot to take in. Yet something about him, about him going around in this very human sack of flesh, helps me to thaw a bit. Those eyes of his, sort of a translucent cinnamon color. They seem to reflect more light than they take in.

A 'trysting place,' he called it. 'A secret meeting place for lovers.' Long ago it meant a designated hunting place. Useless information, residue of my aborted English degree, though it does make me popular on trivia nights. If he's been hunting for me, what's keeping me from wanting to be found by him? I mean, I *have* been found by him, I have been 'saved'.

I think about him looking at my family photos on the wall, now that I know it was him and not a neighbor from down the street—and I think back to the moment I first met him; I've only viewed that moment from my perspective—how he came to me in my darkness, blanketed me with his love—and never from his perspective, what it might've meant to him. He knows I've gotten stuck. There must be more that he wants for me.

He stares across the meadow toward the snowy mountains now dipped in blazing light.

"There are rooms in your heart that you have opened to me, which I have placed in order, made holy, through the work of my Holy Spirit. There are other rooms that you have yet to open to me, have yet to dare to. You have peeked into these rooms, were confronted with the pain that dwells within, then quickly closed them, never to return, and have kept the key from me."

Specific, painful experiences crawl up from the depths, things I haven't wanted to look at. *My worms.*

"Kenny, it is time to consider the condition of your heart."

I stiffen. Now it starts. I *knew* there'd be a catch. I want to run away, to run back home.

"The longer you keep your heart from me, the longer it will take for you to fully experience my love for you."

The trysting place has fallen into gentle shades of lilac as the sun descends beyond the western hills. I'm feeling suddenly, overwhelmingly tired. I am too tired to run anymore.

"That is enough for one day," he says through a yawn. He leads me away from the picnic table. We follow a narrow path that meanders through the trees, emerging beneath a rocky outcrop. In a serene clearing a campfire flickers, illuminating two mats laid out with bedding, hinting at our lodgings for the night. A tapestry of stars will be our covering.

He seems as human as I am, stretching and yawning, sleepy from the day's events. With deliberate care, he washes his hands, whispering prayers in an ancient tongue—Hebrew? Aramaic?—his fingers occasionally stray to smooth a stubborn curl that insists on shadowing his brow. And as he speaks with his Father, the intimate 'abba' falling from his lips, I whisper a quick prayer for Jane and the kids. Anxiety for Kevin gnaws at me; truthfully, I'm concerned for all of them.

"P.S. And God, if you can spare a blessing, then bless my boss-slash-father-in-law, too," who is likely fuming from the loss of the new client—all because of me.

A small surprise— my pillow and the family room blanket, the very essence of our family movie nights, have followed me here, a touch of home in this foreign wilderness. I release a contented sigh as comfort enfolds me. On the cusp of surrendering to sleep, Jesus settles into his own bed beside me, a silent companion under the night's vast canvas.

We're lying here, under the sapphire sky. The stillness of the night carries his words, a whisper barely louder than the rustle of leaves:

"There is a pathway, a sacred trail, from your heart to mine."

I look over at him. He has his arms tucked beneath his head; he is dusted with starlight.

He continues:

"Consider the journey I had with my brother John,
The one spoken of as my beloved.
My love was for all of them, yet with John—

"Like Mary, who sat at my feet and listened to my every word,
So, too, John, rested his head upon my chest
And listened to my very heartbeat.

"John paid the ultimate price.
But oh, the revelations he was entrusted with!
The one whom I could trust with such visions,
Took time to draw near and listen to the visions
That stirred in my heart.

"As with John,
I have a place for you, awaiting,
Near my beating heart.

"As I journey with you,
I will whisper to you,
And cradle you,
As I bring healing and rest to your wounded, weary soul.

"And I, the Author of life,
Will write your story

By engraving it
On the palm of my hand."

His voice gently weaves into the fabric of the night air, a soothing serenade easing me into dreams. Just as his last syllable fades, his breaths deepen into the rhythm of sleep.

6

GALAXIES AND GUIDEPOSTS

Is that coffee? It smells fantastic, and I don't even like coffee. I'm frozen to the bone.

He sits by the campfire with a blanket over his shoulders, silhouetted in the soft pastels of dawn. He looks toward the mountains, holding a metal mug in one hand, stirring a pot over the fire with the other. It's probably oatmeal for breakfast—I detect a trace of cinnamon.

I don't want to relate to him, not just yet. Besides, I like to wake up gradually. Time for my morning ritual: check messages, read emails, catch up on how the Cards are doing, twirl my baseball in my hands.

Rats. I forgot he'd confiscated my phone. And my baseball is gone. What on earth can I do?

The book he gave me! It's in my backpack which is nearly out of reach. I don't want him to know that I'm awake. I'll pull it toward me, slowly, slowly…he didn't notice a thing. Now, where is that book… Yuck! The worms! Look in the other pocket. There it is. Let's see here….

> "*When at the first I took my pen in hand*
> *Thus for to write, I did not understand*

*That I at all should make a little book
In such a mode; nay, I had undertook
To make another, which, when almost done,
Before I was aware, I this begun."*

Bunyan wrote this more than four centuries ago and I can still understand his writing?! It sounds like he was quite a character.

*"As I walked through the wilderness of this world,
I lighted on a certain place where was a Den,
And I laid me down in that place to sleep:
And, as I slept, I dreamed a dream.
I dreamed, and behold, I saw a man clothed in rags,
Standing in a certain place with his face from his own house,
A book in his hand, and a great burden upon his back.
I looked, and saw him open the book, and read therein;
And, as he read, he wept, and trembled;
And, not being able longer to contain,
He brake out with a lamentable cray, saying,
What shall I do?"*

Poor guy, going around with that huge burden, like a backpack. My backpack's filled with toiletries and with a few measly worms, that's all.

He's coming. I fake a snore. *"Snore."*

"Come and eat," he says while ruffling my hair. "And bring your Bible."

"Okay, okay."

I find him sitting on top of a boulder. In the distance, a layer of mist hovers over the meadow, glowing as if from an internal light.

"You and I will start the day by focusing our hearts on the Father," he says, helping me up to the top of the rock. "Look up Psalm 25, verse 5." I sit closer to him than yesterday yet farther away than necessary, with me feeling emotional and vulnerable and all.

I rumble through my Bible. Psalms is near the center of the book. Here it is:

"Guide me in your truth and teach me,
for you are God my Savior,
and my hope is in you all day long."

He begins singing. It is subtle at first, but I swear those birds in the dogwood tree seem to be joining in. No, it *can't* be! Woodland creatures, frolicking in sync with his melody?

My heart feels an invisible pull toward his. Should I add my voice to this choir? But I don't speak his language! My English will have to do. Okay, I'll give it a try. I never sound my best in the morning so it won't be perfect. He just glanced at me with a look of pure encouragement. He's closed his eyes, probably entering his own trysting place with his Father.

Butterflies flit about like notes emanating from an ancient flute, joining in a crescendo of praise to its loving Creator.

He breathes deeply, stealing one more glance at the awakening world. He scoots down the side of the boulder and says, "Come."

We walk toward a circular clearing, cool in morning shadows, behind the wooden bench. We then make our way down a path, toward a stream running through the woods.

What a lovely stone footbridge, arching over the stream!

But he doesn't cross the footbridge. Instead, he leads me down the stony bank toward the deep-flowing waters.

He removes his sandals, gingerly steps over the stones and wades into the stream. His reaction leaves no doubt—the water's coolness is refreshing.

A soulful tune arises from deep within his chest,
"Wade in the water, wade in the water, children—"

It's as if he's listening to the water: with eyes closed, he tilts his head this way and that, like a curious cocker spaniel.

"*Wade in the water, God's going to trouble the water,*" he continues singing.

He dives into the stream.

He resurfaces. His hair flings droplets into the air, crafting a rainbow in the sun's morning glow.

Again, he listens. Changing course slightly, he disappears beneath the water's surface.

Where did he go?

He must be a very good swimmer.

Either he's a very good swimmer, or he's drowned—he's been down there for an awfully long time!

"Jesus! Are you alright?" I yell at the top of my lungs.

He must not have heard me.

This is getting really uncomfortable.

What should I do?

Still no Jesus.

I've got to get these shoes off! Get these socks off! Get this shirt off! Ok, here I go. Wait. Gosh this water's colder than I expected. I'll have to dive in just like he did.

Oh oh oh! I can't catch my breath!

What did I just bump into?

"Jesus was that you?"

No, not Jesus, but something slimy. A slimy boulder.

It's really deep here, I've got to keep my head up! Step on that boulder!

Oh no—the water's dragging me downstream! I'm gulping in water!

"Jesus, save me!"

Wait—I'm supposed to be saving him!

But I've got to get out because my muscles are cramping-up but the current is pulling me downstream and the edge is getting further away and I don't see Jesus and he's been under the water for a very long time!

"Oh God, help! God, please help me—I mean please help Jesus!"

Wait—is that him? Yes! There, farther downstream, I can see his head bobbing up and down in the water. He's really struggling, he must be exhausted. He should've taken off his tunic before diving in, it must weigh a ton!

"Jesus! H-h-hold on! I'll g-g-go find a stick and come r-r-rescue you!"

The current—gurgle gurgle gurgle—I've got to get my head above water. Wait! Sand! Shallower water! I-I-I'm safe! I-I-I'm alive!

He drags himself through the water as if weighted by a heavy burden.

"Oh God! Please! Help him make it out of the water! Yes! Yes! Thank God in heaven!"

"Jesus! Keep going! You're almost there! You can do it!" I shout through cupped hands.

What's that? It looks like he's carrying something out of the water. Whatever it is it's not a fish. What on earth—he just plopped a huge stone into the sand!

And I risked my life because he went fishing for a rock?!

He looks spent, hanging his head between his shoulders.

"What did you go off and do that for? You could've drowned! And me, too!!!"

He looks up at me; his eyes are pools of translucent love.

"Because you were worth it," he says, out of breath.

"What on earth does that mean?"

Humph. Let that hunk of granite keep him company for a while, I need to go back and get my shoes and stuff. Stupid bramble. His sandals are over there, I'll go the extra mile and get them for him. Not that he deserves it.

He bends down and heaves the stone onto a shoulder, plods with it up the bank and disappears between the briar toward the trysting place.

I stumble after him, wrestling with my polo shirt as it clings to my wet skin, bunched up as it is under my arms. He's squeezing water from his locks, twisting his hair into a manbun. He notices my struggle. "Here, let me help you," he offers, reaching to ease my shirt down.

I brace myself for the usual snide remark that never fails to follow, about my lily-white complexion.

"There. Now you're good to go."

But the jibe doesn't come, for once. I'm left uncertain how to respond to this unexpected kindness.

A tray with sandwiches and drinks has been placed by the wooden bench. We eat in silence. I'm still miffed with him. I'd already chosen the title to my autobiography: *The Man Who Saved The Savior.*

It must be siesta time, the way he's stretched out in the shade. Fine by me, I won't have to relate to him for a while.

* * *

"Now, imagine your life as a galaxy, and at the center of the galaxy is you." He's looking more perky after his siesta.

"What? Where am I? What are you talking about? Give me a chance to wake up first, wouldja?" My head is groggy. How am I supposed to focus without a Diet Coke?

He pulls me up, places his hands firmly around my shoulders and guides me to the big stone from the stream that he'd plunked down at the center of the clearing.

"Now, stand here," he says. I have no idea what he's up to.

"Certain relationships in your life have impacted you more than other relationships, would you agree? For example, you remember your second-grade teacher, who humiliated you with the stuffed-animal mascot in front of the class, more than you remember your third-grade teacher, who didn't do much of anything to you, neither good nor bad, right?"

"You remember my second-grade teacher? And you're right, I remember little if anything about my third-grade teacher." I rub my temples to alleviate a throbbing headache. Probably from Diet Coke withdrawals.

He makes a pouch in his tunic by lifting up the front (slightly exposing his tan line on his bare legs) and, with a focused intent reminiscent of an Easter egg hunt, he begins collecting stones of various sizes and hues from around the trysting place. He then drops the stones willy-nilly in the dirt. So, what was the point of picking them up in the first place, then?

He seems satisfied with his work, though completely oblivious to the dirt smudge on his tunic from where he'd been carrying the stones.

He disappears into some bushes. He extracts himself, having found a long stick. A leafy twig is stuck in his hair.

He etches a spiral-pattern out from the center, where lies the hefty stone from the stream, and me. With precision, he's ensured that each stone is found on an arm of the spiral. He catches his breath.

"There are many relationships in your life, some closer to you and some farther away. These relationships make up your heart galaxy."

He's jumped right in front of me! We're standing nose-to-nose and eyeball-to-eyeball and he's smiling this goofy grin. What on earth is he up to?!

He bends down and places two particularly nice stones by my feet. I'll remove the twig from his hair—it's beginning to bug me.

"Oh, thanks," he says, then continues. "Your heart galaxy is made of the relationships in your life that have impacted you the greatest. Now, there are two relationships closest to your heart," he says in a more schoolmarm voice, "your mother," pointing to one of the small stones with his stick, "and your father," striking this stone with his stick. I lose my balance but quickly find it; I'm playing my part. We're standing eyeball to eyeball again. He just pushed away from me with his stick and has begun walking around the open area like Nureyev, a bit too dramatic for my liking.

"Other relationships may include a spouse or partner, or children, or siblings and grandparents and friends, and classmates and workmates and teachers and priests and pastors and sports coaches and scout leaders—these relationships extend almost indefinitely—" he races around the clearing, extending the arms of my galaxy toward the periphery of the clearing, "—as the totality of your life consists of people whom you know or barely know (or haven't yet met), neighbors, salespeople, government agents and healthcare workers—people in your hometown and people beyond your country's borders." He opens his arms wide toward his childlike artwork. "And there you are, in the middle of your universe, surrounded by brightly-colored hearts that nurture you, guide you, and give your life meaning!"

"Uh, not exactly." I'm thinking that, for many people, the closest circle may not include both parents, or just two parents—or any parents at all. The hearts around some people may not be so cheery or nurturing, nor do they always sweep harmoniously around in perfect order.

He stares at me, blankly. He's obviously picked up on my 'exception-to-the-rule' expression on my face. Mom called it my 'know-it-all' expression.

"The bright picture is what people *want* for their lives, isn't it? People near and far who care for them and love them, who wish them well and cheer them on. This is also the heart of the heavenly Father for people, what he'd intended for them, hoped for them. If there is anyone in the universe who's aware of the deplorable condition of human relations on this planet, it is the heavenly Father. Which is one of the primary reasons he sent me to this world. To restore relationships."

"Oh," is all I can find to say.

Jesus looks hot (and not a little bit dusty) in the late morning sun. "Okay, Kenny. Let's take this a level deeper." He airs out the top of his tunic, pulls up his sleeves.

"Imagine the vibrant galaxy of your existence, with you at its core, and witness its transformation." As he says this, he springs skyward, a dancer expressing the spirit of Swan Lake.

"Notice the ebb and flow of connections: observe as a once-close parent drifts from your closest circle, and you feel a sense of loss," he narrates, sweeping his arms away in a grand gesture of letting go, his face contorting to mimic sorrow. "During adolescence, friendships eclipse family, drawing near with the promise of kinship," he picks up some stones from the dust and brings them to me, smiling broadly, "only to drift off again a few years later," he turns away in deep sorrow, clenching the stones to his chest.

"Watch as a cherished heart," he says while lifting a smooth stone, "hurtles towards you," he lunges in my direction, stone in hand, "only to collide with your spirit, leaving the pain of betrayal," a pain he inadvertently inflicts on me by stepping on my foot. "Oh, sorry," he says. With tenderness, he presses this stone against his chest, and with the poise of an athlete, hurls it towards my rock, striking it with a resonant 'crack'. The stone boomerangs away from me. The sudden noise jolts me, yet I can't help but admire the precision of his throw. He concludes with a flourish, bowing deeply.

"Some hearts do not remain neatly in their designated places, do they? They take authority over you that wasn't theirs to take. Some hearts push upon you brutally, aggressively, or press upon you caressingly, seductively. Others battle around you, vying for your attention, competing to control you, creating in you stress, confusion, uncertainty. Another heart, out on a distant arm of your galaxy and still unknown to you, will change the course of your life forever."

I start clapping, realize he's not finished, force my hands from clapping more.

He stops, gathers himself, proceeds with a melancholic leap. "People who have moved on—the absent hearts—cause an aching hole in your heart, an emptiness that you don't always fill so wisely."

I'm not sure why he's looking at me that way.

"A truer picture of your heart's connections would show a mosaic of hearts, each with varying degrees of purity and tarnish, right? Consider how those with selfish aims, or desires to dominate your will, crash against you, sowing discord and tumult; they pull and press upon you, shaping your responses. There are those who oscillate between being your solace and your sorrow, nourishing you while piercing you, the very same individuals capable of inflicting hurt and bestowing kindness upon you in a single breath."

Jesus walks around the open space with his hands on his hips, evidently upset by what he is trying to convey to me. I feel overwhelmed from so much revelation—and by never, ever imagining Jesus performing so theatrically. I've hardly ever thought of these things, people crashing into me, colliding around me, disturbing my peaceful existence. Things are crawling up from the depths, things I haven't wanted to look at: the worms. I sit down in the dust of the galaxy of my life, feeling drained.

Jesus, sweaty, plops himself in the dust beside me, looks at my rock, then looks up toward the sky.

"Do you know what's up there?" he asks, pointing toward the heavens. I don't see a thing. He can't use cloud formations as some sort of Rorschach test, because the sky is as clear and blue as can be.

"What did you see last night, when we gazed at this very same sky?"

"Stars, maybe? I don't know."

He pops up like a squirrel. "Do you know what I saw in the sky last night? Galaxies! Galaxies of universes and universes of galaxies! And they're up there right now, whether you can see them, or not! Get out your Bible, quick!"

"Now? I can barely think—"

"Look up Paul's letter to my church at Colossi—Colossians. Chapter 1. It's just after Philippians, just before the letters to the Thessalonians."

"I got it, I got it."

"Start at verse 16. No, verse 15. Go ahead." He's looking at me expectantly.

"'The Son is the image of the invisible God, the firstborn over all creation.'"

I stop. Something freezes up in me. He's still looking at me. I look at my Bible, find my place.

"'For in him all things were created: things in heaven and on earth, visible and invisible, whether thrones or powers or rulers or authorities; all things have been created through him and for him.'"

My throat feels dry. I feel very unsure of myself, but he wants me to continue.

"'He is before all things, and'—"

"'—and in him all things hold together.'" We finish the verse together.

I look up at him, then look down at my feet. I'm feeling very overwhelmed.

"So, Kenny. We're talking about galaxies and galaxies and *galaxies* out there! You would not believe the joy I've had expressing myself, speaking my creation into existence. Everything is twirling and swirling and whirling around and about and in and through and up and down and all around at this very moment—*and I'm holding it all together!*"

If this person is who this person is, if I look at him I'll turn into a pillar of salt. I better hide my face in my hands.

"Pillar of salt? Kenny, no! You're missing the point entirely! Now, look at me. If I know what's happening inside every one of those galaxies that your eyes cannot see (and in every galaxy the greatest telescopes are nowhere near detecting), how much more do I know everything about your heart galaxy—your heart of hearts! As I'm holding the universe together, I hold you together, even when you think your life is spinning out of control."

He disappears down the path toward the picnic table, comes back carrying a tray with glasses and a pitcher of ice water—and ice cream sandwiches! Which is good because I was starting to feel a bit peckish.

* * *

He's the kind of guy who licks all the edges of an ice-cream sandwich to the point where the cookie layers nearly fall into themselves. He looks out over my heart galaxy; my rock and me are still in the middle of it all. Humming lightly while finishing his sandwich, he drags one foot through the dirt, making lines that radiate out from where I'm sitting, lines that are more-or-less perpendicular to the various arms of my galaxy, joining them together.

I feel the way I do when I've witnessed a magic trick, like my brain's been turned inside-out, because the diagram of my heart galaxy has been turned into a gigantic city map, like the ones I've seen of Paris! I'm sort of sitting where the Arc De Triomphe would be.

He gobbles up the last of the soggy chocolate-cookie layer bits of his ice cream sandwich and licks his fingers.

"Since I know precisely what has happened inside your heart galaxy and you pretty much haven't the faintest idea, as a way of helping you I've placed four kinds of guideposts along your path, to increase your awareness of what's going on inside you. Now listen carefully," he says while absentmindedly wiping his sticky fingers on his tunic.

"One of the guideposts is a memory that intrudes upon your peace at the most unexpected times. It's like an uninvited guest in the midst of a happy moment, a memory you might dismiss as trivial or inconsequential. Yet, this memory could point to a past trauma, no matter how slight, tethering you to an event or individual that has left you bound, or scarred."

This thought jerks me into shadowed corners of my mind. I resurface quickly, pulled back by melting ice cream dribbling down my arm. I hastily lick it away.

"Another guidepost emerges in day-to-day life, when you find yourself overreacting in ways that seem childish or irrational to ordinary situations. Such responses might reveal areas in your life where emotional growth has been arrested, often due to some sort of abuse or neglect—or pride, or unteachability on your part."

I'm not sure what he means by pride or unteachability, but reflecting on recent interactions—with the kids, wife, boss, cashier—my actions have been far from mature.

"Then there are the tempests, the sudden squalls that lay bare the foundation of your character. They challenge how you handle life's upheavals, your thoughts about yourself and others, and where you seek refuge during the storm."

I avert my gaze, my cheeks warming with the admission. I know what he's talking about, even without him saying it.

He pauses before introducing the fourth guidepost, but I think I see where this is leading. I pull myself up off the ground to make my escape. I've had enough of this.

He gently catches my arm and guides me toward him, despite my reluctance.

"Yes, pain," he continues, "it uncovers the wounds within you, the origins of your suffering, and identifies who or what may have inflicted these wounds."

His hand reaches for my chest, to the place where it aches. Memories scatter like shards of broken glass; my heart races.

"But that thing that happened to me when I was a child—it couldn't have been so serious, could it?"

"If it wasn't so serious, why does its sting linger, my dear Kenny?"

7

HEART TRUTHS

He calls them 'guideposts'. I call them 'instruments of torture'.

"It is almost time for dinner," he says, which cheers me up a bit. "Before we eat, though, I have a gift for you." He pulls something out of his pocket and places it in my hand. "It is a compass, to help guide you on your journey."

I learned orienteering in Cub Scouts, locating my specific position in the greater world, but I smile and nod. He gives me a knowing look in return.

"When you come across one of the four guideposts that identifies a heart relationship, this compass will help you know if the relationship has led you in the right direction, or not. If someone has blown your life off course, this compass will also help you get your bearings and then get you going in the right direction."

I look at him, take the compass and hold it up to the sunlight. There's something peculiar about the face of the compass. It changes when I tilt it, exposing a different image underneath, like one of those toys that came in a cereal box when I was a kid. Hmmm. Under the E appears an S, and under the S appears a D, and under the W is a B, while under the N is an H!

"And you want me to guide my life by this thing?"

"As we take a look at your life on this journey, we'll be looking for four truths: the subjective truth, the dark truth, the broad truth, and the high truth."

Taking the compass from my hand he squats down on the side of the trail and motions for me to do the same. The ground under the foliage is moist with early-evening dew. A ladybug is waddling on a blade of grass. In this Shimmering place, even the ladybug and blade of grass are intensified, sharp in detail. I never realized how interesting a ladybug spot could be—

"Now, look here," he says, pulling my attention toward the compass.

"Okay, okay, I'm listening."

He points to the S which is inconveniently located under E for east. "The subjective truth, or an emotional response you've had to something that happened to you, distorts your perception of what really happened, which veers your path away from the real truth."

Look what happens to this row of ants when I block their path with this twig!

"Now, look *here*," he persists, tapping on the D underneath south. "When truth is allowed to deteriorate, it becomes a dark truth, or a lie that has become your truth. Guiding your life by dark truths has caused your life to 'go south,'" he smiles, obviously pleased with his pun.

"Now, the B stands for the broad truth. It offers a wider perspective, helping to counteract subjective truths and expose the lies that lie at the heart of dark truths. In short, broad truths help in forgiving yourself and others."

He completely loses me on that one.

He stands and pulls me up with him, probably to get me away from my little distractions.

"Now, the H here, underneath N for north, this is the most significant truth of all. This is the high truth, which is my Word, your True North. Following what I have to say to you, through my Word and by my Spirit, over time, transforms you to become more like me and more into whom I intend you to be."

"You make it sound so easy." I feel suddenly very tired. All this talk about heart truths and such.

"Yes, that is a good name for them. Heart Truths! One of the most difficult and daring things to do in life is to face the pain dwelling in your own heart. Let's get cleaned up for dinner."

I concur, after looking at his ice cream sandwich-stained, dirt-encrusted tunic, and all the dust clinging to my skin from sitting in the dirt of my life all afternoon. Towels and a clean set of clothes have been set out for us on the wooden bench. We skirt around my heart galaxy, or Paris, whatever, and head through the bushes toward the stream. He talks as we go.

"So, an emotional reaction turns the truth of a situation into something skewed, not fully based on fact, a subjective truth. This turns you inward, often toward self-pity or self-absorption. It holds you emotionally tied to the person or situation, which in turn stunts your emotional growth, at least to some degree."

We break through the greenery and find the stream flowing lazily, shimmering in early evening sunlight. We walk upstream a bit, into the sun, beyond where I'd jumped in to try to save his life. The footbridge is also alit in light. I can see how each stone has been carefully chosen, chiseled, and honed to fit perfectly without mortar with each adjacent stone, creating one, perfect, graceful arch. I could look at its beauty my entire life.

He hangs our towels on a tree branch reaching over the water, and places our clothes on a large flat stone by the water's edge. He walks up to me. "This is my intention for my church," he says, admiring the stone bridge, "and why I work so intentionally on the hearts of my people." He jumps into the water. "Come on in, the water's fine!"

The air is almost hot now. Just beyond, the stream flows; here, waters gather into a deep, still pool. The reflection of the trees upon the pool's surface, the quietness of our surroundings, the beauty of this place is almost too much to take in. He's busy washing himself with a bar of soap; I climb into the pool and wade in the water.

The surface water is warm and pleasant, though the current runs cold around my feet. Something about this place, I don't know, it's bringing something up to the surface of my heart. Vestiges of a memory are making me feel insecure, and small. I put my head under the water, and let out a cry of sorrow. I resurface, wipe my eyes. He's wading near me, not intentionally splashing me. For the first time in a very long while, I feel safe. He hands me the bar of soap.

"Thanks," I say. Is there a guidepost hidden somewhere near this pool?

Without his tunic his upper body is nearly as pale as mine, though not quite as neon. I hand him back the soap. As he washes his hair I notice a deep, rough scar in his side, between his ribs. I've seen this scar portrayed in oil by the Masters; seeing it so up close, so vivid in fleshy detail—I quickly look away.

"Dark truths, or lies that have become true to you, are often formed in the darkest, most secret moments of your life," he says while working suds into his thick hair. "Dark truths hold you captive to your pain, lie to you about your worth, blind you from seeing yourself as I see you. They cast shade on my character, making you doubt my goodness. In the end the last person you think to call on, is me."

Around us the air is mellowing.

Birdsong quietens in response to cicadas' tympanic crescendo, drawing Day toward dream-filled slumber.

Something slimy just swam between my legs! I wiggle and yelp. It's a big old carp, moving lazily in the darker waters flowing near the riverbed.

"In the waters of dark truths, your worms thrive," he says, then wiggles and jumps as the fish weaves through his own legs, lightening the mood. He grabs one of the towels hanging over our heads, wraps it around himself and jumps out of the water.

"Now the broad truths," he says while wringing water out of his hair, "they correct your course, improve your view, reveal a better path for you to take, which is the path toward forgiveness." Forgiveness again. I grab the other towel off the branch as he gets dressed.

"High truths get you going, and then keep you going, in the right direction, toward my heart." He gathers up our dirty clothes. "I'll leave you in peace so you can get dressed. I'll meet you by the picnic table. And don't dilly-dally, as your mother used to say, you'll not want to miss *this* meal," he yells, "probably the best pizza west of the Mississippi—Imo's Pizza! If the Mississippi is still there!" His voice trails off as he disappears into the woods.

The sun dips below the tree line and my lips begin to quiver; he's left me alone with my thoughts. I remember Jessica, when she was little, how her lips turned blue and shivered just like this after swimming in the lake, and I'd warm her up with a towel. There was a time when she still wanted me to hold her.

In the receding light, the green hues of the woods mellow to muted shades of sage. Yet in this Shimmering place even the color sage is brilliant, with every detail of every leaf and blade of grass pronounced in wondrous contrast.

And now I know why I'm feeling blue.

That evening long ago, after playing what would be the very last little league baseball game I'd ever play, I rode my bike to the river. That evening, the woods were dressed in such a light. I had no idea then what would then transpire.

PART THREE

Going Deep

8

THE PLAYGROUND OF SHAME

"Now, before we head out this morning, to get you going in the right direction, find your Bible and turn to Paul's letter to my church in Ephesus." We make an odd-looking set of Bobbsey Twins, me lanky and ginger, he stocky and dark, in our matching cargo pants, blue plaid shirts, and hiking boots.

"Let's see here…Romans, Corinthians, Galatians, Ephesians. There."

"Yes, Then start at Chapter 1, verse 18."

"Okay, I got it. 'I pray that the eyes of your heart may be enlightened in order that you may know the hope to which he has called you, the riches of his glorious inheritance in his holy people, and his incomparably great power for us who believe. That power is the same as the mighty strength he exerted when he raised Christ from the dead and seated him at his right hand in the heavenly realms…'"

"Touch my wound, here," he says, showing me his wrist.

"You're not serious." He nods to me with raised eyebrows, looking at his wrist then looking at me. "Go on, I won't bite."

Like the wound in his side, this wound, though healed, is jagged, revealing the pain he endured. I tepidly touch it, though do so only because he's asked me to. His flesh is left with a brief white imprint of my finger. I just hope he doesn't ask me to put my fingers into his side like he did Thomas.

"Remember that I was not only brutally tortured before being nailed to the cross, but after I hung there, and then died, I was in the grave for three days. You can imagine the condition my body was in."

I do not want to imagine the condition his body was in.

"You can see the condition my body is in now, though. Not bad, eh?"

He makes me smile. "Not bad, no."

"So, my dear Kenneth, the power that my Father used to change this bag of flesh from a pretty miserable state into an obviously good state, is the very same power he uses to raise the decaying and stinky areas of your heart into things of vibrancy and joy, to the praise of his glory. Now turn to Paul's letter to my church in Philippi, Chapter 2, verses 12 and 13—it's just after Ephesians."

"I know where it's at," I say, smugly. I'm not *so* biblically illiterate. "'Therefore, my dear friends, as you have always obeyed—not only in my presence, but now much more in my absence—continue to work out your salvation with fear and trembling, for it is God who works in you to will and to act in order to fulfill his good purpose.'"

"What does that speak to you?"

"I guess it means that I have a part to play in this heart-changing business. Through obedience." I grimace. I've always had an aversion to that word.

"Yes, but for a purpose. My Father is sanctifying you—transforming you into who he intends you to be, as you yield to him—for you to accomplish great things for him in his Kingdom. Think, the best is yet to come!"

But through obedience?

"Read the next verse. Verse 14."

"'Do everything without grumbling or arguing.'"

Sheesh.

★ ★ ★

The trail, bathed in bright mid-morning light, leads us directly north through the meadow. The granite rockface imposingly rises far off in the distance. Life and color envelop us from both sides of the trail. We stop for something to eat. Jesus conjures up, as if out of thin air, homemade chocolate chip cookies as big and round and chewy as any I've ever had the pleasure of eating, complemented with cold, fresh milk. It wouldn't surprise me if he has a mini fridge in that backpack of his. My dietician wife would have a conniption fit if she saw me eating these cookies.

"I agree with your wife; however, when things are tough, it's good to have some comfort. Put that last cookie back," he slaps at my hand.

"Then why did you put so many cookies out, then?"

The trail winds through the meadow, a tapestry of wildflowers in a myriad shades of light and splendor. With cupped hands we gently catch butterflies, marveling at the wonder of each one. He leads me to a stream, the water cool and inviting. I hadn't realized how thirsty I was until now—I'm pretty sure this is the same stream that flows behind the trysting place—.

"Be still for a moment," he says, suddenly.

"What are you doing? I almost ran into you!"

"Hush," he says, and closes his eyes. His face is bathed in peace, as if he is here, but not here, resting in a different place altogether.

I always find it challenging to quieten myself. I mean, I can, if life and limb depend on it. But quietness intrudes upon the chaos of my brain, and I like chaos. Chaos camouflages things inside, things that I don't always want to think about. Too much quiet inevitably leads to my eyes tearing-up, and I don't like it when that happens. It doesn't look like he's going anywhere anytime soon so I might as well do what he's doing and close my eyes, though I really don't want to.

Warmth and coolness play upon my skin as sun and shade dance among the leaves above my head.

The air is laden with the scent of honeysuckle. Wind undulates the tall grasses in the meadow. He's still standing there, eyes closed, listening, as if he's imbued with the essence of joy.

I hear it now, rising from the gurglings of the stream.

"Trust in him–trust in him–trust in him–trust in him."

I open my eyes.

"Trust in me," he says, looking at me. "Trust in me, as you boldly enter into the deepest recesses of your heart."

I nod, basking in this one, eternal moment that quietens my chaos and woos my heart from the shadows.

Placing an arm around my shoulder, he guides me in the direction that we must go.

✶ ✶ ✶

The further north we hike the taller the meadow grass grows, until we find ourselves wading through a field where stalks of corn stand tall and green, exuding the freshness of a farm. Cornfields! One of the best things about growing up in the Midwest.

The long rows of corn stretch far to my right and left, a library of endless shelves of green books.

I should write that one down. Or maybe not.

I'm getting the feeling that a storm is brewing, but there is nary a cloud in the sky. Maybe I'm coming down with something. Maybe I shouldn't have eaten the last couple of cookies.

"Jesus, can we slow down? I'm not feeling so well. Maybe we should turn around, go back to the trysting place."

He keeps walking.

"Jesus, wait up—I know you're new to these parts, but trust me, someone who's nearly grown up his whole life in the Midwest like me has a sense about when a storm's about to hit, even when the sky is as it is today. Which means it's time to high-tail it out of here and find the nearest storm cellar!"

But he keeps going. "Jesus, why aren't you listening to me?" We're obviously going in the wrong direction! If it is the right direction, then why am I feeling so incredibly off-course? It feels like we're approaching a place I've encountered before but would prefer not to return to, thank you very much. And now the cornstalks are receding and the earthen path is yielding to asphalt, and the summer breeze is deferring to a sound that makes my heart sink: the ping-ping-ping of a rubber gym ball being passed around in a game of foursquare. I'm taken straight back to my school days playing on the playground and I don't want to go back to my school playground and I hear kids ahead, laughing and playing and scuffling and I'm feeling very, very wary and one of the worms in my backpack is having a conniption fit.

We step onto the blacktop.

A whistle pierces the air. My fifth-grade gym teacher blowing his whistle is walking straight toward me. He angrily throws a rubber gym ball at me. It stings. The sting of humiliation pierces as the crowd laughs and points at me from bleachers towering like skyscrapers on the world's largest playground.

"The Playground of Shame," says Jesus above the roar of laughter.

The laughter continues mocking me. My stomach churns.

"What are you feeling deep inside you?" Jesus asks.

My mind is blank, my mouth, dry. I look at all these faces, judging me, taunting me. Words bubble up from the pit of my gut.

"I'm not who they say I should be
I am who they say I shouldn't be
I'm not allowed to be who I am.

In a sea of shoulds and shouldn'ts,
I sink, I drown, I die
To whom I am truly meant to be."

I feel utterly drained; every ounce of strength in me is gone. Jesus places an arm around me, a lifeline in a sea of shame. His eyes reflect deep sorrow. As he looks out over the vast expanse of faces, the crowd falls silent.
"Does anyone else have something to share with us?" he asks. A young man steps out of the throng, looking lost.

"What if I
    Say the wrong thing or
    Do the wrong thing or
    Don't dress right or
    Don't act right or
    Don't look right
    To be loved?"

Far, far back in the crowd, a young girl stands up. A spotlight falls upon her from above; everyone turns toward her. She's so far back I shouldn't be able to hear her, but I do, we all do:

"My mother is a famous model—you all know who she is. But I take after my father. And well, you know who he is, too: 'the world's greatest quarterback.'" The crowd is stunned by the implications of being so close to greatness. The young girl continues.

"The women on my father's side are big like he is, big-boned, flat-chested, lovely in their own way, but not in the way my mother is because my mother is perfect. For my last birthday she bought me lip injections and breast implants, then sent me off to a fat farm—and I'd just turned thirteen! I do everything I can to look like her, but everybody can see that I don't, and never will." She weeps bitterly.

Jesus is looking at her, visibly shaken. He's holding around himself.

The girl returns to her seat as the spotlight moves to a high school athlete many rows below her. The young man stands, trying to keep his composure, but breaks. "No matter how much I train, I'm never as strong or fast as my coach wants me to be," he says, wiping his face with a varsity jacket sleeve. "So, I arrive at the sports field at five in the morning, start my routine of running up and down the bleacher steps. I think, 'just one more round, twelve more rounds in the same amount of time, fifty more, and then he'll see how much I've improved.' But he never does. I don't know how much is enough, I don't know how to stop. I could run up and down all *these* steps a thousand times and it wouldn't be enough for my coach. I can't stop. He only says to me, "You better hit the weights harder after school, pal." The young man surveys the height of these bleachers, and bolts up the steps—

"Stop!" shouts Jesus. The entire audience falls silent.

The young man stops. He hangs his head, then looks at Jesus. Jesus looks deeply into his eyes, and says, "Come to me, all you who are weary and burdened, and I will give you rest. Take my yoke upon you and learn from me, for I am gentle and humble in heart, and you will find rest for your souls. For my yoke is easy and my burden is light."

The young man finds his seat and buries his face in his hands.

The spotlight shoots far to the left as a teenaged girl stands to her feet.

"My parents have divorced. They're lost in their own worlds. I found another world, a dark world. In that world we see each other, encourage one another. We watch each other's live streams as we push ourselves to the edge of death. But now they mock me, they say that I'm not taking big enough risks. Some never return from the edge. I don't want to be one of them! I don't know what to do," she cries, sorrowfully.

Jesus is in agony, pacing back and forth.

A young man, hidden beneath a hoodie, steps forward hesitantly. "I've tried so hard to fit in, even swiped the coolest shoes, but I'm still not accepted into the group," he confesses.

An albino man stands, speaks: "They look. They point. They whisper. Every eye is on me when I walk into a room. Or worse: *No one* looks at me when I walk into a room. I'm a nothing, a void, a nada. A zero. I'm different from them. And different must be bad."

Another teenaged girl: "Taunts in the school yard: The jacket my mother worked so hard to pay for, that she wrapped in lovely paper and tied so carefully with a bow, she handed to me with such joy in her eyes—that jacket turned out to be *so last year.*"

A stylish woman, she looks familiar, famous! She says, "I want to crawl under a rug, get out of the picture, get out of the limelight, disappear forever. I want to get away from their stares, their sneers, their cameras. How did they find that picture of me when I was so young, so broke, so desperate, so stupid?"

A man, Asian, says: "My father, with lowered brow, glances nervously toward his father who, sitting in the place of honor at the end of the table, terse and silent, looks at the leaves swirling in his tea bowl but not looking at me, I, who did not pass my medical exams, I who will not become the doctor my father was, and his father, and his father before him. I feel the eyes of a thousand generations upon me, reminding me that I bear upon my shoulders the dishonor of my family name."

Across the playground a million heads nod in silent unison.

"And then there is the real nasty stuff." It is Jesus; he paces the inner circle of the crowd, speaking to all of us, his body a bundle of raw compassion.

"Bullying is like a grim game of darts. The winner is the one who comes closest to piercing the heart. And the winner takes it all.

"Yet bullying is no game to the one whose heart is the target.

"You jab, you spit, you punch—with words, with fists, with tweets. Hiding like cowards behind your numbers, your size, your screens, you do your doxxing, do your cancelling, make others feel like they're the cowards."

He sets himself on a school bench, elbows on knees; the throng pulls closer, hanging on his every word.

"It is worse when you're bullied by someone you're open to—your big brother or the guy you look up to at school. It is easier for such people to find the soft underbelly of your heart."

A little girl steps forward, her voice soft but clear. "Jesus, my group of friends suddenly turned on me for some small thing, freezing me out. I've been banished. I'm no longer on the inside but looking in from the outside, from the loneliness of another lunch table." She runs up to Jesus who welcomes her into his arms.

The playground has fallen silent; something has touched a chord in both bully and bullied alike. Whimpering and weeping break out over the throng of school children, both past and present. Maybe we're all bullies at some point in our lives, I think.

"Then there is sarcasm," Jesus continues.

"Sarcasm is a solution of two percent truth to 98 percent humor, that works like acid on a heart wound, so that it is never allowed to heal."

He pauses, then says: "Sarcasm is 'The Happy Face of Shame': I'm the Big Family Joke! 'Remember the time when he…' and everyone at the family barbecue breaks out into a collective roar of laughter. You find yourself laughing with them, as you always do, at something that happened years ago, one of the most humiliating moments of your life. If you mention that you don't really want to hear about it anymore or make a well-rehearsed funny rebuttal in your defense, you're told you're being overly sensitive. 'Lighten up, wouldja!' The tone at the family gathering changes, turns cold, which they blame on you."

The playground transforms into the world's largest collection of weeping people. The sorrow is disheartening.

Jesus writes something on a piece of paper and hands it to me. "Quick Kenny. Read these verses." I fish my Bible out of my backpack, find the first verse, hesitate, then stand and clear my throat. I've never had so many eyes looking at me in all my life.

JOURNEY INTO THE SHIMMERING

"A reading from the Gospel of Luke, Chapter 6, verses 27 to 28: 'But to you who are listening I say: Love your enemies, do good to those who hate you, bless those who curse you, pray for those who mistreat you.'"

Silence sweeps across the vast expanse of the bleachers; they are listening to the Word of God.

"Good work," say Jesus to me. "Now read the next verse I wrote on the paper."

Emboldened, I find my reading-aloud voice. "A reading from the letter of Saint Paul to the Church in Rome, Chapter 12, verse 19: 'Do not take revenge, my dear friends, but leave room for God's wrath, for it is written: "It is mine to avenge; I will repay," says the Lord.' This is the Word of the Lord!"

I bow. The school children are hanging on my every word! I begin looking up the next passage, in Isaiah 61. He stops me with his hand.

"No, Kenny. That was fine, thanks."

"Are you sure?"

"No, that will do."

He must've memorized the verse ahead of time because he doesn't need a Bible—pretty impressive. He begins:

> *"The Spirit of the Sovereign Lord is on me*
>   *because the Lord has anointed me*
>   *to proclaim good news to the poor.*
> *He has sent me to bind up the brokenhearted,*
>   *to proclaim freedom for the captives*
>   *and release from darkness for the prisoners,*
> *to proclaim the year of the Lord's favor*
>   *and the day of vengeance of our God,*
> *to comfort all who mourn,*
> *and provide for those who grieve in Zion—*
> *to bestow on them a crown of beauty*
>   *instead of ashes,*

the oil of joy
 instead of mourning,
and a garment of praise
 instead of a spirit of despair."

He looks lovingly across the vast collection of people collectively wiping away tears.

"This is who I am. This is my heart for you. And this is what I will do in a heart yielded to my tender mercies."

The school bell rings; the crowd begins to walk off the playground, arm in arm.

9

THE CHURCH BAZAAR OF REJECTION

The playground is now empty apart from Jesus and me. Listening to all those stories of shame was overwhelming. He hands me a tissue for my sniffling nose.

"How do you handle it all? I mean, you see these things happening all the time all over the world."

"And throughout history," he adds. He motions toward a weathered bench under a sprawling oak tree, its branches offering cool shade from the afternoon heat. "Come sit," he says. He removes his backpack and motions for me to do the same. I let out a post-crying sigh. My finger traces the initials and arrow-hearts and childish expletives carved by school children through the years. He produces two metal lunch boxes from his backpack and hands one to me. Inside the box is a peanut butter and jelly sandwich on white bread, a bag of potato chips, an apple, a sugar cookie, and a carton of milk—just like Mom made me when I was a kid. I feel like my legs should be dangling beneath the table like a little boy—like Kyle the other morning. Sniffling, I bite into the billowy white softness of my sandwich, the familiar taste of peanut butter and jelly bringing back a flood of childhood memories.

"I hated playgrounds as a kid," I mutter. "I still don't understand what I did to tick-off my gym teacher." Jesus doesn't seem to be as enthusiastic about his sandwich as I am.

In fifth-grade gym class, the day when my teacher became angry with me. If I'm completely honest with myself, I was being a bit of a clown, the way I wrapped myself up in a volleyball net, rolled on the floor, acted goofy….

"I think I just realized something," I say.

Jesus smiles. "You weren't always the perfect little angel in gym class?"

"Maybe I acted up a bit, looking for attention."

"New school, no friends. Being the class clown helped you cope."

"But still, he should've been the grown-up in the room!" I say this with righteous indignation.

"Yes. But can you forgive him? More importantly, can you forgive yourself?"

"I'll think about it," I say, avoiding his gaze. I glance at the playground, feeling a strange mix of nostalgia and dread.

He rustles around in his backpack and pulls out a gift, wrapped in rustic paper, tied up with string. "Here. This is for you." He hands it to me. I look at him.

"Open it!" he says spryly, brushing away crumbs from our lunch.

Inside is a blue Naugahyde pencil case, brand new, like the one Mom gave me on my first day of school! Inside it are lovely colors and pens and pencils and an eraser, all in perfect condition. I'm struck with boy-like wonder, even at my age. There is a moment of appreciative silence between us.

A memory bomb invades my consciousness. This must be one of those guideposts.

"Jesus, what is this?"

"I would like you to write down this memory, and what you are now feeling."

"But what does this memory have to do with what you've been talking about—what does it have to do with shame?"

He hands me a lovely leather-bound notebook. It has gilded edges.

"Is this for me?"

He nods his head, enjoying my appreciation. I've never owned anything this beautiful. Maybe the words I will fill it with will be just as precious.

"You want me to get these thoughts out of my head, this memory out of my heart?"

He nods again, with glee.

I open to the first pristine page—for me, a moment of awe—and begin.

> We were at a church bazaar, with rides and raffles and refreshments. I had been off playing with some other boys when I wanted to buy a treat at one of the food stalls. I went looking for my father and was happy to find him standing in the crowd. I ran up to greet him. He was in the middle of a conversation with another man.
>
> "Look at him yourself," my father was saying, turning his head toward me, "he's nothing but skin and bones."

It may not be as eloquent as Bunyan in *The Pilgrim's Progress*, but it's my story.

> My father made many remarks that day, but that one, brief comment struck my six-year-old heart with an unforgettable impact. I believed he was expressing disappointment in me, as if there was something inherently wrong with my body, something flawed in my identity as a boy. I found myself questioning why I couldn't align with my father's expectations. Why wasn't I athletic like

THE CHURCH BAZAAR OF REJECTION

him? I lamented my asthma, which felt like a burden. I envied the boys who ran swiftly and hit a baseball with ease, thinking that if I were more like them, perhaps my father would give me the love I yearned for.

I feel a dark truth coming up to the surface.

"Bring it into my light. What has the darkness been saying to you?"

I'm struggling to put words to what I'm feeling, as usual. Jesus is looking off into the distance, not in a hurry, giving me space. I write in my notebook:

That my body is rejectable.

"Which isn't true, is it?"

"So, Jesus, why did this memory pop up just now?"

"Why do you think?"

I hate it when people answer a question with a question. I'll just keep writing in my notebook, then.

I can see how this misinterpreted belief has woven its way into every thought I have about myself. It's grown within me as I've grown into a man, shaming me. I started believing, still believe, that anyone who is more athletic, or better-looking, or comes from that neighborhood or from that family or has that skin tone or has that degree or pedigree or recognition, is more lovable than me, that God loves him more than me. It's become true for me, a dark truth that feeds like a worm upon my heart, a self-inflicted shame.

I slam down my pencil. "Why, Jesus, did you make others easier for you to love, than me?" I know that this can't be true. But it *feels* true. I don't even need that crazy compass to recognize this as a subjective truth.

"I believe that God—that you love me, yes, but only out of obligation, not out of genuine desire. I feel like someone you merely tolerate, perhaps even now."

With the crook of my arm I hide what I'm about to write because I don't want him to see it just yet:

> *How many times have I shaken my fist in anger at the God who, yes, took care in weaving me in my mother's womb, but who seemed to take greater care in weaving others? God must love them more than he loves me. God must be more pleased with those people than he is with me. I've ended up despising God and consumed with despising myself.*

Jesus, not seeing what I've written, looks at me, pained. I close my notebook in a huff and hug it to myself.

The air is heavy with the smell of hot asphalt as the playground turns into a black goo under the afternoon sun. I'm feeling gruff and irritated. At him. He gets up from the picnic table and motions me to sit with him beneath the tall oak tree. I begrudgingly follow him. He props himself against the tree trunk. "Here, lay yourself down next to me. Use my backpack as a pillow." His backpack doesn't have any disturbing worms in it, which is probably why he wants me to use his as a pillow, and not mine. Making sure my notebook won't get dirty, I awkwardly make myself comfortable in the grass beneath the tree, fully aware that ants have a particular affinity to tree trunks.

He asks, "Might there be a connection between how you thought your own father looked upon you, and how you think I look at you?"

* * *

Everything swirls around me in a feverish dervish. I feel like I'm on a nauseating circus ride, spinning uncontrollably in a giant centrifuge. I grip the ground to keep me from flying off into orbit.

"Where am I, now, to you, Kenny?"

"I see you here, now, of course."

"And what else?" he asks. He's chewing on a blade of grass while my entire life spins out of control. He's touching the pain in my heart without even lifting a finger. The then me and the now me are swirling together.

"I see, I feel … I think I see where I am in the now and where I am in the then."

"Very good," he says encouragingly.

"Jesus, I'm in some nameless, lonely place."

"I am with you. Yes, I see you, little boy, standing before your father."

"I'm back in that moment, standing before my father, waiting for something…anything."

"Yes, you are wanting some coins from him for an ice cream."

"Yes, that too, but not quite. Or maybe more." My heart is open. There is something deeper I'm trying to put my finger on. It hits me: "I'm waiting for my father to see me. To affirm me."

"Yes. What happens instead? What do you feel instead, Kenny?"

"I hear my father speak about me to his friend."

"And what are those words?" I feel a dam is about to break and flood my lies toward an ocean of lies.

"He says, 'You can see that he is nothing but skin and bones.'"

"And you are feeling?"

"I can still feel the shame, it sits on my chest like a weight I can't shake."

"And deeper still?"

I stop, tremble, and say, "Rejected."

I watch as the ground cracks open just behind my little-me feet. A black goo, not unlike the asphalt melting under the sun beyond the picnic table, rises through the crack and forms into a pool above the ground. A bubble, viscous, bulges out of the black pool like crude oil. The bubble bursts like a carbuncle! And now—this is really rank—the black goo splats and attaches itself to the base of my little-me neck! It begins feeding on my self-worth like a parasite; it steadily winds itself around my little-me heart. No one sees this happen to me, not my father, not even my little-me me.

I watch as, through the years, the boy within me transforms into the man I've become, the black, sticky string still wound around me, binding me, limiting my movements and growth, influencing my reactions, responses, and identity, initiating the spawning of several of my worms.

How did this sticky mess cling to me if my father never truly rejected me? I don't understand.

"A child does what it can to bring meaning to the adult world around it. It was natural for you to interpret your father's words as having something to do with you—"

"Subjective truths—"

"Yes, when much of what happened in your family had little to do with you, at least directly—"

"The broad truths—"

"Which formed the way you saw yourself and viewed the world around you—"

"The dark truths—"

"Yes, the dark truths."

A summer breeze carries the scent of newness and growth.

Have I really become so broken? "Can you set me free from these bonds, please, Jesus?"

★ ★ ★

The velvety night hums with the rhythmic chorus of contented crickets.

Not a bad description of the evening.

"So, Jesus, what do I do?"

"What have you learned this far?" His eyes reflect the light of a million swirling galaxies.

I fish the compass out of my front pocket, roll it between my fingers. The face of the compass is aglow like a nightlight by the shimmering moon.

"That I was very sick as a boy, and very skinny." The compass needle points to B, a broad truth.

"What else?"

The needle points to the S, a subjective truth: "I must have had a layer of self-doubt that triggered a childish response—"

"—Or a childlike reaction," he inserts.

"Yes, to my father's words. I must've already been questioning my father's love for me and what he thought of me. My father was speaking to a friend. He had every right to discuss his concerns about my health with someone he knew, which might indicate that he genuinely cared for me." And after all, I'm the one who approached them and interrupted their conversation. I keep this revelation to myself, the compass driving hard toward the B. A broad truth.

"Anything else?"

The compass needle jerks south, to the D. A stupid dark truth: "That I let an emotional reaction to one single sentence expressed by my father to another man, maim the course of my life."

My vulnerable, broken six-year-old heart. I'm the one who rejected me. And I rejected my father for rejecting me, when in fact he never had.

"Jesus, I'm sorry for messing things up when I was a kid."

"Oh, if it were only so simple," says Jesus with a sigh, his eyes reflecting a deep well of compassion and understanding. He then says, "Forgive yourself."

"Is that all?"

"It's a start. We'll nurture your heart with my high truths for the next fifty years or so."

I pray silently, asking for forgiveness.

Snip. Snip. Snip.

A particularly unruly worm in my backpack has calmed down considerably, as if acknowledging the light of truth seeping into the dark corners of my soul.

"And what do I do with these worms?"

"As you feed on the high truths of my Word, over time your identity will be less grounded in what others say about you, and more in who I say you are. You'll find yourself responding more readily from a place of wholeness and strength, rather than reacting from a place of insecurity and shame. Shame is a superfood for worms, used by the enemy of your soul to blind you from your true identity in me. There is no-one more threatening to the kingdom of darkness than children of God who know who they are, and the authority they have in me."

"So, my worms won't be shriveling up and dying anytime soon, you're saying."

"Perfect analogy! Your worms shrivel as you live in the sunlight of my Word, though they do have a remarkable ability to rehydrate themselves. Some of them, however, may leave you completely."

A rather unpleasant thought.

"When a worm of shame rehydrates—when you find yourself tempted to believe a lie about yourself—bring it into the light of my Word—trust me, nothing shocks me. As you rest in me, I will ply my truths to your heart as you listen to my heartbeat for you."

"So, it's no more complicated than that." I'm being facetious.

"I wish it were always as uncomplicated as that, Kenneth."

10

THE BRIDGE OF TRUST

The air is moist with morning dew, and so is my pillow. I really should get up but all I want to do is hide under my blankets. I'm feeling a bit vulnerable for some reason.

He bends down and scuffles my hair. "You've gone through some healing. Give yourself time to recuperate. Here, this might help." I scoot myself up as he hands me a brown-glazed mug of hot cocoa with melting mini marshmallows swimming on the surface. He sets himself down, places a breakfast bagel next to my pillow: lox with cream cheese. He takes a bite of his own.

The little clearing is encircled with pink-blossoming dogwood, glistening in the dew.

There! A doe! And there! Her fawn—I almost didn't see it, its speckles blending with the speckling sun. Both mother and child quietly sip from a pool of water beneath the dogwoods. They look up; Jesus bows, they bow their heads in return. Mother and child disappear into the silent woods.

He gazes toward the eastern mountains hidden behind cotton-candy clouds. "Before we set off, let's recite Psalm 23 together. I'm sure you remember much of it.

The Lord is my shepherd; I lack nothing.
He makes me lie down in green pastures,

He leads me beside quiet waters,
He refreshes my soul.
He guides me along the right paths
For his name's sake."

What does it mean that he 'guides me along the right paths for his name's sake?' What does it mean, 'for his name's sake'? I've heard Psalm 23 my whole life but have never understood that verse. I want to ask him about this, but it's probably something everyone understands so I don't want to make a fool of myself.

He settles in closer to me, so wonderfully, uncomfortably near.

"I reveal my character through my names. It is in my character to lead you, like a shepherd, beside quiet waters, to refresh your soul, and to guide you along paths that are good for you—whether those paths seem good to you at the time, or not." I look at him, questioningly.

"I do this not only for your benefit, but for mine, because those right paths will lead you, ultimately, into me."

✶ ✶ ✶

The attire for the day is white T-shirts, khaki shorts, and dark green sweatshirts. The earthen path winds hither and thither through leafy woods under the shadow of the giant rockface. I enjoy the details of God's creation, glory in the vast array of wildflowers along the trail's edge, muse on their petals, pistils and stamens, linger over the scent of each specimen, press them between pages in my notebook. The doe and fawn have given me a new appreciation for the world around me and I'm starting to feel better. The sun has warmed; we remove our sweatshirts, tie them around our waists and continue our hike in our T-shirts.

There is a rumbling sound coming from somewhere down the trail. It builds with every turn we take—I can feel it under my feet. The air has become heavy with moisture.

Through a clearing I see how the stream rages through giant boulders and is transformed into mighty rapids.

He points downstream, to a fallen tree, a makeshift bridge over the rapids. He's not thinking what I think he's thinking—is he?

I shout over the water's roar. "Are you serious? So much for 'leading me beside quiet waters'!"

"This has more to do with guiding you 'along the right paths.' I have something to teach you." He takes a drink from his water bottle. "Shame keeps you thrashing about in the dark instead of boldly approaching my throne of grace."

Why does that matter? He's heading towards a bridge with a curved, slippery surface and no handrails. There's no way I can cross that thing without getting soaked, or drowned, or both.

The log traverses the stream precisely where the rapids are at their most turbulent. I'm overcome by vertigo and we haven't even started yet. Does he show any concern at all that I am on the verge of peril? No. He simply hops onto that log with audacious delight!

I approach the log, place the toe of my hiking boot onto its slimy surface. My grip slips immediately.

"Shame is the source of many of the dark truths you believe about yourself," Jesus calls, as I hesitate on the bridge.

"I'm about to vanish into these churning waters of death and you feel the need to preach?" I scream, petrified by the frothing maelstrom swirling menacingly beneath my feet. I think I'm going to pass out. Instead of coming to my aid he steps *backward* on the log toward the far side of the rapids!

"Shame makes you believe you're not worthy to approach me." He stops midpoint over the stream and prepares to dive into the foaming waters below.

"What are you doing?!" I yelp.

"Shame places your eyes on yourself, to look to your own strength to fix yourself, ultimately leading to greater failure, rather than being empowered by my grace." Now he's doing a little ditty right above those raging rapids!

"Pursue my throne of grace. Don't hide in your shame, Kenny. Run to me." He's standing there on the far end of the log, waiting for me to join him.

I've made it about halfway now. The waters are rolling and boiling beneath me. He's got his arms open wide.

"But Jesus, what if I fall?" I yell over the roar, my voice trembling. "I don't want to fall!"

"You don't want to *fail*, you mean. You're exhausted from trying to live for me, without me. Now, come!"

I am so tired. I am so very, very tired.

"Run to me, Kenny. You can do it. Don't let your fears tell you otherwise."

Oh gosh. The water is swirling right under my feet!

"Lift your head, Kenny. Look at me."

"Jesus…"

"Look at me!"

"But I've made such a mess of things. I don't deserve your grace. I don't deserve you."

"Kenny! I've got you! We can do this!"

I take a step. I nearly stumble!

"Run, Kenny!"

I've got to let go of all this gunk in my life and grab onto him!

"That's right, now you're doing it!"

I don't know what lies ahead, but whatever it is I won't be able to do it without him.

I lift my head. I set my gaze on Jesus. I see his eyes of passion for me. He draws me into himself. With my eyes fixed on his eyes, I take one step, and another, and another…

"I've got you. I've got you!"

His arms. Secure. Safe. I think I'm going to pass out—

But what—he's swinging me around, we're swirling in the air together! He's singing into my ear—

"Stay near me. Stay near my heart, my precious one—"

We've landed on sand, panting, the sun is warm.

"You did it! I'm so proud of you, Kenny."

No one's been proud of me for anything like for ages.

He's lying there contentedly, looking up at the bright blue sky.

I sit up, panting heavily. "What did you put me through that for?"

"How else could I put some backbone into your wimpy faith?"

"You're calling me a wimp? I resemble that remark!"

Jesus laughs.

11

THE DUNES OF CONTROL

It is quiet here on the other side of the rapids, beneath these lovely oak trees.

Here comes one of those memories, tarnishing this lovely moment.

A guidepost!

Maybe I should write the memory down, get it out of my heart and into the open. Do we have time?

"Jesus?"

He's out like a light, snoring lightly.

✶ ✶ ✶

We were on a family vacation; I was six years old at the time. With map unfolded upon her lap, my mother navigated our father, sitting at the helm of our massive station wagon, up and round and down the entire state of Michigan over many miles and many days.

We started by heading north up the eastern side of the state. Mile after mile of I-75 asphalt disappeared beneath our wheels as we drove first to Detroit, up to Boyne Mountain, across the Mackinac Bridge and into Michigan's Upper Peninsula. We stayed in roadside motels on stony beaches bordering a Great Lake, or in quaint, screened cabins in lovely, dense woods adorned with extraordinary clouds of mosquitos. Traveling then west into Wisconsin and then east back into Michigan again, my mother's route finally turned us southward, homeward, along the eastern coast of Lake Michigan.

Whether it had been part of our mother's meticulous plan from the beginning or a rare whim of serendipity on her part, the best was saved for last, our first sight of the giant sand dunes was nothing short of awe-inspiring. And we were going to stop and explore them, too! As soon as our father had maneuvered our station wagon into a parking space, I scampered over a sister or two and shot out of the car to gaze at the biggest pile of sand I had ever seen.

I looked at the cusp of the dune high above, its knife-edge crest blazing against the azure blue of the summer sky. I needed to get up there, to feel its sharpness on the palm of my hand. I envisioned the horizons and vistas and swirling galaxies awaiting me beyond its ridge. If I could get to the top I could see China, I could view the edge of the universe. Approaching the dune with daring and delight, I embarked on my quest.

Climbing the dune, however, turned to be more strenuous than I'd anticipated. Receiving little help from my tractionless sneakers I resorted to pulling myself up the side of the dune, one fistful of sand at a time. Dust soon lined my mouth and nostrils and stuck to my sweaty neck and knees. No matter: my goal was the top and nothing would stop me from reaching it.

Disbelief was painted on my sisters' faces, as if climbing a giant sand dune was the most unnatural thing a boy my age could do. My mother was focused on keeping our baby sister from doing the same. My father stood, hands on hips, looking out over the lake. As I climbed, hot winds carried my sisters' voices up the dune. Stating the obvious, one of them shouted, "Kenny! Come down now, you're getting dirty!" The other one shouted, "Kenny! You're going to have an asthma attack!" This last message carried greater weight, with my regular wheezing spells and frequent trips to the doctor. This message could hold genuine concern for my welfare; nonetheless, I interpreted it as a tactic to get me to return to the car. The winds carried no message from my parents, neither reprisal nor affirmation, no "Kenny! You can do it! Just keep going and reach the top—don't listen to those silly ol' sisters of yours!" Weighted by resistance from my sisters and apathy from my parents, my little limbs did all they could to propel me skyward.

My lungs felt the strain from the thrill and exertion of climbing to the top of a mountain; I needed to stop. The wind swirled around me, forming a sand cove around my little body, and in that cove I retreated. The lake, the sky, the sand dune—the grandeur of it all accentuated how tiny I was, how high up I was, how alone I was. Yet I was so very close to the top! The dizzying heights and swirling wind confused me. I began thinking, maybe I was about to have an asthma attack, maybe I was keeping my mother from her travel schedule, and my father might soon be become angry. Maybe I couldn't climb much higher, anyway.

THE DUNES OF CONTROL

I vacillated in my aspirations.

Leaving my goal behind, I skidded down the face of the dune, my body carving a curvy scar on its face. It took much less time to descend the dune than it did for me to conquer it, and I suddenly found myself at the feet of my family.

I began the laborious job of extracting the sandy evidence of my failed excursion from hair and shoes and pockets. When done, I mustered the courage to survey how far I'd climbed—and how little left I had to climb, as the heady lake winds erased what remained of my boyhood quest.

I was greeted by my family, not with praise that I had listened to and obeyed them, but with scorn that I hadn't done so sooner. And see how dirty I was! Sandy, sweaty and wheezy I climbed into my proper place in the back seat with the help of a clip to the head by a sister.

I remember my father flicking his cigarette through the open window, his eyes never meeting mine in the rearview mirror as he steered the car away from the dunes, away from my boyhood hopes, and toward home. My father never noticed how proud I was trying to make him, high on the dunes of Lake Michigan.

This is what I remember of a memory that never seems to leave me alone.

✷ ✷ ✷

Jesus looks down at what I've written; there's no use hiding it from him, he knows all about it, anyway.

"You write very well," he says to me.

"You probably say that to everybody," I deflect. "When are we getting to wherever we're going?" I ask.

He motions for me to follow him. We walk about fifty paces toward the crest of a hill.

"Kenny, look here," he says. I pull my baseball cap lower to vise my eyes from the harsh sunlight, and scan the terrain. Across the horizon stretches a vast body of water edged by endless mountains of sand.

"It is time for you to return," he says, and descends a steep embankment.

Jesus walks ahead of me, steady and unbothered by the shifting sands. I struggle to keep up, every step an effort.

"You've got to let go, Kenny," Jesus says, his voice calm but firm.

"Let go of what?" I ask, confused.

The stark wind suddenly kicks up, swirling the sand, momentarily blinding me. I've lost sight of him.

"Control," he says through the storm. "You've been trying to control everything in your life, but you can't control these dunes."

"Jesus? Are you still there?" I shout into the scirocco.

No answer.

"JESUS! I can't see you!"

The dunes seem to stretch on forever, a vast desert of challenges I can't predict or control. A shaft of sunlight penetrates the sandstorm and illuminates the crest of a giant sand dune. Is this the same dune of my childhood quest? Visages of that day shimmer in my mind like a mirage: My baby sister, a toddler at the time, was tended to by mom while dad parked the family car. My big sisters were in their teens; I was six or seven. What none of us knew at the time was that dad was six or seven years away from leaving our lives completely. My sisters remember little if anything from the day, so why did it wedge itself so deeply in me?

Attached at the hip through marriage and blood and birth order, our little band of humans travel through the for-better-or-worse of life together, at times packed like sardines in the family car on family vacation. How do these things happen? Pressed by family turmoil and financial woes, we wring ourselves of our unrequited dreams, the longings we suppress for the common good, putting each other's needs ahead of our own—

Jesus isn't here. He's abandoned me at the very moment of my greatest failure. "I climbed this mountain alone the first time," I shout into the wind, "I'll have to climb it alone this time, too."

I embark on my quest—or re-quest.

The lake is out there somewhere, though I can't see it in this sandstorm. I know now that Milwaukee, Chicago and Gary, Indiana, and not China or India or Mars lay beyond that lake. Most dreams temper with reality, eventually.

I'll never make it to the top.

The same old inner message, it knocks the wind out of me every single time. Every personal failure of mine is epitomized by this one giant sand dune. The lofty dreams I had, of becoming an English lit professor….

Each step feels heavier as the sand pulls at my feet, slowing my progress. I'm winded and I'm only halfway up this mountain. I'm pushing forty, I'm winded with disappointment and I'm only halfway through life.

Sand pours from my hand like an hourglass. How many volcanic eruptions and ice sheets and windstorms occurred to grind massive rock into these minute versions of themselves? Appropriate, then, that sand is used to mark the passage of time.

The frictions of life have ground me down to a smaller version of myself.

The more I try to quicken my pace, the more the sand pulls me back, like it knows I'm fighting a losing battle. The wind howls, swirling the sand in a relentless assault to my eyes and nose and mouth and skin. I have to rest. I have to catch my breath! I curl into the side of the sand mountain. A cove of sand quickly forms around me.

Interesting, how the elements overtake anything that stops moving. If I sit here long enough I'll be buried and lost to history without ever accomplishing one damn thing.

The sun is moving closer to its setting. But I need to get to the top! The dune seems to stretch up forever. Just like the vast desert of challenges I can't predict or control. But the more I try to quicken my pace, the more the sand pulls me back! It's like it knows I'm fighting a losing battle!

Maybe I am fighting a losing battle.

An air pocket hits the atmosphere, and I catch a glimpse of Jesus looking up at me from the base of the dune.

I suppose he wants me to come down now. He's probably worried that I'll have an asthma attack. Maybe he's upset that I'm getting dirty, or holding up his plans.

I might as well slide down to the bottom. Again.

I'll never make it to the top of anything.

Jesus—he's scrambling up the side of the dune! Look at him, bounding up the hill like that! He's almost *leaping* through the sand. He's *singing* up this mountain, to greet me!

"Heh! You started the climb without me," he says panting. He's reached my sand cove. He looks tanned and sandy, like a beach bum.

"I lost sight of you! And you didn't answer me when I called! So I thought you weren't interested, or too busy, or maybe too tired to go up with me. Besides, I climbed up the first time alone—"

"Oh, you did not!" he cuts me off with his exclamation. "Even when you can't see me or hear my voice, I'm always near you, okay? That day, when you were a boy, I climbed right there with you. I heard every doubt, heard the slightest of wheezes in your tired lungs. I felt your failure when you ended your little-boy quest in resignation. And Kenny, I saw something happen to you that you weren't aware of, though looking at your string of dark thoughts you've been having, I think you know what I'm referring to."

"You mean that a dark gooey string latched onto me that day—and tied me to this place?"

"Yes! To the place, to the family scenario, to your impressions of what happened that day—your subjective truths. So to help you move on from here I'm going to give you a good healthy dose of high truth. Let me tell you something, Kenny. You have a choice. You always have a choice: to allow others or circumstances to control you, to bind you, to blind you, to make you wither—or not! And let me tell you another thing. I always have a way out for you, to get you out from underneath a controlling person or circumstance. And one more thing while I'm at it: I'm not finished with you yet. I've got plans, dreams, things we're going to do together, working shoulder to shoulder in my Father's kingdom. We're going to get you unstuck, do you hear? We're going to put some spunk back into that heart of yours. Now let's finish this quest together!"

With a twinkle in his eye he shouts, "GO!"

We charge up the dune, slipping and sliding and grabbing the sand, laughing and panting and—

I stop just before we ruin the sharp edge of the crest with our tracks. Jesus stops, too. I've ached for this moment for so many years. The beauty of this edge, so crisp, curved, smooth. And yet so transient. I press it with my fingers and allow the solidness of that memory crumble and disperse with the summer breeze.

We saddle ourselves on this sandy edge, each dangling a leg toward my family memory, the other leg toward the vast unknown. We're here. We made it. We made it to the other side of my mountain, with its dizzying array of lake and sun and summer wind—and whirling galaxies and singing dreams and China far off in the distance—and my heart says yes, we did it! Jesus and me, we did it! And we twirl and swirl and whirl down the far side of the mountain, Jesus and me, laughing with somersaulting glee, and I catch a glimpse of how he truly sees me, knows me, cares for me, even loves me. My heart had been bound for so long but he's doing something new. I inhale this liberating truth and, as we land together at the bottom of my mountain with a sudden, contented thud, we laugh, breathe, and rejoice.

We help each other up out of the sand, remove our shoes and walk in the refreshing water of the lake. Our arms are draped over each other's shoulders like lifelong pals. The sun verges on the western horizon—I deny Milwaukee, Chicago, and Gary, Indiana access to my trysting place.

The aroma of food guides us around a small dune, revealing a charming sight. Smooth stones are thoughtfully arranged along the beach, a leisurely fire crackles to life, glass jars containing fireflies are scattered about, casting tiny, twinkling lights on our faces (thankfully, they've made holes in the lids of those jars so the fireflies can breathe—whoever 'they' are) while the sun bids its final farewell in a spectacular display of dazzling reds.

Skewered little fish roast above the driftwood fire. It might not have been my first choice for dinner, but I suppose he should have a say in the menu from time to time. He is propped up on his elbows next to me, digesting his little fishes. Look at that tan of his. It is only after I've suffered through a series of sunburns, blisters and peelings that my freckles feel sorry enough for me, and merge to give me a whiff of brown. Right now I'm as red as a lobster.

"So, Jesus. What do we do with that black, thick, gooey string that's wrapped around me," I ask while picking at my skin.

"Look up 1 John 5:16–17."

I retrieve my Bible from my backpack. "It's somewhere at the back of the Bible, right? Of course it is. Here. Uh-hem. 'If you see any brother or sister commit a sin that does not lead to death, you should pray and God will give them life. But there is a sin that leads to death, and I am not saying you should pray about that.'" I have no idea what this means, but I don't want him knowing that I don't know what this means.

I ask, "So, Teacher, would you be so kind as to expound on this most valuable of verses? To see if I agree with your interpretation?"

He raises his hands imploringly toward heaven. He can sure be dramatic sometimes.

"Alright," he says, "I will answer your question by asking you a question."

"Please, be so kind as to ask your question, though you are fully aware of the fact that I do not like this practice of yours, answering a question with a question."

"What happened to you, that day, on your family trip to the sand dunes? Did you kill anyone because of it?"

Hmm. Tough question. My sisters, my dear sweet sisters. I've flirted with the thought. Not that I'd ever carry through with it, of course.

"No."

"Some bonds are connected to major sin issues, issues that could cause one to die or be killed. Your control issues, and in particular the dark truth you received that day, were serious, but easily enough fixed by forgiving, being forgiven, and by bathing yourself in my truth. So my question to you is: Do you want to offer forgiveness? So that you may be free?"

"Yes," I answer.

"Then before we sleep, let's do some heart surgery. Let's take a moment, for you to listen to your heart, and what my Spirit would want to say to you."

We settle down. The sunset bathes us in hues of bronze. Gentle waves, rolling across the lake, break near our feet…so soothing…

"Huh? What? Why'd you jab me with your elbow? I wasn't asleep, honest! I was praying!" I don't think he believed me. Alright, let's give it another shot, Kenny. Quiet your thoughts. Maybe my baseball rolled down the basement stairs. But the basement door would've had to have been open, and I don't think it was. Plus, I didn't hear it bounce down those steps. Besides, for the ball to end up there, it would've had to rebound off the front door and bank off the entry wall without rolling into the dining room—unless it did land in the dining room. That's it! But then, I would've seen it when I was hiding under the dining room table—

"Ahem."

"Oh, sorry."

"You could, however, ask yourself what the baseball means to you. But we'll take care of that another time."

"What makes you think I was thinking about my baseball? Oh, all right, I give in. But Jesus, can you help me out here?"

He places his hand on my shoulder and peace fills my soul.

I'm able to see that day clearly now, at the dunes so long ago. I can put two-and-two together, see what happened, why I reacted the way I did, how I got hurt.

"So, Jesus, I forgive my sisters for controlling me. I see now that they were most likely concerned for my welfare, maybe even loved me—and concerned about me not upsetting our parents."

"Very good, Kenny. Anything else?"

"I forgive myself for allowing myself to be controlled by my sisters."

"Very good. And?"

"And what?"

Wait. I know where he's going with this: my mother and father. They were too busy, or too overwhelmed with life then, to see me, to affirm me.

"Jesus? That one goes deep. I don't think I can—I don't think I'm ready to forgive them for that, not just yet. Is that alright?"

He's giving me a hug. "Of course. You've done very well with what you could today."

Clip. Clip. Clip clip clip.

* * *

He nestles in for the evening, pulls a blanket over his shoulders, and says his prayers.

"Thanks, Jesus."

"Thank you for what?"

"For, you know, setting me free and all."

"You're very welcome."

He folds his arms behind his head, gazing up at his galactic creation.

"I've watched you, how you've been afraid of making wrong decisions, afraid of making right ones, never knowing whose toes you might step on, whose wrath you might incur, whose love you may lose."

"One of my worms?"

"Yes, you may call it that, the way you've allowed controlling hearts to form your reactions and responses to various situations in life. The work of forgiveness you've done today will give you umph, to help you protect your heart from the marauding throngs that bang at your door, demanding that you meet their needs. I will be with you, throughout your life, helping you to find ways to get your own needs met as you serve others. You always have a choice, and I always have a way for you."

It is quiet.

"And you have no idea how clever you are at controlling others."

By the time I come up with an objection to this statement he's already sleeping. Or pretending to be.

12

THE TEMPESTS OF INJUSTICE

I have to admit, I'm feeling better already. Nice to find out where that ol' dark truth came from, bring it out in the light, do some cleanup work on the ol' heart. 'Not making to the top.' Ha! If my wife could see me now!

What a glorious morning! New day, new opportunities. I've already jogged up and down the beach, cast stones into the lake just for the fun of it, swam in the morning-calm waters just because I could. I've even had a bit of a 'quiet time'. And he's still lying there like a bump on a log. The Son of Man is looking very much like a son of man this morning, is all I have to say. Is he ever going to get up?

I'll just read a bit from this here *The Pilgrim's Progress* while he snoozes the day away.

> Now, at the end of this valley was another, called the Valley of the Shadow of Death, and Christian must needs go through it, because the way to the Celestial City lay through the midst of it.

Sounds like that man Christian wasn't exactly living the Victorious Christian Life—he should've kept himself on the 'straight and narrow' all the way to the Celestial City!

"Hey, Jesus! Things to do, places to go!"

He yawns, looks around. "What time is it? Running up and down that sand dune yesterday. I feel every muscle in my body."

"Now who's the wimp!"

"Who are you calling a wimp!" He says, and pounces on me like a panther.

"Wait! What are you doing? Heh, put me down!"

"They don't call me The Carpenter's Son for nothing!"

"Okay! I take it back! You're the opposite of a wimp!"

"Too late," he says, as he throws me into the water with a splash.

We were provided with a set of clean clothes—long khaki pants, a fresh white T-shirt (and boxers) and a long-sleeved shirt in royal-purple plaid. Still no Diet Coke. I'm trying to curb my complaining so I don't say anything. Breakfast is leftover grilled little fishes from last night's dinner. He eats them with gusto.

"We have to stop by your house today," he says, sucking the meat off a little fish skeleton.

"You mean, I get to see Jane and the kids?" My heart races with anticipation. "But it could take a couple of days to get back there!" I'm thinking we'll have to hike over the western hills, ford the stream across that blasted log, traverse the meadow and playground and cornfields, back to the Trysting place and then—

"There's a shortcut," he says, sipping from an espresso cup.

"Heh! Where'd you get that?"

"I have connections."

"Then order me up a diet Coke, then!"

"After calling me a wimp? Not a chance."

Silence.

"It gives a nice caffeine kick, I imagine," I say.

"Does a marvelous job clearing the head," he says.

Silence.

"I get the same with a couple of Diet Cokes. Marvelous, though in short supply in these parts. You should try it sometime. Why don't you order up a couple of cans."

"I'm fine with my espresso, thank you."

The valley's perspectives are skewed, shorter on the north side and longer on the south. Despite this, it takes us all day to walk home, though faster than I expected. A car would have been quicker, but this place lacks modern amenities.

I strut in the sunshine, zippidy-doo-da-ing down the trail with flittering birds, imbibing on crisp pears and juicy plums and luscious peaches plucked right off the tree, thankful to be alive. My companion has remained silent nearly the entire day.

"C'mon, man! Let's pick up the pace! I've got to get home!"

He stops me, has me look at him.

"Kenny, what did you read in *The Pilgrim's Progress* this morning?"

"How do you know what I was reading, I thought you were asleep—"

"No matter. What did you read?"

"Something about Christian needing to go through the Valley of the Shadow of Death on his way to the Celestial City. Why?" He's shorter than me, but he's tough. I step back in case he gets the idea to throw me over his shoulder again.

"What scripture do you think Bunyan based this passage on?"

"Well, Psalm 23, obviously."

"Can you quote the specific verse?"

"Why are you wasting so much time!" I take off down the trail.

"Kenny!" he shouts.

I turn around, walk back to him. "Okay, okay. 'Even if I walk through the valley of the shadow of death, I will fear no evil, for you are with me.' What about it?"

He grabs me by the arms. "Kenny, look at me. What you are about to face, both at home and in your heart—it's not going to be easy."

"Would you stop being so glum already? I'm actually in a good mood for once," I almost yell at him. "Besides, it's not long before I'm home!"

These ol' running legs still have some spunk, I'm *smoking* him! Keep running, Kenny!

The sun has fallen behind the western hills by the time we arrive back to Webster Groves, if it were still here, but it isn't.

A strange glow pulses through the woods, from the direction of my house. My steps decelerate with uncertainty. The bubble, I'd forgotten about it. It's the source of the pulsing light. Inside the bubble it's morning; outside the bubble it's dusk. Yet the dusk out here in is brighter than the morning light surrounding my house. Strange.

"Jesus? What is this all about?" He's caught up with me. He glows with the shifting light emanating from the bubble. He does not answer me. He's looking toward my house. I shift my attention from the bubble to my house.

It's like I'm watching a Broadway show, and my house is the stage set.

To the right of the front door, I see a small figure, staring out the bay window in the dining room. He's looking down the street, hiding himself behind the curtains. Startled, he disappears from view. It was Kevin.

Behind the far-left dormer window on the second floor—something's happening in the girls' room. Jessie and Julia are arguing, which is nothing new, but there's an intensity in their gesticulations that I haven't seen before. Jessie storms out of their bedroom holding something; Julia follows after her. I lose sight of them. Wait—they just entered the frame of the middle dormer window, over the landing above the stairway. Jessie storms into our bedroom; Julia is sobbing hysterically and follows her sister into our room.

Julia leaves our bedroom, followed by Jessie. Now they're back in their own bedroom. What? Did Julia just throw her hairbrush at Jesse? Jesse and Julia are tussling—but wait—some guy just stormed out of my bedroom and slammed the door! The girls stop, look at each other, let go of each other. Jesse quickly hands Julia her hairbrush and they begin brushing their hair like nothing has happened between them. The man enters the bedroom, approaches Jesse, yanks something out of Jessie's hands and throws it in Julia's face. The man storms out and disappears into my bedroom, closing the door behind him. The girls are comforting each other.

Wait! From Keenan's bedroom window to the far right—who's that, standing there? Is that Keenan? It can't be, because he'd been out all night! Does he pretend to be out just to annoy me? He backs away from the window, disappears into the darkness of his room. Now he's tiptoeing down the steps to the first floor!

Jessie leaves her room and stands next to my bedroom door, eavesdropping. She quickly backs up against the wall, holds her hands to her mouth. She dashes down the hall as the man storms out of my room and then charges down the steps. The man stops halfway down the steps, turns, then runs back up to my bedroom. Now he's running back down the steps again. The man enters the frame of the living room window to the left of the front door.

It looks like the man is looking for something. He's looking all over the living room, under my chair, behind the sofa. He picks up a vase and throws it against a wall. A framed picture falls off the wall from the vase's impact. The man storms out of the living room and disappears into the back of the house.

Julia, struggling with her respirator, carefully makes her way down the steps to the first floor.

I turn to Jesus; his gaze is fixed on the events unfolding inside my house.

A wave of nausea hits me.

The man opens the front door, carrying a big metal bowl. He looks this way and that, heaves the contents of the bowl behind

the shrubs beneath the living room window. Kyle is screaming in the background.
    The man looks up, then out, then stares in my direction.
    I'm staring myself in the face.
    I back myself into the house and slam the front door shut.
    Keenan begins to play his drums, angrily, aggressively. Why does he always do what he knows I don't want him to do?
    Jane, pulling on a robe, runs down the stairs from the second floor.
    Shouts are coming from the back of the house.
    Jessie runs out of our bedroom and storms down the steps.
    The drumming stops.
    The drumming starts up again.
    The old neighbor enters the scene from the right, his face is lined with concern. He rings the doorbell, then bangs on the front door with increasing urgency.
    I turn to Jesus; his gaze hasn't wavered from the scene unfolding before us. "Jesus, come on, this isn't what happened this morning! I mean it is, but it wasn't *that* bad!" Jesus says nothing, he keeps watching my house.
    The front door flings open; I'm holding a towel to my bleeding face. I grab my neighbor by the collar, shake him, yell in his face, and shove him off the front porch. The man stumbles to the sidewalk. I raise my fist at him, slam the door on him. His wife enters the scene from the direction of their home, runs up to her husband and helps him to his feet. The woman struggles as she helps her husband back to their house.
    "You fed the video of my life into some sort of AI program, didn't you. To make what happened this morning look worse than what it was." Jesus says nothing.
    The front door explodes open. I stumble out the door, pulling on my pants, pulling on my shoes; blood streaks down my cheek from the cut below my left eye. Jane's changed into a running suit, is giving orders, has a screaming Kyle on her hip. Keenan carefully carries Kevin out the front door; I smack

Keenan on the side of the head. Jessie shoves me out of the way, cusses at me, I cuss back at her. Julia pulls her respirator out the door, walks with it toward the driveway and disappears behind the van. I run to my truck, jump in, start the engine, put the truck in reverse. Julia walks behind my truck. She screams, fumbles to the ground, becomes entangled in the cords of her respirator. I stop the truck, jump out of the truck, throw Julia out of the way, get back in, put the truck in reverse, back over the neighbor's flowerbed, shift gears and drive over the flowerbed one more time. I slam on the pedal and my truck screeches down the street toward Elm.

Kyle stands at the front door, crying hysterically, reaching out to his mother.

Jane is also crying; she looks distressed. Jessie places her arms around her mother, sees Julia fallen on the driveway, quickly runs to her sister and helps her to her feet. Julia shows Jessie scrub marks on a hand and a knee; Jessie kisses them, comforts her sister. A wheel on Julia's respirator appears cracked, distressing Julia even more.

Keenan appears through the front door, gently carrying Kevin in his arms. He walks with Kevin toward the van and lays him carefully in the third row of seats. Keenan runs over to help Jessie with Julia who is weeping, kindly helps his sisters into the back seat, then closes the van's sliding door.

Jane, wiping away tears, buckles Kyle into his car seat, soothing him.

The old neighbors return; they comfort Jane. Jane gives them both a long hug before getting into the driver's seat of the van. Keenan gets into the passenger seat, Jane backs out of the driveway, rolls down the window, talks with the woman from across the street, then drives off. The three neighbors watch until Jane is out of sight before returning to their respective homes.

"I don't want to see any more of this." I feel sick.

"You became too angry," he says through the darkness on our side of the bubble. "That morning. Then that night. You became too angry with your family."

"My best friend has betrayed me, my wife has left me, my kids are gone, and you want to talk about *me*?" My mouth tastes like rotten eggs.

"It is painful to watch you let your anger consume you."

"But Jesus! Mitt had no right coming in and stealing my wife, my kids, my family away from me!"

"You've got a problem, an anger problem. And your anger is blinding you from seeing the truth."

"Whaddya mean?"

"If you'd let me examine your heart much earlier, all of this might not have happened."

"So, you're saying all this is *my* fault?! My wife's sleeping around with my best friend—"

"You are assuming that—"

"And my kids don't respect me—"

"You've broken their trust—"

"And now, my entire family, my entire life, has been taken from me!"

My head is pounding. Through the divide I glance at my home. Everyone is gone now. The house looks empty, forlorn. I look away.

Jesus is quiet. His silence is irksome.

"You know I come from a long line of hotheads. Give me a break!" I come to my defense since nobody else will.

"Yes, maybe; but tell that to Jessica, who adores you, but you're rarely there for her and she can't look you in the eyes right now. Tell that to Julia, who feels unprotected by you. Tell that to Keenan, your nearly-a-man son, whose drum set you smashed; he is a much kinder, caring person than you give him credit for. Tell that to Kevin, who's going through something difficult but you haven't been present enough to notice. Tell that to Kyle. You threw him onto the floor during your rampage. Tell that to your wife. It is time for you to own your anger. The long line of hotheads has to end with you."

He's looking at me.

"You must go deep, Kenny. If not, you will end up destroying your family, and possibly yourself."

I step away from the bubble and into dusky shadows. I don't want to face the fact that I hurt my family. *But it wasn't my fault!*

I hear him close behind me. "That morning, when everyone was running late. You could have humbled yourself, asked Jane for help, called your father-in-law to find out what could be done about the meeting, rallied the kids and worked together with them to make a game plan to get them to school as quickly as possible. Instead, you blinded yourself with rage. You just missed running over Jewels. And you didn't stop there."

Driving over the neighbor's flowerbed. The road rage. Tiffany. The blowup at the meeting.

I turn to face him. "But it's her fault! Jane, she just knows how to push my buttons, knows exactly when to push them—when I already got too much on my plate!"

"Do you feel unjustly treated?"

"Boy, you hit the nail on the head. Yes!"

He remains quiet. I've given him something to chew on.

"You've chosen the coward's road, shifting blame and evading the ascent to my cross."

"Get out of here!" I shout at him.

* * *

One weak chirp from a lonely bird announces the arrival of a tepid dawn.

I'm cold under this sorry excuse of a blanket he gave me and my back hurts from lying on this flimsy blowup mat he found somewhere.

"All your immature reactions to everyday occurrences are adult versions of childish temper tantrums."

Jesus. Again. He will not let up. Please, let me die and fade into blissful nothingness. "Why can't you let up already? Don't you think I feel bad enough as it is?"

"Did you feel that you hadn't gotten your way, that you were misunderstood? Did you feel disrespected or belittled or bullied or somehow taken advantage of? Did you feel unseen, unloved? What was it? Look at it, Kenny!"

He's pushing me into a corner and I hate corners.

"The trigger—*think, man*! What was it that made you see red, become blind with rage, throw a vase, make you want to punch, to slam, to break, to kill?"

"I don't know, *man*, okay? What do you want from me? I don't know where these things come from. Maybe from my best friend cuckolding me with my wife, something like that?"

"You got stuck somewhere. You stopped growing, maturing—not in every area of your life, you function well on many levels—but here, you're acting like a spoiled child, embarrassing yourself and embarrassing others. The trigger! Look for the trigger!"

"Just tell me then, wouldja? You know already, Mr. Know-It-All. YOU tell me what Jane said to flip me off, because I can't take much more of this crap!"

He is quiet. Uncomfortably quiet.

He says, "Instead of humbling yourself and saying sorry, you defend yourself. Because admitting to your humanity would confirm that Jane has a right not to love you."

He walks down the stone path and into the woods.

"Oh, so now you're leaving me too? I can't do things perfect enough for you, either? Why don't you just come out and say it!"

I don't hear a peep from him.

I don't need him, anyway.

✯ ✯ ✯

What time is it? It must be mid-morning. I never did get to sleep, and my head feels groggy. I'm tired of this sleeping outside business. And my own bed is right over there in my house! I wish I could get my hands on some booze.

"Do you want to discontinue this journey? You are free to do so." He's sitting next to me, leaning against a tree.

I hadn't expected him to be the one to breech the subject. Maybe we've done as much work on my heart as we possibly can. Or maybe he's had enough of me. But this would be my chance. I mean, I'm home, basically, though how I get through that bubble is anyone's guess.

He picks up his backpack.

"Are you leaving me?" I panic.

He removes a prayer shawl from the backpack. He places the shawl over his head. Facing the eastern mountains, he closes his eyes. A deep, melancholic strain rises from within him in a low, melodious vibrato. His wordless tune rises and falls like sunrise, then sunset.

It is a song I feel I may not enter, since I have yet to taste this measure of sorrow.

He rocks back and forth as he recites an ancient verse in an ancient tongue. It reminds me of something I remember about him, from the book of Isaiah, I believe:

'Surely, he took up our pain and bore our suffering,
And by his wounds we are healed;
The Lord has laid on him the iniquity of us all.'

He removes the shawl, folds it carefully and returns it to his backpack.

"For no one is righteous, not one," he says, then starts down the stone path into the woods.

Relenting, I take one last look at my house, and follow him.

PART FOUR

Going Deeper Still

13

INTERNATIONAL NIGHT

My heart has been heavy all day. There's been too much for me to process, too much to take in, too much to feel bad about. We've walked in silence nearly the whole way, mostly because I'm embarrassed by my recent behavior and I don't want to talk to him about it. And he hasn't produced a single thing to eat yet! On top of it all, it's starting to rain. At least we've made it back to the trysting place—why there are no cars in this Shimmering place is a mystery to me—but there isn't anywhere around here to stay dry, so what are we going to do?

He strides by the wooden bench and continues down the path leading to the stream.

Here we are, back at the scene of where he'd nearly drowned. The rock he pulled out of the stream, nearly dying in those waters—a baptism of sorts, representing his death and resurrection—he did all that to symbolize the price he paid to save me, to die for me. I'm sure he has his regrets now.

The stream runs cloudy beneath the bridge due to the rain. Raindrops splatter on its surface, distorting the image looking back at me. My tears merge with the raindrops. I already know what the stream is going to tell me, that I'm a royal screw-up, how I've royally screwed-up my life. I've already screwed things up on this journey.

I've lost sight of Jesus, but follow his footprints on the rain-soaked trail on the other side of the bridge.

But wait—Jesus' footprints aren't the only ones imprinting the wet dirt! There is a curious collection of footprints—bare feet, the pattern of sandals, the modern tread of basketball shoes, the distinct imprint of high heels—and are all headed in the same direction. What is going on around here? I'm not in the mood to be with people, whoever they are. I'm not in the mood to be with Jesus, either. Maybe they've found a place to get out of the rain, at least.

The trail ascends a small knoll brimming with a purple craze of rhododendron laced with raindrops. Nestled behind a grove of dogwood is a white-clad cottage covered in ivy.

Chimney smoke scrolls through the treetops, joining misty clouds hanging languidly from the dusky sky.

Backpacks are lined up in a row outside a set of French doors, so this must be the right place; some of them harbor very unruly worms, I see, something that makes me smirk.

I peek around a corner, glance through a multi-paned window. Strange, how the cottage looks larger on the inside than it does from the outside. The room is aglow in candlelight, and thrumming with people. I've gotten used to hearing only his voice—or mostly my own, truth be told—so the voices emanating from the cottage are an invasion of my personal space.

Do I smell *kimchee*? No, it can't be. Come on, Kenny, get ahold of yourself. It's probably my extreme hunger playing tricks on my imagination, he hasn't given me anything to eat in *ages*.

The walls of the room are adorned with paintings, while tapestries are displayed on easels standing on the wooden floor. An old-fashioned loom stands grandly at the far end of the room. This must be some sort of artist's workplace, an 'atelier', as I learned in Sister Mary Joan's French class. She'd be happy to know that at least one word survived her efforts.

There's Jesus, standing at the center of a group of people holding plates filled with food. Have I been invited? Does he even want me there? Whatever is going on in there, it'll be better than standing out here in the rain. Besides, the aroma of food is driving me crazy. I'll dart in, grab some food and make my exit. I'll just leave my backpack and its contents out here with the others.

"There you are! I was just speaking of you!" It's Jesus. He caught sight of me trying to sneak in. "Émile, can you hand Kenny a towel to dry himself with? Thanks." A slender, timid-looking man approaches me, smiles nervously, hands me a white fluffy towel, then quickly disappears into the throng.

"Everyone, this is Kenny. Kenny, everyone!" says Jesus cheerily. I feel like I've walked into a support group meeting for international students. All eyes turn to me. How stupid I must look, waving my little "hi, everyone" wave.

With all these people gathered from so many cultures and places, I feel like melted vanilla ice cream on a wilting paper plate. I smile a cheesy smile and gesture toward the buffet table; the others smile politely before returning their attention to Jesus. Is he speaking to each of them in their own language?!

Wow, this is one serious spread! Everything is labelled so nicely. Hmmm…. where should I start…. 'Korean Bulgogi'… 'Japanese Tempura'… 'Nigerian Chicken and Rice'…. 'British Fish and Chips'…. What's this? 'Masai milk with cow's blood served in a calabash gourd'?!

Jesus is speaking so I better pay attention. He's standing by an easel displaying a woven tapestry.

"Your life's tapestry, crafted from countless threads in a vibrant spectrum of colors, is interwoven among the warp, each strand secured to the sturdy wooden frame of the loom."

I stifle a yawn; it's getting late.

He's becoming more animated, using his hands. "Consider the tapestry's creation—a sequence of steps. What, or who, initiates it?" He quickly walks across the room and stands next to the old wooden loom at the far end of the room; the group tags along. He continues his teaching.

"First comes the loom—the wooden frame—built square and strong. Next comes the warp—those vertical strings—attached to the loom. Then comes the weft—the horizontal threads—that are woven through the warp." Jesus surveys the apparatus with a craftsman's eye.

"The Master Weaver meticulously constructs the loom, the very foundation on which the narrative of your life is to be threaded, the framework I intend your life to be lived within.

"Without this structure, grounded in my Word, my precepts and my commandments, there would be no standard to gauge your life's fabric, to discern if it is crafted with intention, or left to fray.

"Without the loving framework of the Master Weaver, everything becomes loose, lawless, relative.

"Look now at the warp, how the strings are pulled taut and straight upon the Master's framework. Your warp is constructed of the countless strings that were already in place before the time of your birth.

"So, the warp of your life is your family and country and language and faith; the DNA for your eyes and your skin (and for things you don't yet see, things you don't really need to know about); and blessings and curses through your generational lines: the victories, the conquests, the sins and the shame; the political climate of freedom or of oppression; the period of human history you share with your fellow travelers. There were literally gazillions of warp-strings already in place when I started knitting you, carefully, in your mother's womb." He runs a hand through his dark mane, scratches his prominent nose—products of his own warp, I assume.

It's time for me to ditch this place. But I'm trapped in a corner and can't get to the door without drawing attention. And there are still some dishes I haven't tried.

An elderly woman, wearing a kimono, walks up to Jesus. They bow endlessly to each other, exchange small, exquisitely wrapped gifts, and bow some more. Jesus locates her tapestry and places it in the middle of the room.

He briefly explains how each thread (whether dark or light, fine or coarse) has been woven into the woman's life by circumstances and by people who have formed her most.

The woman hesitates, looks at Jesus, who nods for her to begin. She speaks to us in Japanese—how I'm understanding her is a mystery. Such a kaleidoscope of individuals, so many cultures—and so much food! Rats, I missed what she said…

"—and the tsunami took my husband, my children, my grandchildren, everyone except for one granddaughter, who remained with me, but in a coma, and I took care of her, for years, until she died."

She looks into Jesus' eyes, then turns away.

"I was angry at times with God for allowing these horrors to happen to me," she pauses and apologizes profusely to Jesus, "but then I allowed you to come into my anger, into my pain, and loss, and into my loneliness, and I have not felt lonely, ever again."

The woman melts in Jesus' embrace.

Jesus invites a man to his side; the man looks startled, wondering if Jesus truly means him. He places his plate of chicken and rice on a table, then nervously stands next to his tapestry. He looks at Jesus with awe. He is from where? Some place in Nigeria. He is wearing a magnificent robe printed in ochre, with a hat made from the same material.

"I am no stranger to sin," he admits, "but Jesus, you came to me with grace, offering forgiveness and salvation." The man bows, takes Jesus' hands into his, bows, and touches them with his forehead. Jesus lifts the man's face, and the man continues. The man's voice carries a weight of unspeakable loss as he tells his tale in his own language.

"Then, Jesus, came the day when the marauders crossed the border, and destroyed my life. They tied me up and forced me to watch, powerless and with clenched fists, as they brought destruction upon my fields with fire and scorn. They dishonored my wife, abducted my daughters, and took the life of my son. My heart, too, they slaughtered that day. All I had was stripped away, my wife succumbing days later to her wounds of disgrace. I have not seen my daughters again. Yet, because you pardoned my own grave misdeeds, I have found it within me to forgive these men, in your name, Jesus."

The group breaks into tearful sobs.

The man adds, looking meekly at Jesus: "Yet though I have lost everything, I still have my King, Jesus. And when I have Jesus, I still have everything."

Jesus envelops him in his arms as everyone in the room gathers around and does the same.

Well, not everyone gathers around Jesus; a few people in the room stand by themselves, looking as uncomfortable as I feel. Is there anything I missed the first two laps around the buffet table? What—can it be? 'St. Louis Toasted Ravioli with Marinara Sauce.' Yes! I hit the jackpot! Looks like it's barely been touched, probably too "foreign" for this lot! Well, that leaves more for me. I'll just take the whole platter, then.

Look at that! That older man Jesus was talking to, what was his name? He just snuck outside through the French doors!

Now those two women are sliding along the wall—and they just darted outside, too!

And that tall, distinguished-looking man is following after them!

I wish I could join them but I'm still trapped on the wrong side of the room. Besides, these toasted ravioli are delicious.

The next person to share is from England, a woman with lovely blond, flowing hair that falls gently upon her face. She seems nervous; Jesus comes up and stands with her.

"I have also done some horrible things in my life," she starts, "but Jesus has made me white as snow." She clears her throat and starts again. "So, when this happened to me," she pulls her hair back, "and I became the victim of an acid attack meant for someone else," she touches the melted side of her face with her fingertips, "the injustice of it, I found it debilitating."

I can't believe what I'm seeing.

"But with Jesus' help I was able to forgive, over time, and at times with great sorrow," Jesus places his arm around her shoulders, "and now I can see myself as Jesus sees me, as his lovely one." She looks up to him as he gathers her into his arms.

Another group hug ensues.

I keep my distance. I can't believe how easy it was for the woman to forgive the jerk who did that to her.

Jesus stands next to another tapestry and then glances at me. It must be my turn.

He gently touches the strands of my weave.

I'm immediately overwhelmed by memories: faces, and odors, and whispers, and terror. A twisted pleasure, an unholy mix of fear and delight.

He looks at me, but in a way that says that he knows that I'm not yet ready to share my story, and that's okay.

I send him an expression of grateful relief.

I watch the others take their leave. A collective affection is shared between them, an atmosphere of unmitigated joy. Though they're sending me polite goodbyes, I feel as though I'm looking in from the outside, perhaps because I didn't share my story with them as they had done with each other.

Jesus is unabashedly emotional as he waves goodbye and throws kisses to everyone as they leave through the French doors. Through a window I watch as the journeyers put on their respective backpacks before heading off into the night.

He looks pleasantly depleted, lingering in the afterglow of guests already missed.

It is just the two of us now. Whether we like it or not.

✶ ✶ ✶

He falls into an overstuffed lounge chair, the kind sold at second-hand stores, worn, comfortable, easy to get lost in and hard to get out of. After a few minutes' rest, he struggles up, walks first to the wooden loom before again approaching my tapestry. He stands for a minute, contemplating. I'm standing next the French doors, planning my escape.

"There are things in your warp that the Master Weaver would have never chosen for you if he'd had his way from the very start: Genetic flaws and birth defects and chronic health problems were never the Weaver's will. Instead, they may be seen as a product of a world that lives outside of my perfect ways, of a warp strung carelessly upon my holy framework."

Much of what he says conflicts with my understanding of determinism.

He finds a wooden stool and sits down, looking pensive. I flip through my mental Bible and remember a story that seems to contradict what the Master just told me.

"But what about the man born blind, the one that Jesus—I mean you—healed? Didn't Jesus—YOU—say that it was God's will that he be born blind, so that God could be glorified through his blindness?"

"Why would I wish that some people be born blind? Just so that I can show off my power as I make them well?" he asks, despondently. "They were looking for someone to blame for the man's blindness. No one was to blame, so they blamed me instead." He sighs.

"I 'allow' blindness and other birth defects in the same way I 'allowed' the world to fall into the enemy's hands. It wasn't my ultimate intention. But I will ultimately make all things new, to make all things right. I already have—it is now a question of seeing the power of my death and resurrection released through my people to a lost, hurting world."

"Which is how you're glorified through someone born blind," I say, trying to cheer him up.

"Yes," he says, "or through children of mine who are born blind, who lean on me until they see, whether they see on this side of eternity, or the other."

He says something, almost to himself.

"Sorry, I didn't hear what you said."

He clears his throat, "Free will," he says more clearly, "I had to allow for it."

He sets himself on the floor beneath my tapestry.

"The weft of your life …. Layer upon layer, strand by strand, the tapestry of your heart is woven. How, and by whom? Your relationships work to weave the tapestry of your life—and you the tapestries of others. What colors have you deposited, what quality of yarn have you used, to weave your impact on the people around you?"

I have no real need to ponder this question.

"It is in the weft where free will truly kicks in: your own free will (when you've done damage to yourself) or the free will of others (when others have exercised their will against your will) to your detriment."

My tapestry is a complete mess.

He stands beside me, places a hand on my shoulder. The gesture irritates me, and I turn to face him.

"See this black yarn there? Where were you then? Why didn't you stop them from doing those things to me, from putting that spot of dank on my life? Where *were* you?" There's been so much dark. So much pain. "You could've stopped it if you wanted to."

"It is time for bed," he says, quietly.

I watch him through a window as he walks toward the footbridge that leads to our trysting place.

My tapestry. Useless. Pointless. Ugly. Get this mess out of my sight!

There. It's smashed to smithereens.

14

THE FOREST OF TEMPTATION

I've got to get out of here. I feel like a caged tiger.

I bang the walls, slam the windows. Smash the weaver's loom? No. Punch my fist through a pane of glass? Yes.

Pain! My wrist!

The blood—the glass, I've got to pull my arm back through the glass!

Now, *do it.*

It cuts. It hurts. It stings!

A shard of glass still attached to the windowpane is traced with my blood.

Grab it, jerk it free!

See how nicely they go together, this sharp edge against my exposed wrist….

But I have to think about my children. And Jane.

I've got to stem this bleeding! Oh God, how?

The first aid kit! In my backpack! Where is my backpack? It's still outside! But what if somebody's taken it? There it is, it's the only one out here. But I don't want to face my worms! My blood, a scarlet, liquid worm, moves down my arm and drips to the ground. There: some cotton gauze! Wrap it around the wrist!

The pain has deflated my rage.

The night air has cleared my head. Where do I go, what do I do?

Jesus is probably waiting for me back at the trysting place. I don't want him to see me like this, I don't want him to see this mess. I wouldn't blame him if he doesn't ever want to see me again.

A voice calls to me, softly. It is the stream, running by the atelier:

"Run to him–run to him–run to him–run to him!"

Yet there are other waters, deeper, darker, drawing me away from him, away from myself.

I don't know what to do with it, this restlessness, this loneliness in me, this nagging sense of incompleteness. It's the way I feel on my business trips, when I'm away from the family, spending lonely nights in lonely hotels. But I'm not on a business trip, I'm on a journey in this Shimmering place and I've hit a dead-end. My world has disintegrated into nothingness. Because I'm a nothing.

"Kenny."

He stands there, mottled in moonlight. His sudden nearness unsettles me, it disorientates my heart and the direction it wants to go.

He steps closer. "Do you remember what John wrote? In his first letter? 'Do not love the world or anything in the world. If anyone loves the world, the love of the Father is not in him.'"

He takes one step closer still. "When your heart craves the world, it is precisely there that you have a deficit of my Father's love for you. It is precisely now, in your craving for garbage love, that you will choose either to turn your heart toward me, or toward that which does not fulfill. Should you turn your heart toward me, you will experience my Father filling you with a love that satisfies beyond your deepest longings."

I want to turn around and tell him that I know that I shouldn't do what I'm about to do, but I don't know how else to meet this need in me. A father's love is an alien concept to me.

I need the familiar right now, and the familiar lies within that forest.

But I can't say this to him. I walk in the direction of the forest without having said a single word.

The stream runs along the trail, its voice more urgent, "Turn around–turn around–turn around!"

If I turn around, I'll have to face him. But I can't face him! I don't deserve him. I deserve to be punished. I deserve to die.

The trail veers away from the stream, the voice of the stream becoming less distinct. I *think* it is saying, 'night on the town–night on the town–night on the town.' Maybe a 'divine appointment' is waiting for me, in the forest. I've heard about those "tavern evangelism" ministries, that would suit me just fine. I'll keep walking then, deeper into the forest.

For some reason the worms in my backpack have become extremely activated.

The stream must be tumbling down some rapids because I can clearly hear its voice—

"TURN AROUND–TURN AROUND–TURN AROUND–TURN AROUND!"

That was pretty clear. I really should listen.

What's that, just ahead, further up the path? I see some lights, hear some voices.

"I'll go check things out, then head right back to the trysting place, alright? Stream, did you hear me?"

The path diverges farther from the direction of the stream, leaving me to my choices. I don't really need the stream on a night out, anyway—there's no need to mix religion with pleasure.

Voices emanate from the woods, and laughter. It's probably just a bunch of losers enjoying stale beer.

I'll keep moving.

I'm sure there are better things to discover, deeper in the forest.

15

'THE TEMPLE OF MY HEART'

The forest looms dark and dense, its thick canopy swallowing the moonlight. The trees close in, their twisted branches clawing at the air. I stumble forward, feeling a strange pull deeper into the woods. With each step a growing heaviness presses down on me.

A faint light spills out from within the forest, casting long shadows onto the path. My heart hammers in my chest. A mixture of anticipation and apprehension is building in me, unsure if the light is leading me to safety—or not. With a deep breath, I step toward the light, unsure of what awaits me.

There: A grove of giant trees like redwoods, evenly spaced, framing a rectangular clearing on all four sides, like pillars of a Greek temple.

Between two of the pillars, branches intertwine to form an archway, an entrance of sorts. Along the archway, as if lit by lightening bugs, are the words 'The Temple of My Heart.' The earthen floor looks as though it's been recently swept clean.

My heart hammers inside my chest as I cross the temple's threshold.

I glance around; the giant tree-pillars, towering over me, hold up the starry night-sky.

'The Temple of My Heart'? It sounds deep, meaningful This must be one of those high-end nightclubs I've never had the pleasure of visiting with all the responsibilities I've carried around my neck since high school. This is my chance…

Wouldn't it be great if this was a fine Greek dining establishment, like the ones in St. Louis? Maybe I could order some moussaka and an ouzo or two. Anything to escape myself.

"Hello? Hello-o!"

No answer.

Ah, well, maybe they'll serve some food later. A guy deserves to loosen up a bit now and then. No need to be spiritual *all* the time, you could lose your balance, become one of those Bible-thumping fanatics standing on a soapbox passing out tracts. "All in moderation" is my motto. Besides, you can't be too "woke" these days, don't want to find yourself "canceled" because of your beliefs. No one will ever get saved if you tow a pious line, would they?

There's a shimmering in the air! Which means this place must be legit, right? They got the dry ice going! And disco lights flashing to the BOOM BOOM BOOM of that sound system! Look at all those dancers coming out of the forest, all decked-out in neon-colored Lycra, their faces covered by mini screens! There must be fifty of them. Talk about moves, dancing in sync with the pounding rhythm! Cool!

What was that? I thought I saw something move between the pillars. Wait, I *did* see something. A giant slug, or worm, maybe. *Man*, it's gross! It's got some nerve stinking up this classy place.

"Get outta here! Now, before I *kick* you out!"

Another giant worm rolls by, its slimy skin branded with 'R-E-B-E-L'. Rebel. Rebel without a cause—that's me!

That worm-thingy, there, branded with F-O-O-L. Fool. *Fool?*

They're showing up in bigger numbers now. That one's got GLUTTON spray-painted on its side. That one says UNFAITHFUL. That one: PIECE OF MEAT. There, on the worm

'THE TEMPLE OF MY HEART'

over there, does it really say SPOILED BRAT? You get rid of one and they come back like rats. Maybe this is one of those reality entertainment shows, or maybe a party game—they'll probably give the answer to the riddle at the end of the event.

Whoa!!! What's that they're lowering from the sky? Whoa-ho!!! Drinks on the house! And other "party favors." Now we're talking! And they've got ouzo after all!

"Hey! Waiter! Over here! Got any moussaka to go with that? No?"

BOOM BOOM BOOM. *Another one bites the dust.*
BOOM BOOM BOOM. *Another one bites the dust.*

One of the neon-thingies is pulling me onto the dance floor. She must think I'm hot. Or he? Zee? Hard to tell these days, especially when they've got digital screens lit-up over their faces. Only one way to find out.

"Excuse me, but what are your preferred pronouns?"

Yowzah! That ouzo just hit my brain.

Those huge slug-thingies seem to be getting bigger. Or maybe it's the ouzo. That one over there says 'SUCKER'!?

"Anyway, all this Jesus stuff, I don't know, man. Or woman or whatever—sorry, don't mean to offend you in any way. I'm sure religion has its place in today's society, you know what I mean? But is it *relevant* for today, is my question. I'm not dissing anyone's right to believe what they want, mind you. Tolerance and all that. But why should an old book filled with unproven, unscientific stories be allowed to dictate today's ethics, is my beef."

I still got the moves! I ain't settling down, no way. "Heh, look at my moonwalk! Michael Jackson, eat your heart out! May he rest in peace—"

"Oh, you want to say something? It's a little hard to understand you with that screen over your face. Not that I object or anything, we live in a free world. What's that? I'm a what? I'm a *hypocrite*? No, no, you got me all wrong! Hypocrites are by nature closed-minded people, and I'm a *very* open-minded person. It's all in the interpretation of the good book, a question of theology.

AAAAAH-HHHHA! Heh—your face screen—it just flashed like a dark angel! Whoa! Now, that was scary, got my heart going! I'm not into that, though I am a freethinker." There's another one of those party wormy slug thingies—it's huge! 'DISOBEDIENT.'

This is absolutely crazy: A giant round disc is being lowered from night sky. I don't know how they're doing it, but on top of the disc has got to be the biggest hologram in the world. The neon dancers, they're doing their robot moves around the disc and it's a bit kinky-like, what's happening in the hologram. People are doing things to each other and it's, it's, wait, I've seen something like this before. Probably on my secret little website, truth be told.

Truth. The compass feels like a hot potato! OW!!! It's burning a hole in my pocket! Pull it out, quick! It's spinning like a top. Probably some sort of electro-magnetic field in the vicinity.

Another massive worm—it just slithered off the dance floor and right into my arms! It spat in my eyes! It's disgusting! I can't see! I've got to wipe this stuff off my face. What's that there, DECEIVED. "Deceived? Me? No way! I was with J-Je-Jes—I can't seem to say his name—just a couple of hours ago! And I just came out to have some fun! Get away from me, you filthy vermin!"

The night is starting to drag on a bit and the music's giving me a headache. All this dancing is wearing me out.

Look at what's going on in that hologram, everyone intertwined, gyrating. How on earth do they—I'll grab a shot off that serving tray over there.

Gosh, that's disgusting.
What on earth?
Huh? What, are they all freaks or something?!
Oh.
Oh my.
No way.
I feel sick.
"Can't somebody make this stop?"

What if that were my daughter? Or son?
But I *can't* stop.
I feel raw.
Slimed.
Somebody's lowering that giant disc into a hole in the ground.
At least that hologram's out of my face.
If I could only have watched one more scene….

16

SHARERS OF THE ROAD LESS TRAVELED

Where am I? My clothes are all damp and I'm freezing to death. I must've crashed on this floor—I probably had one too many party favors. It feels like my brain is trying to kick its way out of my skull.

'Temple of My Heart', all right. A pretty cheesy place when you see it in daylight. *Gawd*, it's bright. Did I really watch that crud all night?

It feels like all that crud's been swept into my heart.

I feel slimed.

I better get back to the trysting place, face the music.

* * *

What, *more* backpacks? No, please, not *another* group of losers to deal with. Can't a guy get some peace around here?

Sounds like breakfast is being served. I'm starving. I'll peek through the bushes to see what's happening.

At the picnic table, two women are seated on the left, and two men are seated on the right. Jesus is seated in a chair at the far end of the table.

Wildflowers are placed in small vases, colorful napkins adorn the table, candles twinkle in jam jars. I mean, who lights candles for *breakfast*?

Wait. Are these the same people who slid out early from the International Night last night? Yes they are! I don't want to have to relate to this bunch of losers. I'll make my exit.

Rats. I stumbled over the backpacks.

The group around the table falls into silence.

Do they have to watch me make my way into the upright position? Sheesh.

What choice do I have now but to join them for breakfast?

I guess that empty chair is meant for me. Not that I asked them to do me any favors.

Jesus is looking at me through the flowers and candles; I avoid his gaze.

"I invited some of my other disciples to share breakfast with us this morning. I hope you don't mind." The others look shyly at him and nod.

Are they all thinking what I'm thinking, that the others are crashing their breakfast?!

"No, no, I don't mind, not at all," I say with a very large dose of sarcasm. Because I *do* mind. My night in the forest is catching up with my conscience and I'm feeling dirty and cheap. I'd rather eat my breakfast in the presence of my own misery.

Jesus seems rather relaxed this morning, the way he's casually propped his Doc Martens against the table leg and rocks his chair back and forth. Wait, *Doc Martens*?

The pain in my arm has returned with a vengeance, and the bandage looks disgusting. I don't want them to see it; I'll hide it underneath the table. But how am I going to eat, then?

Seeing my predicament, the young woman to my left places two slices of fresh bread onto my plate and slathers them with butter. She has piercing all over her face. I feel my smile freeze on my face.

"Is everything alright with you? You look a bit uncomfortable," she asks me in a thick accent. "Maybe you need some water. Here." She receives a food platter from the older woman seated next to her and tops my bread with thin slices of cheese, and meat, and alfalfa sprouts. The young man to my right pours coffee into a tiny cup from one of those European coffee-press things, and hands it to me.

"By any chance do you have a Diet Coke? I'm not a big coffee drinker." The guy holds the coffee cup in mid-air. We make eye contact. I've seen him before. I mean, I saw him last night, weaseling his way out of the atelier, but still, there's something familiar about him. He diverts his gaze from mine. "Just give me the coffee then, if finding a soda around here is too much of a bother."

It all feels European, or at least un-American. These open-faced sandwiches aren't easy to maneuver with just one hand. I'll just plop this one piece over on top of the other, and, voila! a regular sandwich.

I steal several glances at Jesus. He's wearing black skinny jeans and has his hair stuffed into one of those knitted hats, like he's stepped out of a German car advertisement. Or like he's a youth pastor. He looks younger than me, which I suppose he would be at thirty-three, and a lot cooler, the kind of guy my daughters would fall for—or my wife. Jane's always nagging me that I should spiff up my wardrobe, but do I have to go *that* far?

Everyone looks desperate to find some book or magazine to hide behind, apart from the older woman, who's as gregarious as can be.

We go around the table and give a quick introduction.

"My name is Renata, I am from Germany. From Berlin," says the young woman to my left, barely looking up from her plate. I've never heard the name before, so it doesn't stick. Something like a regatta of ships, I think.

"Don't speak with your mouth full, deary," says the woman next to her. The young woman stiffens. The older woman continues, "And my name is Anastazja, from the lovely city of Krakow, in Poland!" she says louder than necessary and with a gigantic smile. She stands to shake my hand and overturns a glass of orange juice in the process. "Oh, dear, I am so sorry!"

"My name is Jesus, from Nazareth," says Jesus while sopping up the spill. This garners suppressed giggles from the group. I still don't want to look at him.

"My name is Émile. I am from Lyon, in the south of France," he says, stiffly. Everything sounds so French with a French accent.

"My name is Simon. I live in Brussels, Belgium, though I was born in a village outside of Kinshasa, the capital of the Democratic Republic of the Congo." Simon also puts a French twist on his name. See-MOAN. *Oo-la-la.*

Everyone is staring at me. I guess it's my turn.

"Hi everybody! Nice to meet you guys. My name is Ken! My mother called me Kenneth when I got into trouble—she passed away a few years ago, may she rest in peace—but most people call me Kenny." I smile around the table. "My father also passed away, long ago, but that's another story." I seem to have lost my train of thought.

"Oh. My grandparents on my father's side came from Ireland, from County Donegal, but they moved to Dog Town in St. Louis, you know, next to the St. Louis Zoo—you've GOT to see our St. Patrick's parade on St. Pat's Day—everybody's Irish on St. Pat's Day! My Dad's work required him to move the family around a bit—until he died, of course. After that, my mother moved us back to St. Louis, which is where I call 'home'. But my wife Jane and I, and the kids—we've got five!—we live in Webster Groves now, though not in the part of Webster where Jane grew up, in one of those fancy neighborhoods next to the university." I roll my eyes.

The group remains quiet, so I assume they want me to continue. "Oh! And you can see the famous Route 66 from our house! And—"

Jesus clears his throat loudly from the other side of the table; he caught me in my slight exaggeration. Gosh, who would have thought he'd know so much about St. Louis streets? "Okay, well, maybe you can't quite see Route 66 from our house—"

"Since it is several blocks away?" he interjects. I change the subject.

"But I'm a huge Cardinals fan. The biggest. Jane, she's my wife, she calls it my 'religion'. I've got the biggest flat screen money can buy, to watch all the Cardinals games. I've got big plans to turn our basement into a sports bar, everything decked out in red and white, sports memorabilia, the works!"

They're still looking at me, still not saying anything. What more can I tell them? Seeing Renata, I remember: "Oh yeah! We're all German on my mother's side. They *all* come from Germany. Somewhere south, I think. A place called Stuttgart, if you've ever heard of it."

Uncomfortable silence. Émile breaks the uncomfortableness.

"And what *country* might you come from, young man?"

I don't fully grasp the question. "Well, from *America*, of course!"

"Of course," repeats Émile dryly, then heatedly babbles something in French to Jesus. Jesus places a hand on Émile's arm to calm him down, for some reason.

✶ ✶ ✶

Breakfast seems to go on like forever, with ensuing platters of fruits, cheeses and nuts, ending with a bowl of fancy dark chocolate of the Swiss variety (invoking a collection of oohs from around the table) accompanied by coffee so thick that potholes could be patched with it. Jesus seems to be in no hurry, dipping a little cookie into his little espresso cup. I wish I could get my hands on a Diet Coke.

Apart from the older woman—Anastazja—who seems to gab on and on and on, the others seem only slightly more interested in engaging in conversation than me. The atmosphere around the table feels a bit glum, if you ask me. Somebody's got to liven things up around here. There's that one joke I once heard….

I stand up, tap my glass. The group falls into even greater silence.

"Eh-hem. So, in *heaven*—Jesus, correct me if I'm wrong here—I hear that in heaven the French are the cooks, the Germans are the engineers, the Italians are the lovers, the Swiss are the organizers, and the British are the police."

I take a theatrical pause. They look at me, dead-panned. Tough crowd.

"In *hell*, however, the British are the cooks, the Italians are the organizers, the Swiss are the lovers, the French are the engineers, and the Germans are the police!" I slap my hand on my leg and snort with laughter.

No one laughs. They just stare at me.

It is the older man who speaks. Émile. I'll need to practice these foreign names. "In that case, what are the Americans doing in heaven, and in hell? Can you tell us?"

Anastazja pipes in: "Whatever Americans will be doing in hell, they will make it into a verrrrry hellish place! Eternal work hours, no vacation time, no maternity leave—"

"Everyone MUST wear button-down collars," chimes in Simon, rolling his eyes, "baseball caps, sports logos on *everything*, khaki pants with those huge pockets—" I look down at my khaki cargo pants with huge pockets and adjust my Cardinals baseball cap.

"We'll be driving around in monster, gas-guzzling SUVs!" Renata perks up from her doldrums.

"And the food! *Sacre bleu!* Ketchup flowing everywhere!" Émile got his two cents in. More uncontrollable laughter.

"Ok, ok, we'll end this here," says Jesus, biting his knuckles to control his laughter. Regular stand-up comedians, they are.

"Hey! What will Americans be doing in heaven, then?" I come to my nation's defense.

"They're the entertainers," says Jesus, wiping away laugh-tears with his napkin.

* * *

He's coming toward me, carrying a basin of water and with a towel thrown over his shoulder. He kneels beside me and removes my filthy bandage. I wince and look away, though curiosity gets the better of me and I look at what I've done to myself. I'm so close to him that I feel his body heat. Like Mom, when she tended to my wounds when I was a boy.

He washes my sores with water, soothes my skin with oil, wraps it up in love.

"There is only room for one in the temple of your heart," he says, looking directly into my eyes.

I can't keep myself from tearing-up a little.

"There," he says when he's finished. And then: "This is what I am about to do to your heart."

I look at him and melt. I'm not ready to say sorry for the night in the forest. Probably because I'm not ready to forgive myself. I feel like dirt.

17

THE ALTAR OF DARKNESS

The others adjust their backpacks, shifting weight and checking straps, since their worms are going absolutely berserk. My worms are only mildly agitated. Not that I'm comparing myself with them.

We walk around the back of the clearing and down toward the stream. We cross the bridge, uncertainty growing with every step. As we pass by the atelier the others notice the broken and bloodied pane of glass, and do a collective gasp. I remain silent. I can see Jesus noticing my tapestry, mangled and smashed in the back corner of the room. He glances at me, saddened, and a tinge of guilt washes over me. "Sorry," I mouth to him.

Uh-oh—is he veering off the trail and taking us on the path to the 'The Temple of My Heart'? If he is, I'm in trouble. I'm going to have to go around with a giant 'A' sewn on all of my clothes like in 'The Scarlet Letter.'

Jesus stops and gathers us around him. He takes a moment to caringly notice each of us.

"I have chosen the five of you to accompany each other on the next segment of your journeys. What you are about to endure will be challenging, so you will need each other to lean on for support. And remember, there is no pit so deep that my love for you is not deeper still."

"Hey! You're plagiarizing Corrie ten Boom! I remember reading that in one of her books," I say, a bit too loudly. I'm glad to catch *him* in a discrepancy, for once.

"Could it be that this was a theme Corrie and I spoke of during our times together?" he asks me.

That gave me something to chew on.

Jesus doesn't take us on the path to 'The Temple of My Heart', thankfully, but continues on the main trail. Strange, I'm not the only one who looks relieved!

Heavy clouds shield us from the sun's warmth, and the air has become clammy and close. I wish I could hang out at the atelier today, eat up the leftovers from the International Night—I'm desperate for some alone time.

The trail follows the curves of the stream. I wish I'd listened to it last night.

Émile walks with a pretty strong limp; I wonder what happened to him. Uh oh, he's slowed down and is waiting for me. I do not want to talk with him—or with any of these losers. I walk right past him. He runs to keep up with me. Can't the guy take a hint?

"Anastazja has quite the story," he says, as if he's telling me a terrible secret. Anastazja is talking up a storm with the young woman walking with her—what was her name again? Renata, that's it! It looks like Renata wants to say something, but Anastazja doesn't give her a chance. Renata looks flustered. Émile keeps jabbering, "I became better acquainted with Anastazja last night, in the forest, at the 'Oktoberfest Tavern'. It was her choice of venue, not mine, I must say." He speaks like Inspector Clouseau.

"So you spent the night in the forest, too? I mean, with that woman?"

"Maybe not *all* night like *some* of us," he says, pointing in the direction of Renata. I thought he'd blown my cover.

Émile walks next to me in blissful silence. The man must be in his late fifties, slender, softly graying. He's wearing wire-rimmed eyeglasses, the kind that make Europeans look European—and a blue-gray scarf only Europeans can wear without looking gay, knotted just-so around his neck. Everything about him, from his heather green cashmere sweater to his impeccable light-blue dress shirt, makes me feel very underdressed. Oh no—he's found something else to talk about.

"All of those stories yesterday evening, about forgiving injustices, and being forgiven, they were not easy to listen to, *non*?" He looks at me uncertainly, comes closer and asks, "Have you ever been unjustly treated, Monsieur Kenneth?"

I need to get away from this guy before I punch him in the nose. The last person I want to think about is Benedict 'Mitt' Arnold.

I hadn't noticed how dark it's become—we're walking in dampened hues of charcoal. Jesus doesn't seem to need a break, so we keep plodding deeper into the forest.

An owl hoots from a nearby tree; Anastazja jumps and yelps. She grabs Renata's arm, giggling nervously. Those black stretch pants are a size too small for her, and I wouldn't say that frumpy sweater compliments her in any way. She's probably in her sixties, though it's hard to tell since it looks like she's led a hard life. Why she's got her frizzy, faded red hair piled on top of her head with that big plastic clamp, I'll never know. Jesus turns around to look at her, then quickly turns back to hide his smile—she obviously makes him happy. I doubt if I do. Jessie might look like Anastazja if she lets herself go in later years—or has lived as hard a life as Anastazja, which I don't want to think about.

Renata—twenty-four, twenty-six maybe? Her hair is a bit like Jane's—or like Keenan's or Kyle's for that matter—straight and black, though she wears hers shaved razor-short on one side, and shoulder-length in the front and back She's wearing Doc Martens, like Jesus, and the sort of thing a ballet dancer might wear when not dancing: black latex pants and a sleeveless strapped top, also in black, that she's covered with a loose, wide-necked sweater in periwinkle blue. Her face is lovely, though old

JOURNEY INTO THE SHIMMERING

beyond her years, with soulful brown eyes peering through a frail complexion—it's hard to see underneath all that piercing. Neck tattoos haven't taken over her face, at least not yet, and I hope they never will!

She pulls at her sweater, attracting my attention to something on her shoulder. It's not a tattoo: she's been branded. With an iron. I feel sick. I think I've seen something like this somewhere before, though I can't quite remember where.

Émile taps me on the shoulder.

"What is it *now*?" I almost shout.

"He is rather well-known," Émile whispers. He points to Simon walking next to Jesus; they're deep in conversation.

"Who is, Jesus?" I couldn't help myself.

"*Mais non! Mais oui*—I was speaking of Simon! He is a famous—"

Jesus looks over his shoulder at Émile; Émile clams up and moves away from me. Honestly, the French accent is beginning to grate on me.

High above us a wisp of shadow dims what little light there is; we flinch as if being dive-bombed by bats. Jesus waves us forward.

Simon must be in his early- to mid-thirties, tall, slender, buff. Amazing, how his ebony skin seems to glow from the inside-out. One thing's for sure: I'd have to wax my thighs to get into those black skinny jeans he's wearing. That white tailored shirt accentuates his ripped frame. I'm hit with admiration. Or envy. Come to think of it, he *does* look familiar....

I jump. There is movement in the shadows. I think we're being watched. I'm feeling the same way I did back in the corn field, when I told Jesus to stop and turn around because we were going in the wrong direction. Did he listen to me? No, and we ended up in that playground from hell. Where on earth are we going to end up this time?

We turn a bend and, in near-pitch darkness, Jesus disappears! Now Simon has disappeared! And Anastazja! And now

Renata! Woah—I'm slipping down a steep slope slimed with wetness! Everyone is screaming! It's dark and slimy and gross! It's absolute chaos!

I land with a thud behind Renata as Émile slams into me from behind. We're like a bunch of kids smashed together at the bottom of a slide. We're quiet as we gain our bearings and figure out what just happened.

Jesus helps us to our feet, then sets his sights elsewhere as Anastazja primps her hair and Simon mumbles something about his clothes being dirty.

My eyes have adjusted to the darkness, and I can see what has caught Jesus' attention: A gargantuan, bulbous dome, as black and rough as volcanic rock, is wedged between two almost-vertical rockfaces. It looks like a meteorite that has plopped out of the sky and skidded into place, half-buried into the forest floor.

I realize our predicament: the rock completely blocks our way forward! There's *no way* we can get around it, wedged as it is between the two cliffs, and there's certainly no way we'll be able to climb up that slippery slope—at least not all of us.

"Jesus, we're trapped!" I express my panic. In the dusky light I see his eyes; he places a hand on my shoulder, which calms me to some degree. I then hear him say, "Come."

In pitch darkness, Jesus and I approach the rock. We walk along the curved surface of the dome, guiding ourselves by touching its course exterior. I hear Renata emit a stifled whimper as the others follow behind us. Ahead of us, a muted, throbbing sliver of red light illuminates the forest floor.

With a shoulder, Jesus pushes hard against the surface of the stony wall. Our senses are immediately assaulted by a jarring scraping sound, accompanied by the stench of meat that was allowed to putrefy for a thousand years. Anastazja wails and walks in circles. Simon stares at the crack in the wall, stone faced. Émile is saying the rosary.

I timidly peak into the crack; the interior of the dome looks gelatinous, gummy and translucent, tinted in a distasteful shade of pig fat.

I have to say something. Anything. Yes! I'll dig out the book and find my flashlight.

"Heah, everybody! Listen up! Here's something appropriate for the occasion, from *The Pilgrim's Progress*:

> *'Why, the Valley itself, which is as dark as pitch; we also saw there hobgoblins, satyrs, and dragons of the pit; we heard also in that Valley a continual howling and yelling, as of a people under unutterable misery, who there sat bound in affliction and irons; and over that Valley hang the discouraging clouds of confusion. Death also doth always spread his wings over it. In a word, it is every whit dreadful, being utterly without order.'"*

"You recited this to encourage us, didn't you?" Simon's words are tinged with sarcasm. He's irritated with me, so I might as well milk it for all it's worth. I moan and groan while holding the flashlight to my chin, shining the beam upward to make me look like a goblin—I taught the kids how to do this for Halloween. Simon slaps my hand and causes the flashlight to tumble into darkness. I want to slap him back, but Jesus motions to us to follow him as he steps through the crevice.

No one looks particularly enthused to obey.

Émile is the first to dare. He wanly pokes the gelatin with a finger, sticks his arm into the glop, then shimmies himself into the glutinous interior. The gel reminds me of the grease that coagulated on top of Mom's cold pork roast dinner. I want to gag. Jesus and Émile converse on the other side.

"I cannot go in there," says Simon flatly, echoing my sentiments.

I shimmy my way past the women, stand next to Simon and, in one fluid motion, push Simon through the opening. He does not look pleased.

"You naughty boy, get your hands off of me," shouts Anastazja before I shove her through to the other side. Simon and Anastazja stare at me through the aspic. If looks could kill.

Now it's just Renata and me.

"So here's my plan," I say to Renata over a howling sound sweeping through the forest. "Now that they're all stuck in there, you and I can find our way out of this place and—Renata? What are you doing?" Did she *really* choose to enter that filth instead of coming with me?

At least my plan worked: now all I have to do is get out of this forest and run all the way home. If I can manage to make my way up that slide.

"Sayonara, losers!"

The edges of the scar on the surface of the dome—they're coagulating around me! I'm being sucked into the slimy goo, like a fly into the dripping mouth of a Venus flytrap! The gelatin, oh how it feels like bacon grease! Oh, God, I'm gagging! I'm going to throw up! I'm being squeezed into the innards of this disgusting organism! I don't want to die like this! I don't want to be found here, coagulated, by some archeological dig a thousand years from now!

"Noooooooo!"

Everything has slowed to a crawl. My eyes are having a hard time adapting to this new kind of murk. The red, sickly light pulses through the gelatin, a *whoosh whoosh whoosh* sound throbs like blood in my ears. Anastazja wails; Renata whimpers. Émile and Simon exclaim a bunch of hysterical French in surround-sound around me. What, is Simon complaining that his clothes might get ruined? We could *die* in here, for crying out loud!

I'm doing alright, apart from feeling claustrophobic and agitated and angry and everyone is getting on my nerves and a dread is building inside me and my worms are going crazy and my face feels like it's going to explode from all this emotional pressure! I've got to get out of this place! I've got to escape! I've got to run!

"Help! Help! Help!"

Jesus comes over and places his hand on my heart. My wrenching innards are instantly soothed. But now it looks like it's Renata's turn to have a panic attack, because she's bent over and can't catch her breath!

Jesus rushes to her, moves her face toward his. "Repeat after me," he says to her, gently but firmly. She's in a daze. "Renata, listen. Though you walk through the valley—"

"Though I w-w-walk through the v-v-valley—" she says in what is most likely German, but for whatever reason I'm able to understand her, anyway—

"Of the shadow of death," says Jesus,

"Of the shadow of death," We join her in our own languages,

"You shall fear no evil," says Jesus,

"I shall fear no evil," says Renata, trembling,

"For I am with you," Jesus has made eye-contact with Renata,

"For you are with me." Renata is quieted, or so I thought: she just pounced to her feet like a cougar!

"But Jesus," shouts Renata, "I cannot do this! I cannot go through this alone!" Her fists are clenched at her sides.

"You are not meant to do this alone, my daughter!
I rescue you,
Not by throwing you a line from a polite distance,
But by entering your sarcophagus,
Into the very core of your pain and humiliation.
As I did with a little girl long ago,
I will rouse you from your death,
Resurrect you with my life
By speaking tenderly, *Talitha cumi.*
I will take you by the hand,
Pull you up from the bed of your withered slumber,

For I am Emmanuel,
Your God who is near."

Renata allows Jesus to place his arms around her, and she buries her face in his shoulder.

Something strange is happening to me.

Am I seeing *things—or am I* feeling *things?*

The murkiness of this gloopy muck hasn't at all brightened, but I'm seeing things I normally only feel, and feeling things I normally don't see. Because I see Renata, stabbed, pierced, bound in slithery strings!

And Simon there, look at him, bound like a mummy in gross, gory gooeyness!

And Anastazja, look at that giant black monster-thing swirling above her head!

Oh, and Émile, he's slashed! Shattered! He's bound by a massive collection of black bonds!

What's happening now?!

There is a writhing-back in the atmosphere, a sucking retreat of evil, a bending of realities, as Jesus is revealed in a different glory.

He is now Jesus, King of Kings, adorned with a majestic crown of shimmering gold that casts light and scatters shadows.

We fall on our faces before him.

How long have I been out for? Minutes? Eons? I am afraid to look around me. I feel a tap on my shoulder.

"Kenneth."

It's Jesus. Play dead, Kenny. Maybe I *am* dead. Maybe I've been turned into a pillar of salt or something!

Another tap. I open an eye. Jesus is bent down, looking straight into that eye. All of his holiness is making me want to hide from him even more. I'd rather lie here in the dirt, thank you very much. Nonetheless, he reaches out his hand to help me to my feet.

His crown is dissipating into the glitter of a million shimmering lights. He is once again robed in modern-day attire, looking at me reassuringly.

"Kenny, as my holiness is clothed in humanity, so is your humanity clothed in my holiness. When my holy Father sees you, he first sees me. Do not confuse my work of salvation with my work of sanctification. On this journey, do not allow the dross rising to the surface of your heart detract you from the truth of who you are in me."

I'm not sure if I understand all this, but I probably won't be turned into a pillar of salt. I'm not so sure about the others, though. Look at them. How can they stand having all of those black strings restrict them like that?

We follow Jesus even though it seems like the stupidest thing to do. Pushing our way through the schmalz, we scoot down chutes and slide down slides and trip up steps and stumble down stoops, whimpering and wailing and muttering and sniveling along the way.

We stop. We look around us:

It is as if we've entered a private balcony in some wicked, twisted opera house.

Far below us, placed at the very core of the dome and guarded by a sentinel of gnarled, ancient stalactites intertwined like gargoyles locked in eternal strife, we see:

A stone, a slab,
Some sort of sacrificial altar,
Adorned with vile carvings
Of goat heads
And symbols, and runes and incantations
In forbidden, ancient tongues.

This stone is
Covered with broken souls,

And silent screams,
The terror of the innocents.
We are standing before
The Place of Secrets,
The Dregs of Shame,
The Heart of Wickedness,
The Den of Demons,
The Incubator of Oppression,
The Tesseract of Tethers,
The Source of Wounds and Worms and Lies.
My wounds. *My* worms. *My* lies.
I am standing on the brink of my own abyss.

I am overtaken by a memory:
Faces and odors,
Pressings, and whisperings. Terror.
Fright imbued with wicked, twisted pleasure,
A nauseating tincture of pain,
Blended with fear and spiced with indulgence and attention.

"Jesus," I can scarcely speak. My pulse is racing, my nerves are titillated. I swerve back and forth between the pain of the abuse I've known, and the pleasure of whatever I've found to deaden my pain.

He speaks to my heart of hearts,

"I journeyed
To hell, through death.
I dwell now in your darkness,
Your paralyzing, terrorizing pain.
Yet I have journeyed from life, through death
To carve the way back for you,
From death to life."

Anastazja has collapsed to the floor. Jesus runs to her and motions for us to do the same. He is huddled over her. His voice, strong and sure, pierces through this hideous grunge:

> "The poison of an evil heart
> Is extracted from your heart
> In the Shimmering
> Of my radiant, holy love for you.
> Which is exactly why
> The Enemy of your souls
> Wants you to hide your pain
> In the darkness of shame."

"Jesus," I say, "I know what you're asking me to do, to forgive the people who've hurt me. But there's *no way in hell* I can let those people get away with what they did to me!" I can't forgive them. They've taken too much from me. It hurts too much.

"No," I say, in case he didn't get it the first time. I want them to pay, to suffer as they made me suffer. Besides, I enjoy wallowing in my own victimhood.

Jesus stares at me. I glare back at him.

"Oh, so now I get it! You think that, because I'm not perfect myself, those scumbags who used me can get away with what they did to me?"

"No one gets away with anything," he mutters.

My worms, now the size of boa constrictors, slither out of my backpack, around my shoulders, down my back, around my waist, and into my awaiting arms.

He grabs my backpack devoid of worms, makes his way down the stoney steps.

"Heh! What are you doing?!"

He approaches the altar. The altar's lurid content writhes back from him, whimpering. He reaches out and uses an arm to scoop the sordid wretch into my backpack!

"Watch out for my toiletries in there! And keep an eye on my notebook, wouldja!"

He returns with my backpack. He stands in front of me.

"Put it on," he says. He does not look pleased.

My silence is my answer. I pet my worms into purrdom. From the safety of my arms they regard Jesus with comfortable disdain, even with their faceless faces.

"I don't want that scumbag on my back!"

He places the backpack at my feet.

"Unless you deal with your wounds, by forgiving and being forgiven, you will go through life with your heart filled with the filth of others, and your worms will feed on that filth until they explode, damaging your life and the lives around you!"

Turning from me, Jesus approaches Émile, Simon and Anastazja, who are huddled together in the gloop—I've lost sight of Renata. He says something to them, probably something about forgiveness, like he said to me. Anastazja, looking determined, shakes her head 'no'. The two men look at each other and resignedly hand their backpacks over to Jesus. Jesus makes his way down steep steps with their backpacks and toward the altar.

The filth on the altar writhes back from Jesus. Jesus stands resolute before it. With an arm, he slides the disgusting stuff squirming on the altar into each of the backpacks. He bounds back up the stony outcrop and hands the backpacks to Émile and Simon. Neither seem particularly interested in receiving them, much less putting them on as Jesus is signaling for them to do, but they relent.

Jesus points toward the other side of the slab, to an arched doorway carved into the hard wall of the chamber. The two men, at first reluctant, scurry down the steep steps, around the altar, and disappear through the portal on the other side of the chamber.

Anastazja is confronted by Jesus one more time. She wears her worms around her shoulders like a mink stole, which would be disgusting enough without that head-monster of hers, its rubbery bonds attached like snakes to her brain. Folding her arms over her chest she enters into a staring match with Jesus. She wins.

He looks at Anastazja, then me, then turns and makes his way down the stony steps. He eyes the altar sternly before dashing toward the portal on the other side.

Anastazja emits the highest pitched scream I have ever had the displeasure of hearing.

"Don't leave me heeeeeere!" she squeals.

Jesus stops, turns around and looks at her.

"Wait! Wait! Jesus, pleeeeese!" she cries as she tiptoes her way down the perilous steps. Jesus meets her before the disgusting altar and gives her a huge hug of reassurance. Anastazja hands her backpack to him, then covers her eyes so she doesn't have to see the festering glop he's scraping into it. She screeches as her worm-goblins untwine themselves from around her shoulders and glide into her backpack. Taking Jesus' hand, Anastazja warbles with worry as the two of them slide around the altar and run toward the portal. A sharp sliver of light pierces the darkness through the portal before being extinguished by the darkness.

A whoop of victory crescendos through the sooty, sticky air of the chamber.

The King has departed.

Am I left alone to rot in this stinking subsidiary of hell? What has become of Renata?

Darkness presses upon the aspic atmosphere. I can barely breathe.

A greenish light pulsates to a booming beat. Tainted by last night's excesses, my body is swiftly, strangely stirred. The beat intensifies. Whoops and hollers erupt as the neon dancers from The Temple Of My Heart appear out of the darkness. They circle the altar while doing their jerky robot moves to the electro beat.

High above me, a disturbance occurs in the gelatinous gloop.

Wow. Just wow.

An electric buzz pulsates the air, punctuated by flashes of intense, wiggly light. Like a gigantic camera lens a huge hole swirls opens in the chamber ceiling. Through the hole a huge, flat disc descends into the cavernous space.

It is the giant hologram I was glued to last night, and it is materializing directly above the slimy altar!

The same people are doing the same things to each other as they were doing in the hologram last night.

Is that it? Is this all they have to offer? It all becomes pretty much same-old, same-old after a while, if you ask me. I hope they ramp up the activity a bit.

And they do! The hologram just collapsed before my very eyes! It is no longer a 3-D video of these people, it's become the *real* people doing *real* things to each other! The room falls into absolute mayhem, a den of debauchery. My eyes are riveted to the scene in front of me. I try tearing myself away from their filthy gyrations but I've got to see what's going to happen next!

Gosh.

Oh.

That's not—

But, when you see it this up-close, it's a bit gross if you ask me, especially with all those gooey black cords wrapped around all of them—can't they see it themselves?!

This is disgusting. I mean, really, this ain't cool at all.

And it has nothing to do with love.

The performers stop what they're doing. They look around as if they've come out of a stupor. They try to cover up their nakedness as best they can as the gaze of a million eyes ogle them from the darkness. They huddle together, shivering, looking exposed and vulnerable.

Now there's yelling, and screaming, because the giant disc is tilting, and the people on the disc are being tipped onto the wicked altar! The people grip the rim of the disc to keep themselves from falling off.

"Stop this!" I yell.

I'm able to reach a young man, he's beseeching me to help him. He grabs onto my arm but his hand is slimy with the filth of the altar and we make eye contact but I lose my grip and I watch him disappear into the altar's wretch.

I see it now:

These people are being offered on that altar.

It hits me, where I'd seen these people before: *on my secret little website.*

But c'mon, man! That's not real!

"It is extremely real for those who are stuck in that 'make believe' world of yours."

A laser of piercing, holy light cuts through the darkness of my heart.

"What—J-J-J-J, God, was that you?"

"And I weep for each one who is forced or trafficked into that industry, or makes their way into that industry out of need, or coercion, or intrigue." His saddened voice resonates through the chambers of my heart. I look around but do not see him.

These are the people I've idolized and gawked at and lusted over in the privacy of my home; now they're in front of me, and I see their wounds, their desperation, their desperate need to be seen, to be accepted, to be loved. I see their hopes and dreams consumed like junk food as their lives are deposited onto the altar of my wonton cravings. This is the altar on which I've sacrificed others for pleasure, in order to deaden my own pain.

I'm tired of looking at the abuse.

There is a brand mark on the back of one of the women falling onto the altar. The same mark as Renata's.

It *is* Renata. *Renata* is being dumped onto that altar.

Now I know why Jesus put the two of us together on this leg of our journey.

The jerky neon dancing-thingies encircle me—they caress me, fondle me, they carry me plank-like toward the slab of the altar.

I'm startled, though honored; I enjoy the attention given me and glory in their revelry.

Now *I'm* the one being dumped onto the altar.

This is the altar on which I have been sacrificed for pleasure, in order to dampen the pain of others!

Slithering tentacles bind me to the altar. My body is pressed into the filth strewn across the slab. I'm slathered in all this smut.

"Get away from me, you filthy parasites! Stop it! Get away from me! Please! Make it stop! I can't take much more of this. Please, just stop. Please."

I push against the bondage, punch against the spirits who mock me, pointing at my shame. I heave against the onslaught. I am so tired. I feel exhausted, and used, lonely and abused. I can't make it stop. I cling to my knees, huddle in the fetal position to protect myself from their gapings and gropings.

Renata lies next to me though turned away from me, and I clearly see the scar on her shoulder from the brand.

The raves, the rips, the hookups, the hooks, spin around me in a cesspool of debauchery.

I've given everything, as they've taken everything.

They're finished with me.

They've already moved on to their next victim.

All of this has little to do with me. I'm just a piece of meat feeding some angry monster.

Oh.

I know who that monster is.

What am I doing here? What on earth am I doing here?! Oh, God! How did I end up here? The old stuff. The same old, counterfeit stuff. Same old counterfeit relationships, counterfeit—

"Counterfeit love," he again speaks directly to my heart.

"Your heart was made for love, for holy love—my love—and my love expressed through the holy hearts of others."

"Please help me, J-J-J—"

Bats bombard me, ravens peck at me to hinder me from speaking The Name.

This rancid, greenish light, the BOOM BOOM BOOM, I'm so tired of this grinding, empty music, and the stench, and these hands, these filthy, groping hands. I can't get them to stop. The others around me, sighing, languish in utter hopelessness.

I can't speak, I can barely pull in a breath to exhale the word, "Jesus."

Stillness.

A release in the tension, an easing in the gloop. The neon dancers quickly skedaddle into the shadows.

Now!

"Renata! Renata! Where are you? Everybody, *we've got to get out here!*"

Sighings, weepings, languishings. No one is responding.

"Everybody, get up, this is our chance! We have to get out of this place, *now!*"

I rip off the tethers, gather whatever clothes I can find and slide myself off the altar.

The swirling activity, briefly stilled, returns in increasing velocity. The bats! The ravens!

"Get away from me!"

I gather my bearings. Toward that portal: run, Kenny, run!

But I *can't* run through all this gelatinous muck!

Wait—my backpack, he wanted me to take it with me. I left it way on top of that outcrop! I have no choice but to choose to obey him, so I need to climb up all those steps and retrieve it.

Oh God! The glowing, groping, gummy hands are back with a vengeance. What if that portal closes before I get to it? I'd be left here to rot!

"Get off me! Get your grubby hands OFF ME! Jesus, help!"

The grubby hands retreat.

I need to run but I can't, but I have to try! I can't give up, I can't give in! Wade through the goop, Kenny! Press yourself through! Now, DIVE!

I'm released from the gloop with a glutinous glop.

* * *

Where am I?

Where is Jesus? I've *got* to find Jesus!

Oh, what a lovely sight—daylight!

How long were we in that chamber? I fear that Renata might still be trapped inside.

Rain! The air is fresh, and clean—no more of that gelatinous bacon grease. Inhale, Kenny, catch your breath. Breathe.

My clothes are torn and tarnished. Even with the rain, filth clings to me. Thoughts of the chamber, that unholy altar, claw at my consciousness. It was a nightmare incarnate.

Am I truly so fractured, so desperate for anything to fill the void? Have I stooped to using others, becoming a leech for fleeting relief from my own torments?

The worms—I sought answers and have been confronted with the painful origins of these loathsome hitchhikers. Must I forever drag them with me through the mud of my life? They've always been my shadow, but now that they've been brought into the light, they squirm for all to see!

"Back off, you vile beasts!" It's time to shed this weight. These worms have got to go!

The forest, menacing in last night's shadows, is quiet, approachable, bright—even in the rain. Strange, how the wall of the dome feels pliable—it certainly is not soft, but not as hard as it was when we first entered.

Which way do I go?

I'm always abandoned, always alone. I'm always contrary and willful, if I'm honest with myself.

Going left would take me back to the trysting place, I think. It would also take me through the forest, and I don't think I'm strong enough to face another round of temptations.

Where will I end up if I go the other way? This is what I get for lagging behind Jesus all the time.

The foliage drips tenderly with cleansing rain, a fugue of worshipful whispers.

"Jesus, which way do you want me to go? I want to be in tune with you again."

"Follow me toward the presently unknown."

It is Jesus! I can't see him, but I know it's him because I can almost feel him near me! He wants me to start on the untested trail.

But this trail: from the crevice in the dome, it's become two trails, plaited together like Julia's braids, crisscrossing, overlapping yet moving together in one direction! I find this is very disorientating. Why wouldn't Jesus want me to join him back at the trysting place?

There's Renata!

"Renata!" I shout to her.

She walks away from the crevice of the dome, biting her lip, looking lost. Mascara runs down her face; her clothes are torn. She's found a vile-looking blanket to cover herself with. She's dragging her backpack in the mud behind her.

"You made it! We made it! But the others on the altar—are they on their way?"

She collapses to the ground.

"Renata! Let me help you—" I reach out my hand to her. She smacks it away.

"Okay, okay! I won't touch you."

She struggles to get up but won't receive my help.

"Have it your way, but we have to get going," I plead with her.

She pulls the ugly blanket tightly around her.

"I think we're supposed to go this way," I say, trying to comfort her.

We start on the trail and step over and around and between the twisting rivulets of swirling mud. Renata follows me haltingly, doing her best to keep up while maintaining her distance.

I'm desperate to find Jesus. Renata has her own reasons for remaining behind, but I should've gone with Jesus when he asked me to. After all I've been through with him, after all we've shared on this journey, the distance between him and me has become unbearable.

Yet the pain I bear has also become unbearable.

Painful, humiliating images invade my mind like ghost lights from a migraine. Inside my backpack the worms fight for attention.

"Knock it off back there!"

Renata lags far behind me; I motion for her to catch up with me, but she stays distant. She looks like a lost little girl. I slow my pace, let her catch up with me. Again, she keeps her distance.

Will we ever catch up to Jesus?

We follow one strand of the trail, stumble, follow the other strand, which takes us back to the other, back and forth, back and forth. I can't see with all this rain; I find my baseball cap in my backpack, put it on—it hardly helps in this downpour.

Behind me, Renata lets out a scream as she trips and falls into the mud. She winces from a gash on her knee as blood mingles with rain water and trickles to the ground. I run to her; she finally lets me help her. Her body falls limp as I lift her into my arms. She looks helpless, frail; her face, her coloring is not unlike Jane's, though with brown eyes and not Jane's blue. I should've been there for Jane.

The black rubber bands I saw on Renata, I can't see them now but I know they're there. Renata turns her face from me.

"Heh, I think I saw Jesus—about fifty paces away!"

"Jesus!" I shout.

"Sorry, Renata, I know this isn't easy, but I've got to jog a bit, okay?"

She rests her head on my chest.

"There he is! He's talking with the others. Oh wait. The others just disappeared!" Where on earth did they go?

Jesus, standing alone on the trail, sees us, bolts back toward us.

"Renata, you're going to be okay, okay? He's almost here."

His clothes are soaked; his hair is matted and dripping around his face. He takes Renata from my arms and bundles her into his own.

He marches with her straight down the middle of the trail. He's already far ahead of me, even with having to carry Renata—maybe because I have to stumble over the stupid braids of this stupid trail!

They've disappeared. Couldn't they have waited for me to catch up with them?

"Jesus! Wait!"

Stupid trail. And all this mud. I'm going to sprain an ankle if I have to keep this up much longer.

Wait, what's that? Strange, how the two strands of the trail have conjoined. And where they conjoin is a tall hedge of greenery.

Within the hedge is a stone archway covered in ivy.

Within the archway is a heavy wooden door, ancient and wrought in iron.

I approach the archway, and the heavy door creaks open.

Trepidatiously, I step over the threshold through to the other side.

PART FIVE

Pilgrims' Progress

18

SIMON

"There you are!"

"Wait, what? Simon, is that you?"

"We've got to get moving—I'm a sitting duck in the open, even in the evening."

I remember now, how I walked through the archway and arrived at this city park. It was still light then, but now the park is lit by streetlights and filled with the din of city nightlife.

"Where am I? I didn't know which direction Jesus went with Renata, so I thought I should just sit on this park bench and wait. I must've doze off," I say, shivering in my wet clothes. I struggle up from a bench. "How long was I out for?"

"Long enough to make the Master dispatch me to go find you. And you should have noticed their wet footprints leading to my apartment, just over there. Sit much longer on this bench and you might get snagged for loitering, especially around here."

I'm confused. "Where is here?"

"Le Sablon. In Brussels."

"Brussels, as in the capital of the Netherlands? Got it."

He lets out a dramatic sigh. "*Mon Dieu*, you Americans. Brussels is the heart of *Belgium*! Come now, we shouldn't linger!"

He leads me through wrought-iron gates to the entrance of a grand French-style building just outside the park.

"Wow, what a door! Mahogany?"

"Please close it behind you. The alarm is set. There is a lift—an *elevator*—but it is just as easy to take the stairs."

Calling it a 'stairs' doesn't do it justice. A black lacquered banister spirals upward, winding like a sleek serpent beside pristine white marble steps. There are two ornate doors on each landing, so this must be an opulent apartment building masquerading as a mansion.

"Couldn't we have just taken the elevator? I'm really wiped-out from what I went through in that chamber back there."

Simon flings around and looks me directly in the eyes. "Do you think you are the only one who suffered in the chamber? *Non*? And now I must open my very private home and life to the likes of *you*," he snaps. He turns and pounces up the final steps to the top floor and out of sight.

"Aren't we a bit testy," I say, but not until I'm certain that he can't hear me. He's bigger than me.

I drag myself up to the top landing where a single, grand open door marks the entry to the topmost residence. Filthy, jiggling backpacks line the curved wall of the landing. I find a spot for my own travel-worn pack. My worms are presently docile; they're probably just as tired from the evil chamber as I am. I slip off my boots and place them next to my backpack. My weary feet almost raise a shout of hallelujah from their sudden freedom. Leaving the world's grime behind me, I step into a lavish dream.

The foyer is octagonal in shape, the pattern of its black-and-white marble floor culminating in a delicately-wrought golden inlaid fleur-de-lis at its center. A modern crystal chandelier drips light from above, illuminating gilded mirrors that magnify the room's splendor. An ornate stairway, its champagne-colored carpet rich and plush, spirals to a yet unseen level.

Something catches my eye: Renata, adorned in a white robe, peeks at me from over the balustrade above, her head wrapped in a towel like a turban. Her beauty catches my breath.

Her presence is a grace note on this symphony of architectural wonder.

"Heh, Renata! Glad to see you're okay! Renata?"

Renata quickly retreats; she probably isn't ready to see me yet, after everything we went through together in the chamber.

From the doorway of a powder room, Simon jumps at me like out of a jack-in-the-box.

"Shhhh!" he shushes at me, "it is nearly *midnight*! The others have taken baths and are on their way to bed. Which I have not been able to do as you can plainly see. Since *I* had to go out looking for *you*!" He says this while looking at the condition of his clothing, and not at me. He looks like a million bucks even when he's splashed with dried mud and grime. I look exactly like I've walked out of an evil chamber.

He leads me down a long hallway—more of an art gallery, really— adorned with eclectic paintings, highlighted with muted lighting. My soggy socks inadvertently smear wet prints across the polished floor.

"Heh, look! I'm adding my own artwork to the place!"

Simon does not look amused.

I wonder what's behind these closed doors…I really want to do some snooping! Maybe I'll just peak into this door here…

Simon stares at me from the other end of the hallway. His arms are crossed and he is trilling his fingers on a forearm.

"You will sleep in this guest room," he says crisply. "The others are settled in rooms upstairs, which I am not. Please, avail yourself of the bath—indeed, I *insist*," he snaps. With all the black bonds I saw wrapped around him back in the chamber, he could benefit from a good cleansing himself, is all I have to say. Which I don't say, because he is bigger than me.

"A bell will awaken you for breakfast, but not too early as we are all fatigued from our journey. I have assembled a wardrobe for you I believe will suit your frame, draped there on the chaise lounge." He darts a glance at me and, with arms still folded, bends to give me a quick peck on the cheek. Both cheeks. "*Bon nuit*, Kenneth. Sleep well," he says sprightly, and closes the doors behind him. The guy is about as stable as a feather in a tornado.

He calls this a guest room? A luxury suite in a five-star hotel is more like it. This place is *dripping* in luxury—it even puts my parents-in-law's house to shame. Look at these walls, what a color—I think they call it 'chartreuse'—is this genuine silk wall covering? Yes. I learned all about this during my summer gig hanging wallpaper in high-end homes around St. Louis. This must lead to the bathroom—

Oh my goodness.

Bubbles crest above the rim of a free-form tub filled with steaming water. This will be my first real bath since entering this Shimmering place, not that I'm complaining or anything. Since Jesus knows my every thought.

Every bone in my body aches as I peel away the vestiges of the chamber, the grime, the damp, the bruisings, the pain.

How did I get here? What am I doing here? Why do I have to be with these people? Why am I so far away from home?

I sink into the warm embrace of the bath, and let out a muffled cry.

✶ ✶ ✶

Light conversation drifts from the living room, down the hallway and to my room. It's time to join the others. But I don't want to join the others, I want to go home. I thought another round in the bathtub when I woke up would help with my sadness, but it didn't help at all. Besides, they're going to make fun of me dressed up in these fancy clothes. But I am getting hungry and I can't stay in this room all day, even though I'd really like to. I just want to crawl back under the covers and hide. Look at me, sitting so stiff on this chaise lounge, because I don't want to mess up these clothes!

My window overlooks the park I fell asleep in last night. It really is lovely, but it isn't home!

SIMON

"God, I think I need some help down here right now." I sigh. That's it! My travel Bible! Of course! I can go for days without even thinking about picking it up my Bible back home. I'm not one to play Bible roulette, but I don't know where to start. "God, can you show me? I could use some encouragement."

Outside my window, tree branches rustle in a gentle breeze.

"Holy Spirit, can you move through the branches of my heart?"

Strange, I just thought of Psalm 45. What do I have to lose?

Let's see here… 'For the director of music. To the tune of "Lilies." Of the Sons of Korah. A *maskil*. A wedding song.' Hmm. Interesting. A wedding song.

> '*My heart is stirred by a noble theme*
> *as I recite my verses for the king;*
> *my tongue is the pen of a skillful writer.*'

Something about these words, I don't know, but they 'stir' something in me. A skillful writer. That's all I've ever wanted to be. To write about 'noble themes.'

> '*You are the most excellent of men*
> *and your lips have been anointed with grace,*
> *since God has blessed you forever*'.

This must be talking about Jesus or the coming Messiah. Although it does say here that it was written for a wedding, probably Solomon's, who was a man. But nah, God wouldn't see me as 'the most excellent of men', not me.

> '*Gird your sword on your side, you mighty one;*
> *clothe yourself with splendor and majesty.*'

That's funny. This is probably the first time since my own wedding that I'm literally clothed with splendor and majesty! In

Gucci, of all things! That hit the mark! But there are probably a thousand verses in the Bible about being clothed nicely....

> 'In your majesty ride forth victoriously
> in the cause of truth, humility and justice;
> let your right hand achieve awesome deeds.
> Let your sharp arrows pierce the hearts of the king's
> enemies; let the nations fall beneath your feet.'

This sounds a lot like the quest he has me on. But more: this gives purpose, and a future hope. Man, this is speaking to me.

> 'Your throne, O God, will last for ever and ever;
> a scepter of justice will be the scepter of your kingdom.'

Something about lifting God up, remembering who he is, I don't know, but it helps to put my problems into perspective.

God can't be speaking all this to me, could he? Of course, it's about Solomon, and most likely about the Messiah. Then again, I wasn't the one who came up with Psalm 45! I'm feeling a bit overwhelmed.

"God, I *think* it was you that wanted me to read this psalm—not that I want to assume anything. But if this is for me this morning, then I know you see me, and that you're with me on this quest. If I'm completely off the wall, well, then I'm sorry."

I walk into the living room.

A wave of impressed murmurs greets me as I step into the living room. Clothed in Gucci, I catch my reflection in a gilded mirror. I don't think I've ever looked this good, or will ever look this good again in my life.

Simon stands coyly with one hand supporting his chin, leaning against the doorframe into the dining room.

"Oo-la-la, you are a born model," exclaims the man in a magenta fluff top and stretch black bellbottoms. Peeking at me from over the back of a sofa, Anastazja wells up in tears, while Émile nervously looks the other way.

With a book in hand, Renata is reclining on a chaise longue upholstered in champagne velvet. Clad in a form-fitting black dress, one of its straps has casually slipped off her shoulder. Her gaze lifts and briefly meets mine, a knowing look passing between us. "Too bad he is married," she says demurely before returning her eyes to her book. This must be her way of breaking the ice between us, which I appreciate—or did she mean it?

Jesus enters from the dining room carrying a silver tray of tall, fluted glasses filled with bright green gloop that had been poured from a blender. He stops, places the tray onto the coffee table, and looks directly at me. He says,

"You have clothed yourself in splendor and majesty, oh most excellent of men! Let your heart be stirred by noble themes, and may you ride forth victoriously in the cause of truth, humility and justice!"

I don't know what to say! How on earth did he know? Oh. Of course he knew! But that means—

I notice that Jesus' outfit is uncannily similar to mine: a dark gray cashmere turtleneck paired with charcoal woolen trousers—in subtle plaid. Our matching outfits provoke a burst of laughter in the room.

"The Master did hint at your similar taste in clothing while in the Shimmering. I couldn't resist playing along!" Simon admits, an amused look on his face.

"As the King is clothed in splendor and majesty, so are you," says Jesus.

It's as if he said this for my heart only. The room falls silent, lost in translation.

Out of the loop, Renata's eyes flicker between Jesus and me, a warm smile playing on her lips before she adjusts the strap of her black dress.

Twin sofas rise from the center of the room like marine-blue leviathans, their velvety upholstery a testament to lavish comfort. They frame a glass coffee table as vast as an ocean. A flurry of exotic birds of paradise burst from a giant crystal vase placed perfectly at the center of the table among tall white candles held in the air by lead crystal holders.

I look at Simon and wonder, Who is this guy?

Clutching my fluted glass, I peruse the grandeur of this vast corner space with tall ceilings that are crowned with intricate moldings. Exotic zebra-skin rugs interrupt the herringbone pattern of the polished parquet floor; the arched windows frame a quiet tree-lined upscale street subdued by the partly-sunny sky. Suspended in the air, a funky chandelier glimmers like a gilded blimp above our heads.

Large portraits adorn the walls of the living room. To my right, near the entrance into the dining room, is a heavily framed portrait photograph of Simon—depicted with a regal bearing, draped in a swath of turquoise and adorned with a massive, intricately crafted silver necklace, his bare chest a statue of chiseled perfection. Framed between two windows, I spot the imposing monochrome of an old woman whose African lineage is etched in the proud lines of her face; there is something about the woman's firm jawline that resembles that of Simon's. Above the marble mantelpiece, toward the foyer, is an oil painting of Jesus, looking buff and brawny, as if his days were spent as a football quarterback rather than walking the shores of the Sea of Galilee.

"That one is a picture of my great-great-grandmother," says Simon, nodding to the black-and-white photograph of the old woman. "It was taken in the 1950s in our ancestral village, by a Belgian photojournalist who was recording the atrocities performed against my people at the hands of King Leopold a half-century before. My grandmother mentioned once that this photo existed of her grandmother. It took time for me to hunt it down, search in archives, gain permission to acquire it, but here it is."

The woman's right hand's been cut off! I revile back at the shocking sight.

SIMON

"I now live in Brussels, a city that rose from the wealth of my ancestors' toil. Each day is a journey in forgiveness, as I seek to bless this place I've come to call home," Simon shares reflectively.

"Seventy times seven," murmurs Émile from the depths of a plush sofa. He casts a fleeting, uneasy glance at Anastazja reclined beside him, both draped in colorful robes emblazoned with the 'Versace' signature over black stretch bellbottoms similar to Simon's. In this touch of casual luxury, Anastazja has taken on a certain voluptuousness. Émile looks stiff and uncomfortable, more likely from Anastazja twiddling her fingers absentmindedly through his thinning hair.

Simon gestures towards the portraits lining the walls, his voice tinged with introspection. "My faith and my heritage, I wear them with pride, though my current path I've struggled with," he comments introspectively, motioning towards his own image on the canvas. Seeing the older couple sitting on the sofa, he says, "Your clothes are being prepared for you and will be ready by dinner."

"I certainly do hope so," asserts Émile, his demeanor rigid. "I have my preferences, which have nothing to do with haute couture, " he asserts.

"I thought as much," responds Simon formally. "Your clothes are being carefully cleaned and pressed, though their condition after recent events have made the work challenging. However, I do have something special in mind for *you*, madame," he says to Anastazja with a wink. Despite the shadows of the chamber, her spirits lift visibly at the prospect. Realization dawns on her and, with a sharp intake of breath, she retracts her hand from the unintended intrusion into Émile's hair. Émile lets his offense be known by gruffly folding his arms and looking the other way.

"Breakfast is served," says Jesus sunnily, wiping his hands on an apron. He looks nothing like his portrait above the mantelpiece—especially decked in the splendor of Gucci.

Breakfast is served buffet-style from the massive marble kitchen island, fresh croissants and butter and jams in fancy little jars, and cheeses that really stink. There they are, jovially sipping their little espressos. Not once do they ask me if I'd prefer a Diet Coke.

* * *

We're back in the living room. Simon has changed into something less glam—I guess he finally read the room correctly—from magenta fluff into a soft V-neck sweater in robin's egg blue, mathematically pulled up at the sleeves. He looks even better in real time than he does in that Dorian Gray portrait of his—at least on the outside.

"This is my trysting place with Simon," explains Jesus, while lighting the candles on the coffee table. "Because of his, uh, current circumstances, Simon prefers to remain in his apartment, so we meet here."

"I'm not sure what 'current circumstances' you're referring to, but if my home looked anything like *this* home, I'd be happy to have our trysting place at home, too!"

By the time I regret my loose tongue, and this isn't the first time it's gotten me in trouble, Simon already has tears streaming down his face. He collapses into one of his oversized sofas and buries his face in a golden throw pillow. I did it again.

Renata places her book on a gilded end table and quickly rises from the chaise longue. She is about to sit next to Simon on the sofa, but is outmaneuvered by Anastazja and lands abruptly on the floor. Renata is the picture of controlled seething. Jesus reaches out to Renata and helps her up. She calmly sets herself on the other side of Simon while throwing an agitated glance toward Anastazja, who is motherly doting on Simon. Jesus settles in front of Simon, a zebra rug under him and the coffee table at his back, anchoring the circle of comfort around Simon. Simon rests his head in Anastazja's arms, and begins to sob.

I keep my distance. This is all getting a bit much for me. Good—a magazine I can bury my nose in. *GQ*—never been my thing. What? Simon is slathered on nearly every page? Oh my gosh, he really *is* a fashion model. Look at this photo shoot, all dressed up like Genghis Khan. And this one, clad in some androgynous short plaid skirt. High heels? Hunting jacket with matching hat and gloves? With a bow and arrow over his shoulder? Weird, but ripped. I realize I'm gawking at him. No, Kenny, you will not run up to him for his autograph.

Émile stands behind Simon, visibly trembling. His hand hesitates before finally landing on Simon's shoulder. In an instant Simon whirls around, bolts over the back of the sofa and knocks Émile to the ground! His fingers tighten around Émile's throat!

Jesus springs into action, vaulting the sofa to intervene as French curses and pleas for calm fill the air. Simon's rage erupts, his torment raw and unfiltered as he bangs Émile's head against the parquet floor. It looks like Émile deserves what he's getting because he doesn't fight back—just like Mitt back in my kitchen.

"Get him, Simon! Give him what's coming to him!" I cheer from the sidelines.

Jesus reaches Simon, his hand finding its place on Simon's shoulder. Simon halts, meeting Jesus' gaze, realizes what he is doing and he breaks, Simon, he crumbles, and now they're hugging each other, Simon and Émile, and they're sobbing, and Jesus kneels beside them and enfolds them in his arms.

My cheers fall silent. Honestly, I feel like I've missed something, like I've lost the plot. Somehow I overlooked some crucial aspect of their connection. Simon reaches out a hand, offering to help Émile up from the floor, who receives the assistance. Simon, shaken, uncomposed, slumps back into his place on the sofa between the two women.

The women look unsure as to how to proceed. None of us are moving, acting, doing. Within this silence, Simon's heart reverberates with echoes of the past, memories casting shadows upon the canvas of his life.

✶ ✶ ✶

"I was a boy in Kinshasa, my mother's constant companion, as we were alone." Simon's voice quivers, choked with emotion. "My mother's endless line of lovers became my transient, one-night-stand fathers. I was a boy longing for attention, the affirmation of a father—" Simon can barely speak now, "—because my mother never knew which of her suiters became my father." He pauses, exhaling a heavy sigh. He looks at Jesus. Jesus has seated himself on the zebra rug directly in front of Simon.

"Must I?" asks Simon.

"Share what you feel comfortable sharing," answers Jesus.

Outside, the sky has become overcast.

"I was a pious little altar boy in the mission church," Simon's tone grows distant, slipping into the recesses of memory, "groomed by the revered man of God, for his exclusive pleasure. I know now that I wasn't his only target, I was not singular in my suffering; yet when you are nine, ten, eleven, twelve years old, in the innocence of youth, you think you are the only one going through it," he reflects, his vulnerability laid bare, "because he made me feel seen, chosen." Simon's essence is transported to that of an open, impressionable, fearful, helpless young boy.

"I imagined him as my true father, which he couldn't have been, but the mind of a little child looks for hope where no hope is found." Émile's muffled sobs echo through the room. Simon continues.

"He bestowed upon me the honor of assisting him with his vestments before Mass," Simon recounts, his voice tinged with a mixture of bitterness and yearning. "Placing the stole around his neck brought me in close proximity to his face. He would allow his whiskers to graze my cheek. It was like sandpaper, but it was still touch, *oui*? When I was home with my mother, I would find myself thinking about his whiskers," Simon reminisces, his mind wandering to distant recollections.

"He would help me with my white surplice, putting it over my head, looking at me, pleased. And he favored me with the task of carrying the censer, stoking envy in my peers. You know, I enjoyed their looks of envy. I've received the same enjoyment as a model; it is also a kind of attention, *non*? Okay, being a model has given me *a lot* of attention," Simon admits with a smile, acknowledging the complexity of his emotions. His smile breaks some of the tension in the room, allowing Renata to release a subtle laugh while dabbing tears with a tissue.

"After the service, he would usher me into the sacristy," Simon continues, his words heavy with the weight of experience. "Assigned to clean the chalice, I found myself ensnared in a cycle of subservience. He'd strip off his vestments, lift his cassock, offer me attention. Or, perhaps, later, I would offer it to him." Simon's gaze flickers towards Émile. Émile withers like a salted slug. The others turn toward Émile whose discomfort is palpable. I still feel left in the dark about something.

"*Non, mes amis, it was not Émile!*" Simon interjects hastily, dispelling any misconceptions. "But a man of God who bestowed upon me the touch and attention I longed for, in reverent measures. What honor," he scoffs bitterly. "What twistedness, what rot. The scent of incense still carries his ghost."

"Oh! I understand now! Émile is a priest!" I say, excitedly. No-one acknowledges my discovery.

Simon's expression darkens, as if he's reached the limit of his emotional endurance.

Jesus steps in for Simon: "The devastation this has brought you, the humiliation, the entrapment, the shame—all of it belonging at the feet of the perpetrator, and not inside your heart."

Simon summons the resolve to continue. "I, once the innocent altar boy, grew into a beautiful, sullied, resourceful young man. I escaped my entrapment, fled my homeland, bartered my body along the way. I found refuge in Europe, here in Brussels, with an uncle who later exploited and then sold me. My mother remained oblivious. That uncle is no more, nor is my mother."

The women gasp in shock, hands flying to cover their mouths.

"The little boy within me lingered, here," he thumps his chest with rhythmic insistence. "Bruised, isolated, searching, adrift. A beautiful, empty shell. No pearl nestled within its depths. Desperate for love, I sought solace in fleeting affections, losing myself in the arms of endless encounters, each leaving me emptier than before. I have looked for love in ways that have at times shocked me. Years of one-night-stand daddies."

Simon looks small and vulnerable sitting between the two women, who draw closer to him, an affectionate wall of protection.

"I ascended to Paris, selling my way to the top. They ogled me, objectified me, devoured me. My image became a commodity, traded for vast sums of money. And I reveled, even gloried in it," he waves a dismissive hand around his living room. "Then came the film offers, of course."

Film offers?! Not that I've seen much in the way of French entertainment—it's a bit too esoteric and melancholic for my liking. And it's all in French.

Simon continues: "The abuse persisted, veiled in sophistication, in refinement, I was sacrificed on the altar of youth, of beauty, in the sumptuous offices of my handlers. It ravaged me. I concealed my anguish behind designer labels. I drank too much. I did everything too much. Despite the adoration of the masses, I felt grotesque. This façade, this cocoon, cloaked the decaying butterfly within me," Simon rises, stretches, adjusts his clothing. "I became nothing more than a desecrated chalice."

The room falls silent.

He walks over to a window, stares out over his neighborhood. "I fled here, to Brussels, where earlier I'd helped my mother settle with relatives, relatives who truly cared for me, and who hid me. I vanished."

"So *that's* where I've seen you! On the cover of Julia's teen magazines! I remember now—the big story of you disappearing, the international search. Hey! Can I get your autograph—for my daughters, I mean?"

Everyone turns to me and stares. I guess I disrupted the flow. "Until Jesus, you, the Pearl of Great Price, came to me and—" Jesus walks over to Simon and places a hand on Simon's shoulder. Simon looks blankly at Jesus, and collapses to the floor.

The six of us are transported back, back, back to the now of Simon the boy, back to where the abuses started. I notice Jesus, who is here and not here, as he enters the very pit of Simon's darkness. Jesus kneels by Simon, takes Simon's face in his hands. Simon stares wide-eyed back at him, present in a different dimension of himself, as the beautiful altar boy is guided by the priest in removing his vestments. Anastazja gasps before a fluttering like angels' wings covers our view.

"Oh gosh, what was that?! That string of goo, it's really gross—it spewed out of the priest and latched onto Simon's chest! Hey, did anybody else see that? Anybody?"

Jesus glances at me, turns his attention back to Simon.

"Simon, do you see me?" Jesus asks the now-Simon. On the screen of Simon's heart, we see Jesus, in the sacristy behind the altar of the mission church, enfolding Simon into a disappearing cloak. What happens to Simon, happens, yet there is this shimmering veil he is enclosed in, with Jesus enclosed in it with him. He is weeping bitterly. The yesterday Jesus is now the today Jesus as he places his arms around Simon, draws him into himself, where Simon spills out years of humiliation and sorrow, like wine from an overturned bottle.

I'm not used to seeing so much pain. It makes me feel sick to my stomach.

As the storm within Simon subsides, he rests, exhausted, in Jesus' arms. His transformed face, now free of anguish, radiates a genuine, heartwarming smile. The women give him a huge hug-sandwich before everyone finds their seats on the sofas. I remain standing.

Jesus walks to a window, listens to the rain now falling gently upon the city. "Has my Spirit placed anything on your hearts to share with your brother Simon?" he asks.

This is all new to me. What am I supposed to do? I'm feeling out of my depth. The others have closed their eyes, so I'll do the same. It's like we're waiting for something.

The air seems to thicken around us.

"Jesus?" Anastazja says, quietly. She looks unsure. Jesus encourages her with a nod and a gentle smile. She remains quiet for a moment, then turns to Simon sitting next to her.

"I, I feel I should say something to you," she looks bashfully at Simon, who has turned his open face toward her. "You see, I also am a mother. I have done some terrible things to my children—I didn't protect them when they needed me. I feel to ask for your forgiveness on behalf of your mother." Streams of tears run down Simon's face; Renata removes a tissue from a bronze tissue box on a side table and passes it to him. Anastazja continues:

"I am so proud of you, my son! You are my precious one. But I did not protect you, no. I knew something was wrong but I did not know what to do. I should have seen the signs. I mean, I did see the signs, but I was afraid. Afraid of the man of God. And of my lovers. I needed the money. But I did not trust God to provide in his way for us. Please forgive me for letting these things happen to you, my son. Please forgive me." Simon disappears into the bosom of Anastazja.

"I forgive you, maman, I forgive you."

"We do this at times, when an offender is unable to do it themselves," explains Jesus to the group.

Jesus looks at Émile. Émile looks startled, realizes that it must be his turn. Jesus makes room for Émile in front of Simon, though Émile remains standing. He bows his head. "On behalf of the priest at the mission station in your village, I am sorry for what he did to you, and as a priest, I ask for your forgiveness."

Simon looks at Jesus, looks at Émile, stops, starts, stops again, looking confused. An awkward silence falls in the room. Jesus kneels in front of him.

"Jesus, I am not sure if I can. I mean, it is not so simple."

Jesus leans his back against the coffee table, stretches his legs, rubs his knees. "Forgiveness, it can be such a trite, empty word. 'Just forgive,' they say. As if it were merely an act of the will—which it also is. Yet pain this deep, for an atrocity this heinous, is only relinquished through a forgiveness that is derived, not through human will, but through a revelation of how high, how wide and how deep my love is for each of you—even for you who have sinned greatly."

"Forgive the one who has trespassed against you, as I have forgiven yours. This is accomplished by appropriating a love only my heart can generate. By allowing me to extend my holy, unconditional and thoroughly divine love through you, you may indeed forgive someone who has harmed you—just as I forgive you when you harm others."

Jesus places his lips near Simon's ear. He whispers words meant for Simon's heart only. Simon physically reacts to these words with raw spasms of grief.

Through receding sobs, Simon looks at Jesus and says,

"But Jesus? I know what you are trying to tell me, and I do feel a bit of your heart for him now. But I still cannot do it. I simply am not able to forgive the priest." Simon looks pretty discouraged.

I certainly can't blame Simon for not forgiving that priest. You wouldn't need to pay me to pummel that scumbag.

Oh gosh. I just got this thought. It came like out of nowhere! What am I supposed to do with it? Should I share it with Simon? What if I'm just making it up? What if I ruin the guy? And who am I to "minister" to this world-famous celebrity? My palms are sweating and my mouth is dry and my heart's banging like a washer out of balance!

Jesus nods to me; he must know what's going on inside me. I return a look of 'are you sure?' Jesus looks sure, so I meander toward the sofa with my hands in my pockets. Simon is blowing his nose. Jesus scoots over a bit to make room for me on the sofa; I remain standing. I clear my throat.

But I can't get it out. I feel like I'm supposed to say sorry, kind of like if I were his father, for abandoning him, and that I should give him a papa-hug. Jesus is waving a "keep going" wave at me. I get down on a knee next to Jesus, position myself in front of Simon and awkwardly try to put my arms around him. With an open face Simon looks at me trustingly as he wipes his snuffling nose with a wadded-up tissue. Actually, everyone is looking at me.

But I can't. I can't seem to do it.

Jesus looks at me with kindness. But I feel like I've failed him.

Everyone's attention is diverted to Renata as she shares with Simon, with childlike wonder, a picture she saw in her mind, of butterflies being released into joy. Anastazja smothers Simon with a hug. Which is probably the hug that I was meant to give him.

✻ ✻ ✻

The sweet jingle of a silver dinner bell echoes through the apartment, rousing me from my nap; it must be early evening. A soft din rises from the city, not unlike the sound I hear coming from Route 66 back home, though the police cars sound different here. I must've crashed on this amazing sofa. Jesus is laying on the other sofa, curled up with a plush brocade pillow, looking at me. He adjusts his position to engage me in conversation.

"When your father taught you how to ride a bike, did he expect you to get it right the first time?"

"Actually, now that you mention it—"

"It's not about what you didn't give Simon, but the reason you chose not to. Do you understand?"

I have to think about this for a minute. I feel a dark truth rising to the surface.

"It's just that, well, Simon's experienced some similar things to me. Maybe even worse." Or better. "But yet, well, he's become so successful. And I haven't."

"You look at Simon's exterior self—his wealth, fame, successes, his looks—people are handed different talents in life. But do you know how Simon sees you?"

I have no idea.

"You should ask him. He sees you first as this man with a lovely wife and children and a stable family life, something he's never had and truly longs for. He's been dealt a unique hand in life that he has learned to play cunningly."

The bell rings again, a bit more insistently. Jesus gets up from his sofa and stretches. "You have no idea how messed up that man is inside—okay, you did catch a glimpse of it. You think I've got my hands full with *you*? You have no idea what I go through with that world idol over there! *Oy vey!*" he says, throwing up his hands and steps toward the dining room.

Simon's story, and what happened to him today, weighs heavy on me.

Jesus takes my hand and helps me up from the sofa. "We'll talk more after dinner," he says. He places his arm around my shoulder and we enter the dining room together.

We find Anastazja doing pirouettes around the table, showing off her flowing, floral gown in rich red tones that complement her complexion. "It is an Oscar de La Renta," she bubbles, coaxing us to feel the silk. She obviously feels beautiful. And that she is.

"It is something I acquired in Paris for my mother," Simon tells the group from the kitchen door while wiping his hands on a towel. "She passed away nearly a year ago." Touched by the gesture, Anastazja runs up to Simon and smothers him with kisses. Simon looks refreshed, both inside and out; he's changed into a dazzling white form-fitting shirt in silk, printed in gold and black.

Émile enters from the living room donning a Band-Aid over his left eye. He looks happy to be back in his own muted sweater and pants. Simon approaches him and kisses the bandage, an act of regret, then invites us to seat ourselves around the massive, funky, freeform table. I'm not the only one gawking mildly at the candelabras and roses and fine china and crystal glasses and the gold-plated cutlery.

Simon has us join hands, then asks Jesus to pray for the food. It is a holy moment. As the room is aglow from dimmed light and candles, we are aglow with God's love. Jesus looks particularly pleased.

Simon fills our plates with a dark, rich stew. I take a bite, and stop.

"What is this? This has got to be the best stew ever created in the history of the human race. It's fantastic!" I say with my mouth full.

"It is Flemish beef carbonnade, made with the best beer in the world—Belgian, of course!" Simon tells proudly. I'm about to tell him that St. Louis is the home of the *real* king of beers, but I'm distracted by the carbonnade. Amazing stuff. And it's served with French fries—how cool is that?

While the others engage in after-dinner conversation over dessert plates emptied of their fresh raspberries and crème Brulé, Jesus leads me through French doors and onto a small, wrought iron balcony overlooking the evening street scene below. A slight overhang protects us from a heavy mist. I've never been to Europe. Jesus fits right in.

"When in Brussels," he grins, reading my thoughts again. The only thing needed to round out his bohemian style is a cigarette. Or a joint.

We're leaning over the iron railing, watching passers-by on the sidewalk below. The way he's smiling, it's like he's recognizing old friends.

"It must be challenging for you to have so many people show up on your journey."

Boy, did he hit the nail on the head.

"This is your journey; this is my journey with you. Yet I often use the crowbar of other hearts to open a heart that remains closed or hidden. It's about relationship, one of my primary purposes—and pains—of my church."

The sky has darkened from dusk into night, echoing my mood. An ambulance drives below us, lights flashing, its siren piercing the neighborhood. The flashing lights echo in my heart, when I was a boy, that fateful night…. We remain quiet until we can hear each other again. Even ambulances sound different than the ones back home. It makes me feel foreign.

"You saw something today," he says to me.

My body stiffens. All those black gooey strings I saw attached to Simon that bind him. It's been bothering me, and he knows it.

"One of the gifts my Spirit has given you is discernment. You see things. Quite clearly. You see what many people only feel, if they feel anything at all." That's what I thought was happening!

He leans against the wrought iron rail; I join him. At the end of the street, toward a bustling intersection, is a fancy French fashion boutique. Is this area upscale, or what?

"What did you see today?" Jesus asks me.

"I saw this black string, this goo, eject from the priest, attaching Simon to him."

"Is that what you saw, or what you *thought* you saw?"

I don't quite understand his question. It was obvious what I'd seen.

He comes a bit closer.

"What you saw was the birth of one of Simon's worms, and a major one at that. Until the iniquity is cut off between Simon and the priest, and between everyone else who has used and abused Simon through the years—and his wounds healed by my truth—Simon's worms will have plenty of fodder to feed on. But don't share this with him, it isn't time. You saw it so you can pray for him—and for you to understand something about the origins of your own worms."

"Whatever problems I might have, they pale in comparison to Simon's problems, is all I have to say."

It becomes a bit uncomfortable between us.

"When we were praying for Simon today, apart from you feeling unworthy to minister to him, did you also think that he was unworthy to receive my blessing through you?"

Isn't that obvious?

He reaches for the handle to the tall French doors.

"When my Spirit gives you something to share with someone else, it is because I want to bless them through you, which then becomes a blessing to you—and to me. If you do not, everyone misses out on a blessing that may take time for the Holy Spirit to set up again. Those who love me, obey me." He steps into Simon's residence, stops, then adds,

"Though the others may not have the same gift of discernment as you, they can still see that you are struggling with things in your life. You may want to humble yourself and admit this to yourself."

He leaves me out in the cold with my own lousy thoughts.

After searching high and low (and doing more snooping around the place) I find Émile, Simon and Anastazja lounging in the cozy library. They look like they've popped out of a scene from an Agatha Christie novel. These 'suspects' have their Bibles open or their noses in the book Jesus had hidden in their backpacks. Is that—no, it can't be a *real* Monet hanging over the mantle?

Jesus and Renata enter through elaborately painted pocket doors from the music room; I stumbled upon them plunking on the harpsichord together while on my expedition.

"But Jesus. Everyone in all of Brussels has a cell phone. Why must we be stuck in this place without one? It just isn't fair!" Renata mumbles something in German as she slumps into deep despair next to Simon into his cognac-colored leather sofa. I've got two such girls at home. Jesus winks at me while setting himself next to Anastazja in an intricately embroidered love seat. Anastazja blushes, primps her dress. Gosh, this really is a real Monet. But then why on earth does he have that cheap-looking painting of a can of Campbell's soup hanging behind the loveseat?

Simon gets up from the sofa and serves us brandy in crystal sniffers from a drinks trolley and passes around a tray of perfectly-aligned Belgian truffles. I probably took more than my share of truffles, but they'll make a good midnight snack. Look at that, over on the fireplace mantel—a candy jar!

Émile, relaxed in Simon's comfortable reading chair, peeks over his glasses at Jesus, sips his brandy, and points to something in his book. "Seigneur, have you read this? I'm sure you have. 'The Blessedness of Winter.'" Jesus nods in response. Simon walks behind Émile's chair and gives him a warm hug. I guess all is forgiven between those two.

"You mean by Jeanne Guyon?" asks Simon while returning to the sofa next to Renata.

"*Mais oui*. I will attempt to translate this into English. For obvious reasons," Émile glances at me over his reading glasses. I've got this gumball in my gob so I can't defend myself. He begins reading. "'I see the season of winter as an excellent example of the transforming work of the Lord in a Christian's life …' Let's see here. Winter 'reflects the image of the purification which God does in order to remove imperfections from the life of one of his children.' *Captivant, non*?" He puts down the book, removes his glasses, thinks, returns his glasses.

"Is there anything else we can do? I'm bored," yawns Renata as she gathers a throw pillow into herself and curls into the sofa's sumptuous leather. Simon places a cranberry-colored blanket over her and pats her gently on the head.

Émile perches himself on the edge of the lounge chair and looks around the room. "You see, the storms of winter remove the dry leaves, revealing the defects of the tree that were already there. Guyon writes here, 'As with the tree, so with you.' And then: 'The Christian, now spoiled and naked, appears in his own eyes to be a denuded thing; and all those around him see his defects for the first time: defects which were previously veiled, concealed by outward graces.' Émile looks over at Simon. "I suppose this is what you've just been through?"

"I wouldn't have designated what Jesus took me through as a mere winter storm, it was more like a category five hurricane!" answers Simon dramatically. This invokes a bout of sniggers from the group.

"Why am I the only one who's never heard of this Guyon woman before?" I ask, flustered. No one answers.

"I assumed you meant that as a rhetorical question," says Émile, dryly.

"The storms of life! One of the guideposts you told us to look for, Master!" blurts Anastazja, looking very pleased with herself. Jesus lovingly leans into her in response. He joins in the discussion. "Guyon goes on to say that the tree looks quite dead during winter. Yet what is truly happening is that in winter, 'The source and principle of life is more firmly established than in any other season.'"

Émile removes his glasses. "*Bon*! The storms of winter expose the tree's defects, so they may be healed, *non*? *Femme incroyable.*" Replacing his glasses, Émile returns to the book in wonderment.

Jesus sets his gaze on Émile. "Ah, but one never knows precisely when a storm will hit, is it not true, *mon frère*?"

A heavy silence falls upon the room.

Émile looks up from his book and hones onto Jesus' gaze. They remain staring at each other for an uncomfortably long time, as if they are transmitting a private dialogue within that connection.

Breaking his interaction with Émile, Jesus looks around the room and says. "I believe it is bedtime, my dear brothers and sisters. Tomorrow will be a full day—for all of us."

19

ÉMILE

Dazzling sunshine streams through the four tall windows adorning Simon's master suite. Simon and Renata take what seems like ages going through Simon's vast fashion collection, giggling and gawking and prancing and modeling everything from haute couture to modern grunge before a full-length mirror. Looking closely, Renata would be a dead-ringer for Audrey Hepburn if it wasn't for the face piercings and the tattoos beginning to climb up her neck. The rest of us recline among piles clothing they've already tried on, enjoying the two of them enjoying themselves. They decide on matching black jeans with black hoodies for the day. Simon found something for Anastazja, a denim pants-and-jacket ensemble with a floral blouse in autumn hues, complementing both her figure and her color palette. Anastazja looks absolutely thrilled. Jesus and I get to keep our Gucci, everyone agreeing we look too good to wear anything else.

Frivolousness has its limits; it's time to depart. As to our destination, Jesus remains mute. None of us are particularly enthused about having to put on our worm-and-filth-laden backpacks.

We promenade down the grand stairway and through the impressive mahogany doors as genteel as courtiers, then break character and strut into the sunshine, hip-hopping to the urban beat of Brussels. I'm sure I'm not the only one that is tempted to break free from the group and do some touristy things—I mean, it's my first time to Europe, after all, if this really is Europe and not some illusion in this Shimmering place. I really want to get my hands on a beer and another giant plate of beef carbonnade and fries! But no, Jesus leads us directly to the archway hidden behind lush greenery, through the open wooden door and onto the twisting muddy trail still in the throes of Noah's deluge. Simon, thinking ahead, had handed each of us our own Chanel umbrella as we left his apartment ("Chanel's flagship boutique in Brussels is just around the corner, they were handing these out for free—at least to me!" he says, gleefully). Even with her umbrella, Anastazja is worried that her clothes will be ruined and her hair will flatten from the humidity. I offer to add my umbrella to hers, but she stiffens.

"Sorry, I was only trying to help!" I say, more offended than contrite. What's up with her, anyway?

We dash through the rain. Jesus runs straight down the middle of the trail, while we must be content with fumbling back and forth between the two muddy braids of the trail.

We come to a wooden door to our right, nearly hidden in the foliage—again, exactly at a point where the two braids of the trail conjoin.

How on earth does this keep happening? Go through one door, we're in one world, go through another door, we're in another world. I went through my fuchsia-colored front door and look at all that's happened since. I shouldn't be surprised at anything anymore. Because now we find ourselves on a broad, sloping hill overlooking a verdant valley resplendent with vineyards and bejeweled with manors and ancient castles. Which I don't think exist in central Brussels. Simon confirms my suspicions: We are now in France!

We gesticulate like mime artists at the scene set before us, twirling and swinging and dancing with our umbrellas as an expression of our amazement.

A subtle mist fills the dips and dales of the undulating landscape, the valley shimmering in creamy silkiness, the sensuous color of French lingerie.

I should be recording these bursts of literary genius into my notebook. Not that I would show this entry to Jane, necessarily.

If this is indeed France, and we just left Simon's trysting place, then it is logical to assume that we've arrived at Émile's meeting place with Jesus.

A wooden bench, not unlike the one back in my own trysting place, wherever that is, overlooks the vast expanse of the valley below. Jesus comfortably sets himself down on the bench.

Émile remains standing; he surveys the valley he undoubtedly calls home.

He points far off into the distance. A French manor, grander than the others adorning the valley, appears like a visage through the dissipating mist. It's like he's forgotten that the rest of us are even here. My gosh, look at the ruckus happening inside Émile's backpack!

"I sacrificed others, yes. Yet I...."

Émile looks lost. I walk up to him and pat him a couple of times on the back. I've done my bit so I join the others who've made themselves comfortable on picnic blankets on the soft, green grass. He continues speaking.

"I come from a prestigious family in France. Our bloodline can be traced back to Charlemagne—through one of his bastard sons. My family name may not be familiar to you, though our family enterprises would most certainly be. I changed my name to distance myself from any association with *La société*, as we refer to our family.

"I was the second of three sons. We were given everything that money could buy—the schools, attire, toys—and given nothing that money cannot buy.

"My older brother, charismatic, charming, commanding, was destined to rule the family dynasty. Consumed by the corporate machine, I rarely see him anymore.

"My youngest brother, the darling, was killed in a skiing accident, in Les Diablerets, in the Swiss Alps. Though we were in the charge of two governesses that morning, our mother, before heading to the spa, placed me in charge of my brother on the children's slope. I did my best, keeping him near me, while our governesses sunned themselves beneath the lazuline alpine sky. I was not in charge, however, of the snow mobile that careened out of control, taking my brother's life and nearly taking mine."

We hang on Émile's every word.

"Émile, come, please sit next to me," says Jesus, tenderly. I remember him doing the same with me. Émile seems to awaken from a trance; he turns toward Jesus' voice and moves stiffly toward the bench; I'd forgotten about his limp. He sets himself into Jesus, as if he belongs there, and much closer to him than I had when I first arrived at the trysting place. I suppose Émile has walked far with Jesus? Émile continues:

"I was nevertheless blamed by my mother for not reacting sooner, for not running swifter, for not being stronger to protect my brother from harm. My mother, a master at emotional distancing, distanced herself further from me after the accident. I was eleven years old at the time.

"I convalesced in a private Swiss hospital for weeks while doctors tended to my multiple fractures. My mother never visited me, though my father did, once, with his entourage, handing me a bouquet of flowers for the photo op before abruptly leaving. When I was finally allowed to return home, I was nursed by private staff on the third floor of our manor, sequestered from my family and hidden from public view."

Émile seems to return to the present. He looks at us, nervously smiling. He pulls his leather wallet from his pants pocket and removes a photograph. It was evidently taken sometime in the late 70s or early 80s, based on the picture's pantone, the hairstyle of the woman in the picture, and the sideburns of the men. "This is my mother, this is my father, this is my older brother, and this is me. I was once handsome, *non*?" He points to the tall, slender teenaged boy in a turtleneck and dark thick-rimmed glasses staring tepidly from behind the woman. The name of a French company appears on a sign above the entrance to a brutalist building complex. Émile smiles nervously, his eyes dart back and forth to see if there is any recognition of the family empire. Our faces express shock. Jesus glances at him. Émile quickly returns the photograph to his wallet and continues, nervously.

"Father tired of his unmerited riches, finding thrill in the roll of the dice—and quietly amassed great debt. Out of fear of retribution or shame, he kept his misfortunes from my mother. To protect the family reputation, my father was not able to approach the seedier sides of French society for financial assistance, so he was forced to consider more creative solutions. One of his yachts inexplicably caught fire off the Amalfi coast, which was handsomely covered by insurance. The insurance company was not nearly as understanding when another of my father's yachts suffered the same fate soon after. Of course, these are just two of a long list of financial faux pas that ultimately made my father a laughingstock around the gambling tables of Monte Carlo.

"My mother caught wind of the rumors, of course. It didn't help when she discovered one of her Tiffany necklaces missing from a locked drawer that my father suggested was swallowed by the family dog. She threatened to divorce him, to cause him public ruin, to leave him penniless. My father fell into drink and despair.

"About this time, someone approached my father, someone from a competing family. A deal was made. My father agreed to its conditions, and his gambling debts suddenly, blissfully vanished. I knew nothing about any of this at the time, of course, especially the detail that it was my mother who had orchestrated the transaction.

"I did notice the young man who began visiting me on the third floor of our manor not long after." Émile stands to his feet, then turns his back to us.

A tap on the shoulder. There is a whisper in my ear. "I have a feeling I know where this story is heading." It is Simon.

"What do you mean?" I whisper over my shoulder.

"Just wait and see," is the return whisper.

Émile continues, haltingly, pensively. "Jean-Pierre, he called himself." Émile hides his face with his hands. "Jean-Pierre was charming, handsome. Athletic." Émile stammers, gathers himself to continue, "He was everything I wanted to be but couldn't be, with me stuck in a wheelchair."

Émile turns toward us, uncovers his face. His gaze looks distant, coming from somewhere within him.

"Jean-Pierre would be by my side when the physiotherapy was particularly difficult, encouraging me that I could do it, comforting me when I couldn't. Jean-Pierre made me laugh. He'd sneak me out of the house and race me in my wheelchair around the gardens and I would laugh with glee. He seemed genuinely interested in me—in whatever was left of me as a person. He met my longing for companionship, for friendship. For attention."

An alteration occurs in Émile's demeanor. It's as if he's become the boy he is speaking of.

"Hidden deep within our gardens, he did things to me."

"There it is," says the whisper over my shoulder.

I turn to look at Simon. "What?" He gives me a knowing look.

"Afterward, I wouldn't see him for days, and I wondered if he would ever come back. I felt confused, tense, abandoned. There was also a part of me that had hoped he would never come back," says Émile. "But then he'd return out of the blue, with a gift, a book he liked, he'd pat me on the head and told me a joke. And he would give me attention again."

Émile's body tenses. He flexes, then releases, then flexes his fists before hitting himself repeatedly in the head. Jesus rushes to him.

"Émile, look at me. Stop. Shhh. Look at me. I'm here. I'm here with you. Breathe." Émile's eyes, wild and panicked, gradually soften. Jesus guides him back to the wooden bench, offers him a flask of water. Anastazja hurries to his side, while Renata stands, looking lost. Simon is sprawled on his back on the picnic blanket, with an arm covering his face.

"Pardon me," says Émile, patting his forehead with his ironed white handkerchief. "I apologize for my behavior." I'm barely hearing his words. Too many feelings are being stirred up in me.

"A year after his first visit," continues Émile after taking a sip of water, "when I was twelve," he stops, looks at Jesus. "Should I continue, *Seigneur*?" Jesus places his arm around his shoulder. "When I was twelve Jean Pierre brought me down into the cellar of our manor, where he prepared me, placed me on a bed." Émile stops for a very long time before he continues.

"Men were waiting in the shadows—I'm not sure how many there were, I didn't hear their names and never saw their faces. Jean-Pierre remained present in the room. It was he who tended to me afterwards, who held me as I wept—*C'est difficile, Seigneur!* This continued for two years. It was woven into the rhythm of my weekly schedule, until my body began to mature and was no longer of interest to these men.

"One time I resisted this ordeal: I kicked at the men, scratched at their faces; they beat me mercilessly. Jean-Pierre left me alone in the cellar for two days. No one heard my pleas for help. Jean-Pierre bore no smile when he returned to clean me up. When he brought me upstairs, no one inquired about my appearance, nor about my disappearance. I knew that my parents knew, yet they said nothing, did nothing. I began despising them from the pit of my heart." He speaks this with contempt.

"Jean-Pierre disappeared completely from my life and, when my body had healed from the accident and from the abuses, I was allowed to lead a normal life—normal for those living in such circles of French society—at least for a time. But I began to notice that my longings were—how should I say—not normal.

"I did not understand the renovations I heard occurring in the cellar of our manor—I was too terrified of my previous experiences to go down there by myself to find out what was happening. When the construction was completed and the manor again fell into silence, that is when it started to happen."

Émile falls off the bench and slumps to the ground, unconscious. Jesus kneels beside him, places his hand upon his head. Émile's backpack is bulging—maybe the worms in there are about to explode!

"Unspeakable things have happened to you," Jesus says gently to Émile. "You were forced into silence." Sitting beside him on the green grass, Jesus continues, "You were sacrificed to satisfy others' wicked cravings. Their evil seeped into your heart, filling it with secrets, shadows, lies."

We fall into a vortex, all of us together! Arms, legs, screams, terror are bashing together as if we're in a giant clothes dryer. Oh God, my vertigo! Stop this circus ride! Bam, thud, ow!

Quiet.

"Where are we?" asks Renata as she disentangles herself from Simon and Anastazja like a game of Twister gone awry. I lend a hand to Anastazja, she brushes it away.

"I was just trying to help!" I say. She distances herself from me in a huff. What's gotten into that woman?

"*Mon Dieu*, what is this place?" Simon yelps. It's like a refined version of the wicked chamber: a circular stone slab, within a dungeon of sorts, in a room ringed by thick candles on tall pedestals. Are we in the manor Émile had been pointing to? Where is Émile?

Oh God, what's happening now? Hooded beings wearing blood-red robes enter the room, moving rhythmically toward the stone altar, chanting dully. We fling ourselves against the stone walls. And now: I see a teenaged boy, chained to the altar, looking sedated. Could it be Émile?

What are they going to do to him?

A fluttering of angels' wings. My eyes are covered.

"Jesus!" cries Émile from the altar. "Where are you, *mon Dieu*?"

"I am here, my child," responds his God. "I am with you, here, now, even as it happens to you over and over again, there, then."

"Oh, they've cut out my heart," weeps Émile bitterly.

"Yes, they have cut out your heart," says Jesus, quietly.

"I feel empty, disconnected, shattered…"

"Shards of your identity, pieces of your reality fall from you, are stepped on, crushed."

It is difficult seeing Émile in so much pain, though I'd already seen this about him, back in that wicked chamber. Anastazja and Renata have collapsed to the stone floor, holding around each other, sobbing desperately. Simon stands with his face to the wall, praying.

Upon the altar, Jesus tenderly shrouds young Émile within a veil as thin as muslin.

"If I had been stronger, I could have saved my brother! It's my fault! I let go of his hand. I lost her little boy. I deserve this, I deserve what she lets them do to me!"

Who is he talking about?

A beam of light focuses on a hooded figure. "*Ma mère*," cries young Émile, chained to the altar. His mother is *leading* this ritual, letting this happen to her own son?!

Black goo is ejected from the souls of the hooded people, attaching themselves to Émile, sapping him of his life force. The room is filled with a foul stench.

What am I seeing? Émile the boy, wrapped in muslin, is growing into Émile a young man right on that very altar! How many years did they do these things to him?

"I became a priest to requite my pain," screams Émile, "to earn your forgiveness, to daily offer you my penance, my sacrifice—"

"Hoping to be purified from the impulses driving you—" responds Jesus.

Émile begins to sob, "—and I ended up doing the very things I vowed never to do, the things that were done to me—"

"—from your own slashed core," responds Jesus, tenderly. "You could not live, can never live, a holy life without my resurrection power."

Oh. I think I know what they're talking about.

"Over and over and over and over again—" whispers Émile in hopelessness.

"Until you met the One whom you'd been so desperately trying to appease."

"You revealed to me that I may never work to earn your absolution, may never earn your forgiveness, I may never sacrifice enough, because—"

Jesus takes over: "—Because I have already sacrificed myself, taking your punishment, your wounds, your pain and your iniquity, upon myself."

Jesus climbs on top of that wretched altar, removes the shackles from Émile's wrists and ankles, embraces Émile into himself. Jesus speaks, "You are now enfolded into my Sacred Heart, where truth and mercy meet."

Dark, thick clouds begin swirling above the altar like a cyclone—and the clouds are filled with faces! Children's faces. Faces filled with anguish, confusion, woe. Black strings tether Émile to each child.

Émile's countenance has turned dark, like he's fallen into a black pit inside himself. Yet a strength seems to be rising up within him, like he's facing his own storm. He says, "Jesus, I am sorry for trying to meet my twisted needs in twisted ways, instead of looking to you to fill my love-deficit," and begins to quiver.

I can't believe it. I simply cannot believe it! To think of the atrocities this man has done! He's not a man, he's an *escargot*, a sniveling, slimy slug! Look at him, dissolving into Jesus' arms from the salt of his own tears. He deserves everything coming to him, is all I have to say.

"You are washed as white as snow by the blood I shed for you," declares Jesus.

"I am sorry," shouts Émile to the faces swirling above him in the cyclone, "please forgive me!"

A mountain of guilt and shame lifts off Émile's heart, and he is able to rest in Jesus' arms.

"Émile, repeat after me," says Jesus,

"In the name of Jesus
I break off every soulish bond
That binds this child to me:
I let you go. I release you into the loving heart of Jesus.
And I pray that you will find grace, over time,
to forgive me for what I have done to you.
So that you may be free of me."

Émile speaks this out, over and over, adjusting it to specific individuals in the storm cloud swirling above the wicked altar.

Clip clip clip. Clip clip.

A blood-curdling scream erupts from the depths of Émile's heart.

Oh gosh, what else can happen?

A thick, black cloud pierces the eye of the cyclone, halting just above Émile's head, ready to crush him, revealing the faces of a hooded woman and man!

"No! I will never forgive those monsters, '*Mes parents*.'" Émile spits this out with contempt. "I will never forgive them for using me as a bargaining chip with the devil, for sacrificing me for their business advancements. I will never forgive them, not *ever*!"

I'm kind of feeling something for Émile. Should I give him a papa-hug? I'm not sure, I don't want to make a mistake like I did with Simon. Not that I really want to give that sorry excuse of a man a hug, though it's probably what's expected. I'll go up to him and get it over with—

Jesus grabs my arm. He shakes his head 'no'.

"What? Why not—?" He pulls me next to him, says in my ear, "He is not ready for it—and neither are you."

Jesus goes up to Émile instead.

He bends down, chooses a piece of shattered heart. He finds its counterpart, welds the two together, finds the next piece, aligns it with the first two, glues them together with his blood, finds the next piece, over and over and over and through the years, until one day, in the end—

"I see a jewel-heart!" exclaims Renata. "A beautiful, precious ruby, cut, polished, shining!"

"I got the same picture!" bursts out Anastazja, "On a golden chain, worn over the heart of the King!"

Émile sobs in the arms of his Master, releasing years of pent-up guilt and shame.

Just don't let that *escargot* get anywhere near me with those feelers of his. I've had enough of that in my life.

Between rows of maturing grapes, Émile and Jesus rest on a picnic blanket beside a wicker basket filled with baguettes and cheeses and grapes and honey and walnuts and wine. The rest of us huddle together under a spindly tree and share a dry crust of bread. We do not want to have anything to do with that pedophile.

A mutant worm slashes its way out of Émile's backpack. I watch it slither for its life in the direction of the manor far beyond.

"There shouldn't be forgiveness for the likes of him," says Anastazja to me, standing with arms crossed. She looks at Émile with disdain. I nod my head in conspiratorial agreement.

I can't reconcile the abuse done to Émile with the abuse Émile has done to others. I mean, I kind of felt some warm-fuzzy feelings for him, but that doesn't mean the slug shouldn't get what he deserves.

I've got to get out of here.

I've got a sudden, insatiable craving for a bacon double cheeseburger, fries, a vanilla milk shake and a diet Coke. If I can only find my way out of France. Maybe the magic door out of this place is down this row of grapevines….

"Where truth and mercy meet." It is Jesus. I stop and turn toward him; he stands further down the path. Flecked with sunshine escaping through leafy vines, it is as if he gazes upon me from behind a wooden lattice. I feel myself blush.

"Do you think I am unaware of the pain and devastation Émile has wrought on the innocents?"

Guilt rises in me with each step he takes toward me. I find myself lashing out at him. "Why are you so buddy-buddy with him, then? Letting him off the hook like that!"

"Do you believe I did not witness the horror each child experienced at his hand, the heart scars each carries within—and the horrors of your own abuses?"

"Don't mix my stuff with his!" I think of all those faces swirling in the cloud above Émile, and shiver.

"You have met your storms. Émile needs you to get through the storm that is about to batter his life."

"He needs *me*, you say? He needs me to strangle him!"

Jesus is quiet. Which makes me feel uncomfortable.

"Back there, the Father gave you a taste of his heart for Émile. This made you despise Émile all the more, which is why I stopped you. Soon you will understand the reason why I brought the two of you together on this part of your journeys. If it'd been possible for you to have grown up together with Émile, you would have been ideal brothers for each other, with you modeling masculinity to him—and true fatherhood."

This stuns me.

"Underneath that rough exterior of yours, is a heart made to know the Father's love. Through your sensitive heart and lanky arms that are good for hugging, the Father will be able to convey his love for another through you. And you are a much better father to your children than what you're able to see right now."

Within me the grapes of wrath wither beneath the light of this high truth, and I don't like it. "Simon should've finished Émile off when he had the chance," I say, kicking at the French dust. I don't know what is real and what is make-believe in this Shimmering place anymore.

"There is mercy, and there is justice," he says to me, quietly. "There is sin, and there is criminality. Émile has agreed to turn himself in to the French authorities for his crimes. Which is why I'm drawing him deeper into the Shimmering, into my presence, to prepare him for what lies in wait for him when he returns. And why he needs a brother like you by his side."

"And what does Émile possibly have that he could remotely model for me?"

Without giving an answer he turns to rejoin the others, and I feel justified.

20

ANASTAZJA

Is that Simon? I thought I'd never find my way out of this blasted vineyard. I missed lunch because I just had to go off in a huff to make a point. I'm starving.

Simon leans against the stone archway to the wooden door, using a stick to clean mud off of his Converses. He looks sullen. "You took your time," he says, not looking up from his mud-caked shoes. "Look at this mess. What am I doing, trying to clean these when we must go down that trail again! And why is it always raining on the trail? I do not understand," he quips. "But the Master told me to come back for you, *again*, so here I am—why he gives me the honor of rescuing your tardy butt all the time, is a mystery. We'd already reached our next destination—I hope you are fond of sauerkraut and sausages."

He casts the stick into the vines and splatters his white shirt with mud in the process. "Now look at me! I brought a clean shirt, it is in my backpack, but I am tired of always having to face my worms! Come. The others are waiting," he says and turns toward the door. "I have no idea where I placed my Chanel umbrella!"

"My umbrella is right here—the one you gave me, I mean. We can share, if you like," I offer, a bit star-struck. Besides, Jesus mentioned that Simon sort of appreciates me. I walk up to him, lean nonchalantly against the stone wall.

"*Merci*," he says, grabbing the umbrella from me.

"So uh, what did you think about Émile's sob story? He certainly tried to tug at our heart strings, didn't he. That escargot."

Simon stops wrestling with the umbrella and stares at me. "What is it you are saying, Kenneth?" he asks, blankly.

"I mean, it's one thing to learn that he had a rough childhood and all, but that doesn't justify all the rotten things he did, does it." It'll be good to get Simon on my side. Comrades united by a common enemy.

Simon becomes tersely silent, as if he's funneling his energy into comprehension, then forming his thoughts into words.

He nearly erupts. "What are you thinking? That Jesus had us visit Émile's trysting place right after mine, so I could flippantly forgive the priest who abused me?"

"Well, yes—I thought that was obvious—"

"You know nothing about me—okay, you know a bit more about me after what I shared with the group—but you still cannot make assumptions about how I should think or feel," he says, gruffly.

"Gosh, sorry!" I say, maybe a bit defensively.

"Did you not hear a word that Jesus said? That no-one can force us to forgive another person—not even Jesus himself? Émile's story offers a broad truth about who Émile is, which in some general way I can transfer to Father Étienne—the priest who hurt me back in my village. But I need to feel how Jesus feels for Father Étienne, and I'm not sure if I want to know what Jesus feels for him."

Simon begins pacing.

"You see, I want to at least *try* to forgive Father Étienne—Émile's story has helped. Yet I feel that the Lord is doing something deeper in me, giving me a deeper revelation: that I am to lay the sin of Father Étienne onto Jesus—onto the cross. It is Jesus who died for the priest—not me. I will never be able to muster up enough love to reach the depths of that man's iniquity. And that is the point, Kenny! Only God has that much love! I am perceiving this truth as in a mirror, dimly, yet it is enough to make me shiver at the enormity of Jesus' love—for Émile, for Father Étienne, even for me."

Simon takes a deep breath; he returns to where I'm standing, rests against the stone wall. "I wish I had a cigarette," he admits to me. Basking in the sunshine, he continues his pondering.

"You see, I am counting the cost of forgiving. The priest hurt me badly. I still think he owes me. I think, because he did such and such to me, my life changed course. If he hadn't done these things to me, I might be in a different place in my life today. Maybe my desires might have been different, who knows? My tapestry is complex—I had no father, and the priest was by no means my only abuser. I've resented my attractiveness at times, while flaunting it at other times. And what about original sin? It all gets muddled in my head and heart and I've felt entangled, but Jesus is untangling me. No matter. What counts now is that I live a holy life before a holy God in God's holy power and love. I can't do it on my own. And I know I will keep failing, I will mess up. I will sin. But since my healing time with Jesus back at my apartment, it's like I'm starting fresh, at least in some areas of my life. I have renewed hope. But it's still my choice. I can blame the priest and my uncle and the industry for using and abusing me, but it is still my choice to lean on Jesus. To be honest, I do not want to give up my victimhood completely—so much of my identity has been formed around being hurt, in being offended. If I forgive those who have hurt me, I must find my identity in purer sources, even in God. And I'm still a bit suspicious of God—can you believe it? I have given my life to Jesus, yes, but the Heavenly Father—"

Simon's bottom lip trembles. He wipes his face with a shirt-sleeve. "We should be going," he says quietly, walking toward the stone portal.

Wow. That was an earful.

Simon grabs the wrought iron latch and pulls open the wooden door. He stops and turns to me.

"Maybe you needed to hear Émile's story even more than I did. I see it all over you—your smugness, the way you stand there in haughty self-righteousness." There was nothing malicious in his voice, which irks me. He disappears into the rain.

The white noise of the downpour and the metallic scent of ionized air vies with the rich, sun-drenched earth of France. Both feel foreign to me; I want neither of them. I want to leave this place; I want to go home.

The conversation didn't go the way I'd planned.

* * *

We're back in the deluge, back on this muddy, criss-crossy, double-braided trail. I can't say that the rain is uncomfortable—it's warm, soothing almost, like the rainforest showerhead at my parents-in-law's house—but it's the *amount* of it that is irksome, not to mention the mud it congers.

Look at Simon, running so fast. He probably wouldn't be in such good shape if he had a wife and five kids and a mortgage, is all I have to say. He disappears through a hedge on our left, and through another arched wooden door.

Where are we now?

It's like we've walked into an enchanted fairy tale!

Here it is autumn.

Leaves pave the way before us like a crimson runner.

The stream gurgles happily behind trees painted in vibrant hues of yellow and orange. Bluebirds flitter with gilded butterflies, brown-tailed squirrels frolic with adorable skunks. It's only a matter of time before townsfolk leap forth and break into song.

Simon was right—the air is thick with the smell of sauerkraut and sausages and it's making me salivate. But in a place like *this*? My stomach pulls me forward like a dog on a leash, leading me over a drawbridge, through a tall stone archway and into an ancient town square. In the center of the square is a delicately detailed pavilion encircled by merrily-dancing daffodils. And lying on a gilded chaise at the center of the pavilion, is Anastazja.

Anastazja is lovely in a bejeweled gown in shimmering white lace; her hair is quaffed and fitted with a medieval headdress in white satin. Her Prince Charming, sitting beside her and clad in royal purple velvet, is gobbling up sausages with gusto. Émile and Renata are sitting at a little outdoor table, chatting while gazing at Anastazja, eating their sausages. Renata is in a long, goth-looking black velvet gown. Émile is in dove gray pantaloons and tights, and slippers curled at the toes. He looks miserable.

It feels like we've walked into a cosplay convention!

Trumpets announce our arrival; Anastazja catches sight of me. Squirrels crash into skunks, bluebirds collide with butterflies, as mustard drips down, down, down, and plops onto the shimmering gown of the princess. A communal gasp ensues. Anastazja bursts into tears. The Prince looks at me through a forkful of sauerkraut.

Renata glances at me then whispers something in Émile's ear. Looking at me, Émile relays the message to Simon. Simon ponders what he's heard.

"What? What's this all about?" I ask Simon. Simon hesitates. "Tell me!" I insist.

"It's just that Anastazja has been disturbed by something, and that something has something to do with *you*."

"Can't you tell me anything more?"

Before Simon can answer, two knights in shining armor approach me, grab me under my arms and drag me out of the village!

"Heh, wait, stop! "Where are you taking me? What did I do wrong?" I feel like a guilty boy accused of another boy's misdeeds.

"Anastazja! What did I do wrong? Anastazja!"

The last thing I see is Anastazja crying uncontrollably on Prince Jesus' shoulder as he watches me being dragged away. I'm not even trying to offend people, and look what happens.

I wish I'd grabbed a sausage on the way out.

✯ ✯ ✯

If the only thing the knights wanted was for me to change into this cosplay outfit, they didn't have to drag me away like a common criminal! Then again, I probably wouldn't have gotten into these ridiculous clothes willingly, especially into these tights. Look at these puffy arms and pantaloons—and the feather in my hat keeps falling into my face!

The others have gathered under the pavilion, sipping from mugs, reading from books. Look at Simon, all decked-out in maroon velvet—as if he's walked out of a scene from *The Bridgertons*! Anastazja has changed out of her mustard-stained dress and into a long flowing gown tailored from the same dark green velvet as my outfit; it complements her ginger hair, so I guess it complements mine, also, which is probably the reason we're the only two wearing dark green.

Jesus motions for me to join them. I'm surprised he's able to keep his curls from springing his hat into the air. He hands me a cup of warm apple cider.

The pavilion is encircled by armored knights wielding menacing lancets, their faces hidden behind metal helmets; I sense their steely gaze on me. I'm still feeling a bit ruffled from being man-handled by them. I keep my distance.

"They are angels, protecting Anastazja's trysting place," whispers Émile, pulling uncomfortably at his tights. I find myself recoiling from Émile, like I've seen a snake.

"Why did they treat me that way? And why don't the angels reveal themselves to me like that?" I quip.

"Because you complain too much," remarks Prince Jesus in royal purple.

The cider must be spiked with rum; it sure is warming on this autumnal afternoon but I can hardly feel my arms anymore.

From this angle I can see how the castle towers lay in ruins, as if they'd been hit by cannon fodder; a series of wooden scaffolds have been built around their outer walls.

Émile leans into me and points to the damaged towers. "It is similar to Isaiah 61, is it not? 'They will rebuild the ancient ruins and restore the places long devastated; they will renew the ruined cities that have been devastated for generations.'" Mostly to get away from Émile I sit next to Renata who is touching up her black lipstick.

The town square is filled with the soft tones of harp and lyre. Anastazja sighs, then drops her book upon her lap.

"What's troubling you, sister?" Renata inquires.

"I don't know. This passage. In the book the Master gave me," says Anastazja, sorrowfully.

"Which book?" asks Émile as he sets himself in a chair next to hers. Anastazja crosses her arms and looks away. She says coldly, "It is by Saint Faustina Kowalska, a Polish nun. Her diary, *Dzienniczek*."

"Oh, yes. *Divine Mercy in My Soul*. I've read its French translation a number of times. Magnifique," says Émile.

"Have you read that one, too?" I ask Émile, surprised.

"Yes, of course. Anastazja, please read the passage to us."

"All right," says Anastazja, bashfully. She clears her throat and reads a snippet of the book in Polish.

Anastazja looks lost.

"What does it mean?" I ask.

Jesus rises and approaches Anastazja to translate the text for her. "'Let the greatest sinners place their trust in My mercy. They have the right before others to trust in the abyss of My mercy.'"

Anastazja looks at me as tears stream down her cheeks. Do I always have this effect on people?

She rises from her chair and gazes beyond the castle walls, toward the surrounding hills painted in crimson. She speaks.

"I was caged in my own home,
Not by bars,
But by beatings,
My screams rewarded

With more beatings.

"Express a need for school supplies?
A smack on the face for my wastefulness.
Scrape the fork on the dinner plate?
A kick to the shin under the dinner table.
Sit quietly with a book in the living room?
A swat to the back of the head for simply existing.

"There were too many mouths to feed,
Too many bills to pay,
Too many pressures to bear,
So torrents of rage were hurled upon the innocents.

"I learned to scream,
Silently,
To contain my rage
Politely.

"My mother, trapped in her fear-dungeon,
Turned a blind eye, held her tongue.

"I married young.
My husband, my knight in shining armor,
Rescued me from the dragon-father.

"When I was finally free from the dragon's lair,
I found myself shackled by my own temper,
Trapped in the same cycle of rage.

"One morning I blacked out with rage," Anastazja confesses, tears streaming down her face as she looks at me.
"My oldest son, he would be about your age now. He had red hair, like yours, like mine. My precious one! My baby." Her

voice quivers as memories of her son flood her consciousness, each word heavy with the weight of her grief.

"When I came back to my senses, my son lay lifeless."

The revelation lands like a heavy blow, plunging us into the depths of shock.

"My parents never visited me in prison," she continues, her voice trembling with anguish. "I did not understand the abandonment, their coldness. It took time for me to understand, that what I'd done to my son had also deeply affected my family: the shame, the public scorn, the television cameras, the media crews parked outside their home. Our family story was exposed in tabloids of half-truths." Émile passes Anastazja a white starched handkerchief. "The other half of the story was worse. My siblings and I shared strands of light and happiness as well—I don't want to paint my family too darkly—but the happy times did not keep me from doing what I did to my son, did they?" She looks at the castle's damaged parapets.

"My other children grew up, not by knowing me through my embrace, but by knowing me through rumors and playground taunts. They carried a load too heavy for any child to bear. They were confused: How could they ache for the warmth of a mother who killed their own brother? By the time I was released from prison my children had grown into adults. They no longer needed me—at least not in the way I needed them to need me. Healing has occurred between us through the years, which I am grateful for, but I felt alone," says Anastazja tearfully, looking at Jesus. He nods for her to continue.

"After prison I resettled into a different community, started fresh, turned a new leaf. Not long after, a neighbor recognized my name on the mailbox and warned the other neighbors about me. Again, abandonment, coldness. I'm never free!" She turns to face us with handkerchief in hand, like a plaintiff before a jury.

"Yes, I snapped, I blacked out with rage." Anastazja admits, her tone laced with regret and self-reproach. "And yes, I tried to cover it up, shift the blame, point fingers in other directions," she exposes the depths of her guilt and the destructive aftermath of her actions. "But how could I admit to the police what I couldn't admit to myself, that I'd taken the life of my son? When I was finally released from my father's house, finally released to express my anger, caused by my father's anger, well, look what happened." She weeps bitterly.

Who would've thought that Anastazja could do such a thing? And to her own child!

It's happening again. There is a shift in the atmosphere, a bending of realities. A massive cyclone, an inverted black hole of a million black tethers, twists around the head of Anastazja! She gasps for air, her eyes are wide with terror. "But I forgave my father years ago!" cries Anastazja from the midst of her storm.

"He who is forgiven much, loves much." It is Jesus.

"Jesus, you know I have asked for your forgiveness, I have served my time in prison. But I still feel bound. Please, Savior, *set me free!*"

I glance at the others—don't they see what's happening to her? Simon sits there, filing his nails, while Renata twiddles her nose ring like she needs a fix. Émile must sense something, because he walks over to Anastazja and places a hand on her shoulder. She sees who it is and shrugs it off. Émile backs away but remains near her. There's some backbone to the man now—what happened to the slithering slug?

I say, "Jesus, why aren't you calming the storm?"

Renata glances at the clear skies, then looks at me like she thinks I'm crazy.

Jesus is also looking at me.

"Wait—Jesus—I can't! Besides, that's *your* line of work!" What I don't say to him is, there's *no way* I'm going to minister to someone who's killed her own child!

But I *am* feeling something for Anastazja, to be honest, and it won't let up. There's like an artery running from Jesus' heart through my own heart, like I'm feeling all this compassion for her. I almost can't take it.

Jesus approaches Anastazja first, enfolding her into himself. He invites me into the fold, encouraging me with his eyes to do what I feel he's placed on my heart to do. Reluctantly, I acquiesce, kneeling beside her.

But I can't find a single word to say to her! Nothing! Nothing at all!

Anastazja looks at me, sees that it's me. The recognition triggers in her a torrential outpouring of grief. Her cries pierce the air, escalating into despair. Jesus holds her tight, her head buried into his chest, and he looks up at me.

I just don't know what he's asking me to do! I look helplessly over at him. I'll do just about anything to make this uncomfortableness go away—but wait—

"Anastazja! What on earth are you doing?!" She's fallen on top of me, causing me to fall backwards onto the pavilion floor!

"Stefan! Oh, my Stefan! I am so sorry for what I did to you! Oh, Stefan!"

I struggle to breathe as she clings to me, her anguish palpable in every sob. "Oh, how I miss you, my son!" She's making a big mistake because I'm just Kenny!

"Anastazja, wait! I'm not—" I begin to protest, but Jesus catches my eye. In this one, wordless moment, I know what Jesus is wanting me to do. Anastazja somehow needs me, who resembles her son, to be her son for her, for one, sweet, brief, eternal moment, in order to be able to forgive herself. A sense of peace sweeps over me, and I allow her to slobber all over me.

She sets herself next to Jesus and me and wipes her nose on the sleeve of her green velvet gown.

And Anastazja prays:

"In the name of Jesus,
I forgive myself
For taking the life of my own son
Out of my own anger.

"I cut the ties that bind me
To any spirit of wickedness,
That attached themselves to me
By my act of murder.

"I close the door to any dark power
Opened to me by my sin,
And I cover that door
With the blood that Jesus shed for me.

"I now allow you, Holy Spirit, to fill me,
To continue to strengthen me,
Restore me, tend to me, purify me,
Love me.

"I now stand forgiven
By Jesus,
For Jesus,
And in the name of Jesus,
Amen."

    The black hole of Anastazja's swirling pain is quelled in the pools of Jesus' mercy. I hear a *clip clip clip* sound as Jesus frees her from her tethers, speaking tenderly to her, calling her his own.

    Again, Émile approaches Anastazja, though cautiously, extending his hand to pray for her. With a mischievous glint in her eye, Anastazja grabs him by the arm and pulls him down on top of us, with Jesus somehow landing at the bottom. And Simon stage-dives on top of us as we embrace each other in the castle of Anastazja's heart.

    I see, yes, I understand now: that Anastazja's million tethers (well, many, certainly not all) were able to be released from her when she was finally able to release herself.

In the peaceful wake of Anastazja's receding storm, we eat all the sausages and potatoes and cabbage and apple strudel our stomachs can handle.

I catch sight of blood trailing along the cobblestones. A disquieting realization dawns.

"Has anyone seen Renata lately?" My question hangs in the air.

With a solemn nod, Jesus leads us forward. "Come," he beckons, "We must find Renata."

21

RENATA

We trudge along the double-braided trail, the relentless downpour soaking us to the bone. Our spirits feel as heavy as the rain-soaked ground beneath our feet. Jesus leads the way, his figure a beacon of determination. Of course, *he's* able to avoid these muddy ruts, nearly gliding above them!

Ahead of us, to the right, stands a metal door, stark against the backdrop of the wooded surroundings and protected from the rain by an ivy archway—again, located at a point where the two braids of the trail come together.

We huddle behind Jesus as he grapples with the stubborn latch, his efforts allowing us to finally come out of the rain.

We find ourselves in what appears to be a ticket booth, in disuse, its circular shape reflecting what I've been feeling about this journey: Am I really getting anywhere?

Jesus leads us through another door that ushers us onto a raised train platform. An arrival announcement, in German I think, reverberates through the station.

There, unmistakably, is a track of blood.

With swift determination Jesus races down broad steps leading to an open area adorned with quaint cafes, pubs and restaurants. There is no sign of Renata amidst the bustling crowd of posh patrons. People are staring at us. No wonder, since we didn't have time to change out of these medieval clothes before leaving Anastazja's trysting place! We must look like a rain-soaked troupe of traveling troubadours.

A ripple of surprise passes through the onlookers as a young woman gasps, pointing and whispering excitedly to her companions. Simon retrieves a pair of dark sunglasses from the front pocket of his backpack and slips them on.

"Too late," Simon murmurs, scanning the crowd.

Jesus, sensing the urgency, quickens his pace, leading us to the left and across a bustling street. We scramble to keep up. My heart races with anticipation. Émile lags behind due to his limp, as does Anastazja, disoriented by the chaos.

A horn is blowing!

"Anastazja! WATCH OUT!" I shout.

A streetcar!

She looks confused.

"ANASTAZJA! WATCH OUT!" I shout even louder. That young man on an electric scooter nearly plowed over her! She's stumbled to the pavement!

"Simon! Help Anastazja!" shouts Jesus. Simon walks past her, preoccupied, adjusting his sunglasses. Émile, however, stops and helps Anastazja to her feet. She looks dazed, but is out of harm's way. Aware of the eyes upon her, she smooths her hair and straightens her dress. She's safe now. We're all safe for the time being.

Look at all these swanky shops—and there's a sign pointing to the Golden Arches! Wait: Jesus is motioning to us like a military commando, pointing toward the left into a dark alleyway—and away from the Golden Arches. Sad, but Renata needs us.

This has got to be the craziest, grungiest, most kaleidoscopic scene I've ever seen. I mean, who's ever heard of an entire alleyway painted in street art?

"Where on earth are we?" I ask the group. Everyone is gobsmacked by sensory overload. Of course, it is Émile who answers me. "This is Haus Schwarzenberg, just off Hackescher Markt," he says, rubbing his bad leg. Seeing my confusion, he adds tersely, "In Berlin." Émile seems less nervous and more confident than what he was before our visit to his past, but I still don't want him anywhere near me.

Though the blood trail has ended, Jesus confidently navigates the way.

The vibrancy of the street art is overwhelming. "Wow, look at this one!" I exclaim, my gaze fixed on a particularly vivid mural. A rather unsettling piece catches my eye. "That artist could use some therapy," I quip.

Chants of "Si-mon! Si-mon!" fill the air. A crowd of onlookers gathers at the entrance to the alleyway.

Oh. *Now* I understand the frenzy.

The crowd runs toward us—there's no way we'll escape them! We duck under a dark, graffiti-covered archway connecting two buildings; Émile motions to me to help him knock over a couple of dumpsters to block the passage.

It worked! We stopped them! Feeling pretty cocky I give Émile a high-five, who awkwardly returns my gesture. Simon glares at us from the other side of the barrier.

The screaming mob catches up to him, their adoration turning physical as they tear at his clothes.

"JESUS!" Simon yells, panic edging his voice.

With amazing agility, Jesus leaps over the dumpsters, grabs Simon, and hauls him to safety. I never imagined Jesus moving so fast.

A paparazzo's flash catches Simon off-guard, momentarily blinding him, causing him to trip and fall. He quickly scrambles to his feet as the mob closes in. The mob lifts the dumpsters up and over their heads, like at one of those stage-dive concerts I've never been to but have heard about. Simon is in serious danger. We use our bodies as a shield but we won't be able to keep them from him for very much longer.

Wait—what's happening? There is a shimmering in the air, a bending of realities, a faint rustling sound of wings. A translucent barrier manifests between Simon and his adorers. The groupies pause, bewildered, then slowly disperse.

"Cool, man!" I can't help but express my admiration, mixed with a hint of envy at the attention Simon receives.

Simon appears shaken, his breaths labored. "This face is insured for one million Euro," he says somberly as he dabs blood from a scratch on his forehead with a paisley handkerchief. "I hope you never have to experience what this kind of fame feels like."

Jesus helps him up to his feet, then checks on all of us before directing our attention to the back of the alley. We make a dash through a courtyard, then through another covered walkway leading us into a smaller courtyard, everything decorated with a wild menagerie of street art. A small crowd gathers nearby, signaling the opening of an open-air grunge bar gearing up for the evening. We rush past them and through a doorway leading to an old stairwell whose walls are overlaid with years of graffiti. Jesus bounds up the steps ahead of us.

"Wait for me!" cries Anastazja, her voice echoing through the stairwell. Émile promptly turns back to assist her while Simon and I scramble up the steps in pursuit of Jesus. By the time we reach the top of the staircase, my leg muscles have cramped-up and I'm having to hoist myself up by the greasy handrail. Simon has barely broken into a sweat.

We find ourselves on a musty landing beneath a low ceiling. A solitary, grimy door stands ajar, beckoning us to enter.

Jesus steps inside. "Renata?" His voice echoes slightly, met with silence. We follow him in.

The room is tiny, a cramped space tucked beneath the rafters of the old tenement. Graffiti sprawls across every inch of the walls and ceiling. The only light in the room glows from a retro lava lamp, its blobby-orange balls glopping up, and then down.

A framed picture of Jesus the Good Shepherd holding a lamb rests on a small table. Next to the picture is a used needle. Next to the needle is a worn, ancient book.

Émile enters the room with Anastazja, and notices the book immediately. Dabbing his forehead with a handkerchief he reads the German title of the book. He is silent for a moment, then says, "In English it is called 'Following the Poor Life of Christ,' commonly known as *The Book of the Poor in Spirit*. It is attributed to Johannes Tauler, a fourteenth-century German theologian, though some dispute this claim." His eyes catch mine and, seeing my curiosity, he explains, "I am a scholar. I am a Jesuit. Now, let me see that piece of paper there." He points to a torn scrap nestled within the book's pages, a rough bookmark. "Renata must have written this quote from the book. Looking at me, Émile resigns himself to translating the passage into English.

"Thanks," I say, and I mean it. Émile proceeds.

"'You have within you many strong and cruel enemies to overcome. There are a thousand ties you must break. No one else can tell you what they are; only you can find them by looking within yourself and into your heart.'"

"Up here!" Simon shouts, looking down through an open skylight. A step ladder is propped underneath it; blood is smeared on the skylight window. Jesus must've already climbed up there. I follow Simon while Émile attends to a very stressed Anastazja.

We navigate a narrow ledge that hugs the slanted roofline high above the city. I'm blinded by the intense late-afternoon sun shining freely up here on the roof. My vertigo kicks in, my head is swimming in circles and I think I'm going to fall over the edge. Jesus meets my worried gaze, we're suddenly together back on that treacherous log over the rapids, and my scattered thoughts are steadied.

The ledge leads us to a rusted fire escape, which leads us to a tall painter's ladder, which leads us, finally, to Renata.

From a short distance, Jesus, still in his purple-velvet medieval outfit, quietly observes Renata, elegant in her black-goth velvet gown.

Renata mindlessly removes her backpack, its contents agitated, and slumps it beneath a tall painter's ladder leaning against the brick wall of her tenement building. Her self-inflicted wound on her left arm is in definite need of attention. She doesn't seem to notice this, maybe it's nothing new to her, maybe she's lost in her own world, a world that includes a large wooden box filled with spray paint canisters in many colors.

She stands before an immense display of street art, her canvas a brick wall, the pointed, top-most section of her tenement building. We overlook an old graveyard, far below. Her painting appears unfinished as its foreground remains empty.

Renata has painted the blank brick wall with a picture of a tenement building—a tenement building painted on the wall of her tenement building—and has painted the top-most section of the wall in blue—a sky of sorts. Floating languidly in the sky are caricatures of three clouds, resembling wilted balloons tethered to earth with strings.

Renata has painted three larger-than-life windows. In one window, a little girl is seen being slapped across the face by a male figure; in the second window, a young woman is being fondled by an older man; in the third window, an old woman leans upon the windowsill, cigarette in hand, looking despondently over the city. The woman is painted so realistically, it is as if she is gazing directly at us.

Below these windows Renata has painted a rough urban courtyard scene. Against the wall of the tenement stands a trash can overflowing with garbage. On top of the garbage is a broken doll, a tattered school diploma, a crumpled, soiled wedding veil. Hanging on a clothesline above the courtyard is a little girl's dress in periwinkle blue, sullied and torn.

Renata scans her box of spray paint. She chooses a particular color.

It is probably the mother instinct in Anastazja that causes her to call out to Renata; Jesus holds up his hand for Anastazja to remain where she is. The disturbance has done its work. Renata, as if waking from a trance, notices for the first time that we are by her. She looks distraught, her countenance has darkened.

She turns from us and exchanges her spray can with a different color. Approaching her canvas, she splays her art with a long spray of black!

A collective shout of "No!" rises from the group, followed by an elongated "Oh..." as Renata gashes her artwork with darkness.

Jesus rushes toward her. He attempts to make eye contact with her by gently grasping her arms. At his touch her bleeding wound comes together and heals. His act of kindness seems to shift her pain inward as she shivers, breaks down completely, and collapses to the ground.

"You have been too hard on yourself," Jesus approaches her carefully, "and too forgiving to those who exploit you. You are exploited again and again by each person who watches you online." His gaze finds mine. I want to jump off the side of the building to get away from him looking at me.

He holds her, whispers tender words to her that are for her heart only, soothes her fragmented spirit.

Renata's scream pierces the urban din.

Jesus speaks gently, "I will never, ever harm you."

"If I'd been a good little girl, this wouldn't have happened to me," Renata whispers, her voice shaky.

"You were not a good little girl, no," Jesus responds softly, "but you did not deserve what happened to you."

"It goes on for so long," she whimpers. "This must be normal, right? This must be right, right?"

"If it were normal," responds Jesus, "why did it make you feel Sick?
Used,
And not affirmed?
Abused,
And not loved?
Split
And not whole?"

Renata gasps, struggling for breath.
"Daddy. Don't."

Jesus gently wraps her into himself and says,
"You've punished yourself,
Humiliated yourself
For circumstances you were powerless to control.

"You disappear
As you disengage
From what is being done to you.
You hide so deep within yourself
That you cannot find your way back.

"You are consumed like a piece of meat
For the pleasure of others.
You want to run from the movie set,
Escape the stench, the dead, jarring music.
But you need the money, the attention.
So you stay, do your tricks,
Endure the shame.
You scream soundless screams,
Until you hear,
'That's a wrap, be back on Wednesday.'"

And then I see it—legions of black, gummy tethers binding Renata to each person she has had sex with, to each person who has viewed her films, to each person who has connected with her through a screen. Thousands upon thousands of dirty hookups with faceless, dirty scumbags.

I look down: One of those tethers connects Renata to me. One of those dirty scumbags, *is me*.

"Jesus, the stench—it sticks to me," cries Renata. "I can't wash it off. I am scum, scum, scum, scum."

Jesus lifts her chin, his eyes filled with compassion,

"Yet I call you Reborn, Renewed, Redeemed."

I've never looked at any of those people on my secret little website with the purity Jesus looks upon Renata. He sits cross-legged next to the paint box, takes her hands into his.

"Certain relationships
Have intruded upon you,
Overstayed their welcome,
Entered without your permission.

"Once, you were soft, open, wistful, carefree.
But in your search for love, money—or just a good time,
You were pricked and pierced.

"A needle from another's heart:
Pushed into your own heart,
Brutally, deeply, abruptly—
Or twisted in, finely, intentionally, sweetly:
The infliction of affliction.
"When the wound scabs over,
The pain inside is trapped inside you.
You've got to let it out,
You've got to make a release valve!
You've got to deaden the pain,
Rip at it, cut it out."

I don't know how to deal with so much pain. I don't like pain. I don't like my own pain. Jesus keeps going but I wish he'd stop:

"The irremovable bandage—
The scar you're left with—
Becomes your own silent scream."

He pulls Renata into himself, she folds herself within his arms.

"The blade, the pill, the joint, the sex—they've become your trusted friends," says Jesus to Renata.

"They understand me," says Renata, "they know my depths, my twistings, my defeats."

"Yes, they purge and deaden and console you,
They bathe you in a soothing sea of lovely endorphins.
How lovely, that oblivious floating, carefree, gone."

Renata has buried her face into his arms and is sobbing deeply. He strokes her hair.

"You wake up the morning after, only to discover a new needle that cuts into your flesh like a dagger."

Sunset has turned the sky a soft shade of rose. Jesus adjusts her position on his lap to get the blood flowing in his legs. Émile sets himself behind Jesus, rests his back against Jesus' back to support him as he holds Renata. Jesus looks over his shoulder, gives Émile a smile of appreciation as Renata rests.

"How feckless and faithless your blade-friend was," says Jesus softly, stroking her hair.

"Yet I, the King of Hearts,
Call to your bruised and battered heart.
See how my body was pierced for you.
There is healing in my wings for you.
Let me cradle you with my kindnesses,
Lavish you with healing oil,
Flowing from my cross, my sacrifice for you.
Oh, Renata, my Precious One,
My Shimmering Jewel."

Jesus motions to Émile that he wants to get up, Émile quickly stands and helps Jesus and Renata to their feet before standing next to me and resting an arm upon my shoulder. Émile looks at me as a brother. I stiffen, being so close to this 'person'.

We watch as Jesus and Renata rock back and forth, back and forth, slow-dancing to a tune only they can hear. Renata nuzzles her face into his shoulder as he speaks over her again and again, "The lover of my soul...the lover of my soul...."

I'm not sure what I'm supposed to do—go up to Renata and apologize? In order to do that, I'll need to take a good hard look at why I look at those images in the first place. And be willing to stop. But I'm not there yet. No, I'm just not there yet.

* * *

We're eating *currywurst* acquired from a little takeaway place around the corner and down the street from Haus Schwarzenberg. This sausage is so good I've forgotten my desperate need for a Big Mac. The others are sitting shoulder-to-shoulder on the fire escape, leaning against the brick wall overlooking the nightlife below. I stand alone overlooking the graveyard. The night sky of Berlin is bathed in light from the windows of a million, longing souls.

Pointing over the ledge, Émile says to me, "That is a famous Jewish cemetery." Turning to Jesus, Émile says, "You were once in a Jewish cemetery." I think about what Jesus had shared with me earlier, about the condition his body was in after the crucifixion. This very-much-alive Jesus is absorbed in Renata completing her artwork, as if understanding that with each stroke she lays bare her soul to him, to us, to the world. And I notice how the wound on his wrist is not altogether different than the one healing on Renata's arm.

He gets up to assist her, handing her specific spray cans at her request. Renata works fervently, attacking the wall with color, her movements revealing an inner vision with startling force. Though I am abhorred by her utter disrespect for private property, the subtle artistry Renata wields from a simple spray can is absolutely astounding.

The two of them step away from the canvas. Placing their arms around each other's shoulders, they admire Renata's completed work. Covered in so much paint, they nearly blend with the finished scene in front of us:

Prominently painted on the foreground of the street art: a little girl, swinging on a swing. She wears the same periwinkle-blue dress that hangs tattered on the clothesline, though this dress is clean, and fresh, and renewed.

The little girl, safe and free, is in utter glee as her swing is pushed by two giant, fatherly, shimmering hands reaching down from heaven above.

22

KENNETH

"Kenny, could you pass me a few more *serviettes*—what you call napkins—*s'il vous plait*? This food is *magnifique!*" declares Simon. We're back at the picnic table where the five of us started our journey together. Today there are no awkward open sandwiches or fancy finger food: the angels pulled out all the stops this time, decking the table with the best St. Louis has to offer—spareribs grilled to perfection, pork steaks, brats and burgers, beans, slaw and potato salad. Everyone is up to their elbows in barbecue sauce. And look! Cherry pie for dessert!

While the others sit comfortably around my picnic table, I stand at a distance, with paper plate in hand. I still can't quite look Renata in the eyes. Besides, I definitely need some private space after last night. We were *way* too close for comfort, all of us squeezed together on Renata's floor, sleeping on old futons that had definitely seen better days. I'm feeling irritable from hardly getting any sleep, with all the gabbing and giggling and the snoring and turning and elbows in my back and the grunge music blasting from the pub in the alleyway downstairs.

It sure is nice being back at my trysting place. Aside from maybe Simon's, I've got the best-looking trysting place of the lot. Who would've thought the distance between Berlin and St. Louis would be so short? If there'd be anyone who'd know about tesseracts, it would be Jesus. But Jesus' chair remains empty.

"Where's the Boss?" I ask the others. They quickly turn and look at me. It's the first thing I've said to them all day.

"He's probably avoiding having to put on this silly baseball uniform," grumbles Émile. Émile does look shriveled and glum under the Cardinal's red and white, I must admit.

"Look at me! I look utterly ridiculous," chimes in Simon. Simon is the only one I care to interact with since he's the only one in the bunch I feel even remotely safe with. "If you only knew the sponsorship deals you'd get looking that 'ridiculous' in a uniform."

"You have a point there, dear Kenneth," smiling broadly. He looks good even when he's smug.

"Besides, I had to wear Gucci in your trysting place, so it's only fair," I say.

"You should have seen the other outfits I'd planned for you," he says, dreamily.

"This food is just like home!" Anastazja is lost in a world filled with bratwurst with mustard and potato salad.

Renata brings the chatter to a deeper level. "We have experienced many things together, have we not? Jesus has taken us to the depths of our hearts, to bring us into the heights of his love." We descend into that place within ourselves where experiences are kept, and nod in agreement.

The group has gotten pretty quiet with all this pondering; I need to stir things up a bit.

"I remember the first time I saw all of you, sneaking out of the atelier thinking you weren't being seen! I should've known even then that there was something strange about you guys!" I hope they know I'm jesting.

"Why do you call us all 'guys'?" asks Renata. With her striped Cardinals shirt tied to expose her midriff and her red cap turned backwards, she looks like a punk Marilyn Monroe. And certainly nothing like a 'guy'.

"Sorry—it's just an expression, a Midwestern way of pluralizing 'you'—"

Renata gives me a demure grin.

"Oh! So, you were pulling my leg!" I exclaim.

"What does 'pulling my leg' mean?" she asks innocently.

"Well, uh—Oh! You just pulled my leg again!"

Renata giggles the sweetest of giggles. It's nice to see her so light-hearted. "I noticed you, too, that night, hiding behind the food table!" she says, coyly. Her words 'I noticed you' make my heart pound. Her purity of countenance pulls my emotions back from the brink.

Émile smiles at me. "And we saw you trying your own escape, at the entrance to that wicked chamber! You were almost smashed to death between those closing rocks!" Émile's humor must fall under the category of 'dark'. I can still feel that narrow escape in my bones.

"We still do not understand why you and Renata chose not to leave the chamber with the rest of us," comments Simon. He must be representing the consensus of the others; they're looking at us for an answer. None of them witnessed the trauma we experienced on that terrible dais. Through her eyes, Renata signals to me to keep what happened there between the two of us. Looking at her I say, "We don't need to share everything with everyone, do we? Jesus knows what happened to us, and that suffices." Renata expresses her gratitude. How pure she seems now, even with her Cardinal's shirt tied-up like that.

Anastazja pipes in. "And that intolerable, disgustingly muddy, slippery double trail! I am so tired of it, and of the rain! I will be glad when all that is finally behind us. I do not understand why it has to be that way! Doesn't he think this journey is hard enough?"

"And he floats over that trail without a care in the world!" I remark.

"'Graciousness and truth have met together; righteousness and peace have kissed each other,'" says Émile from his end of the table. "From the eighty-ninth psalm. These come together only in Jesus."

"Yes, but Jesus becomes just as wet and muddy as we do," Simon interjects. "Why is it so?"

No one seems to know the answer. We chew on this and on our food in silence, for a very long while.

Simon speaks first, turning to me. "So, why is it that your trysting place does not look like you?"

"What do you mean? Look out over the valley. It's obvious that it looks like a baseball mitt," I answer in my defense. The others turn around, look out over the valley, and shrug their shoulders. They return to their eating. They evidently don't see what I see. Which makes me feel edgy.

Simon continues: "It does not make sense, non? I mean, it's baseball this and baseball that with you, but here we are, sitting in this most beautiful place surrounded by all of these lovely flowers. It looks like an impressionist painting. Like my Monet!"

I protest. "Would you stop pushing me? It does not look like a Monet!"

A gentle breeze douses us with wisteria blossoms.

Émile interjects. "I would say that it looks more like a place where a writer would go to receive inspiration." He says this while cutting a small piece of barbecued pork steak, using his left hand to lift his fork to his mouth without letting go of his knife in his right hand, European style. It does seem more efficient than the American way of using a fork and knife. Not that I'd admit this to them.

"This place doesn't look like you at all," confirms Anastazja. Her eyes well up with tears as she looks at me, her voice trembling. The sudden shift in her demeanor leaves us all uneasy. "I so wish my Stefan could have experienced this valley!" Renata comforts her with a hug while Émile grasps her hands across the baked beans.

Renata gently lifts her eyes toward me, soft in the afterglow of her healing time with Jesus. "Or maybe it perfectly reflects you, Kenneth. Maybe you do not know who you truly are. Or how creative you are. Maybe you're hiding things. Or lying to yourself. I mean, we've been at your very beautiful trysting place all day and you have yet to share anything deep with us. Why is this?"

"Have you been talking with my wife behind my back? I talk all the time!"

"Yes, but about nothing deep."

"Jane! Come out, come out wherever you are!" I shout dramatically. "And what lofty position do you hold that I must share my deepest thoughts with the likes of you? Besides, I've got things under control," the vision of their bondages is still fresh in my mind. I stop, think, weigh the risk, and add: "And I'm in a whole lot better shape than all of you losers."

"Who are you calling a loser?" Simon throws his napkin down for emphasis.

"Well, I don't go around in women's underwear, for one thing."

"How dare you say that in front of the others! I shared that with you in confidence!"

"Your secret is obviously no secret. What about that hint of eye shadow I see?"

"This is not eye shadow, it is eye *enhancer*, you buffoon! You will never know what it is like having to look perfect every day of your life."

"So, under all that 'enhancer' you're just a normal bloke like the rest of us?"

Simon looks me up and down. "Hardly," he says, dryly.

"I bet you're so perfect your farts smell like lilacs." I couldn't resist.

"You, who waste your life away on pornography!"

"I may *watch* it, but I certainly do not *perform* in it."

I went too far. Renata is beginning to cry.

Émile stands and addresses us. "Brothers and sisters, we are all weary from our journey, missing our loved ones back home—"

"Ah, so your money and power gives you the privilege to play Mr. Diplomat, I see!"

"I, I gave all that up, for Jesus!" His humility irks me.

"Monsieur Pedo-Escargot. Keep your antennas away from me, is all I have to say. I've had enough of that kind of stuff in my life."

"Oh, so finally the man is honest!" It is Anastazja. "You have experienced some things—some things done to you, and maybe some things you have done you are ashamed of?"

"That's rich, coming from *you*," I say, with a knowing smile.

"Enough!" I hear someone shout.

"How *dare* you!" spits Anastazja at me. She stands up from the table and slaps me across the face—just like Jessie!

"Ow! What did you do that for?"

"If you were truly my son, I would teach you the importance of respecting others!" Anastazja's coming in for another slap. I push her away, causing her to stumble into Émile, who falls on top of Renata, who screams.

Simon rushes to their aid, his face a mask of anger. Before I can react, he punches me in the gut, knocking the wind out of me and sending me sprawling over the picnic table. I'm looking down into a bowl of German potato salad. One of my arms has landed in overturned apple sauce, while the other arm is swimming in a lake of melted Jello mold. My St. Louis feast lays in ruins.

I unstick myself from the tabletop and swiftly turn around to look at Simon. "Look at what you made me do, you *imbecile*! You have no respect for my culture—and yes, I have culture, too!"

"But it was *you* who pushed me!" he says in protest. I race toward him.

"No, Kenneth, don't hurt him!" Renata beckons as I'm about to punch Simon in that million-euro face of his.

"Enough, I say!" Jesus' voice cuts through the chaos, commanding and authoritative. Everything stops mid-air, the tension palpable. Jesus stands before us, his expression a mix of disappointment and resolve. I see now that he has changed into his Cardinals manager's uniform.

He is carrying a tray with a torn-up loaf of bread and a flask of red wine. For communion.

He lets the tray fall to the ground.

Émile gasps.

"Quickly get yourselves cleaned up and ready to leave," says Jesus, sternly.

"I ain't going nowhere with that bunch of losers," I say, as I grab the cherry pie and storm off.

PART SIX

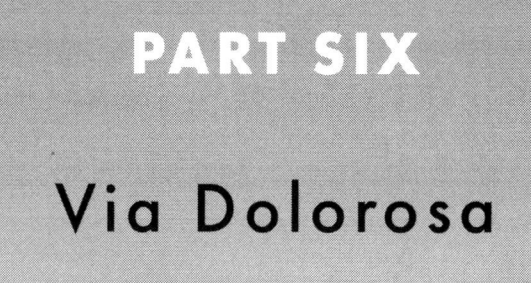

Via Dolorosa

23

ASCENT TO THE DESCENT

Jesus must be far ahead of me by now, as are the others. It was my choice to storm off, indulging in my cherry pie in the privacy of my own pity party. He could have at least looked for me, or waited for me. And nobody bothered to clean up after Simon ruined my love feast!

Strange to think that my trysting place has a back door, people coming and going without the least bit of respect for my welfare and privacy! Think about all those people at the International Night and how they trudged right through without a wink and a nod! And how *could* they forgive their 'trespassers' so flippantly—even for the most unforgivable of crimes!

I could stay here, at my trysting place. But it was created for him and me together, and not for me alone. It isn't the same here without him; I'm already feeling lonely. It's either staying here, alone again, or enduring this confounded trail. Look at that—the double braids have turned into gullies of trickling, liquidy mud! What choice do I have, really?

"*You've chosen the coward's road, shifting blame and evading the ascent to my cross,*" Jesus had said that evening when we revisited my house.

Toward the left, the trail leads to the portals to my fellow-journeyer's trysting places. And back into the dark forest.

Toward the right lays the road less traveled.
I'm standing on the threshold of my own Via Dolorosa.
I make my choice.

The braids have gotten so wide and far apart I'm no longer able to straddle them. I choose one braid, switch to the other, stumble where they intersect.

Simon's story, filled with people who used him, abused him and monetized him, vexes me. In the end he allowed it for his own career advancement! Yet, his words haunt me: *"The little boy within me lingered... bruised, isolated, searching, adrift. A beautiful, empty shell. No pearl nestled within its depths... I sought solace in fleeting affections..."*

Renata, letting herself be compromised and filmed, to be ogled by millions of unseen eyes. She ought to be ashamed of herself! And yet, what Jesus had said: *"I weep for each one who is forced or trafficked into that industry, or makes their way into that industry out of need, or coercion, or intrigue."* What was it that Simon said to me? *"You, who waste your life away on pornography!"* His words resonate with what I realized, back in the chamber of darkness: *"This is the altar on which I've sacrificed others for pleasure, in order to deaden my own pain."*

Émile, the sob story he told us, looking for sympathy for his own twisted rot! *"Jean-Pierre helped me with my crutches... he pushed me in my wheelchair around our gardens... he made me laugh... he appeared interested in me... he met my longing... for friendship... for attention... hidden within our gardens, he did things to me...."* But then, his story echoes my own story: *They see me... the lonely boy... how open I am, longing to be seen... they play with me...* And what was it I thought, back in the chamber of darkness? *"This is the altar on which I have been sacrificed for pleasure, in order to dampen the pain of others...."*

And what about Anastazja! She killed her own son! She said, *"Yes, I snapped, blacked out with rage... I tried to cover it up, shift the blame, point fingers in other directions... but how could I admit to the police what I couldn't admit to myself, that I'd taken the life of my son?"* Oh, how I judge her! But what about the consequence of my own anger? *Jewels walked behind my truck… she fumbled to the ground… I threw the truck in reverse… she became entangled in the cords of her respirator… I jumped out of the truck, threw her out of the way….* I almost ran over and killed my own daughter.

I can't bear the truth.

That memory again! It punches me in the gut every time it hits! They say that what happened to me happens to a lot of boys. But it doesn't make it right. And it doesn't take away the pain. But how can I face it? How can I face my pain when it's mixed with so much shame?

I look up into the weeping sky, tears from heaven dripping on my thoughts, pounding on my heart.

My backpack is filled with filth from the filthy altar. I'm carrying on my back the filth of each person who's hurt me. My worms thrive on the filth attached to my heart-wounds. But I refuse to let those people go. I *can't* let them go!

How did I arrive at the base of the rock face so quickly? Another tesseract. A dream.

This confounded trail weaves its way up the face of the cliff, its double braids carved into the granite like two colossal, warring serpents slithering their way to the top!

There's Jesus, way up there!

He turns to look at me. I can't even see his face and I know he's telling me that I went too far with the others, back at my trysting place. I'm ashamed of myself.

Up, up, I zigzag up these two twisting monsters toward the top of the cliff. I'm so far behind him yet I can't climb any faster but I can't take much more of this agony. My throat is parched, my feet have blisters, my lungs are burning, my legs are exploding and I'm drenched to the bone, but I've *got* to catch up with him!

Why is he taking us up here?

"Just let go. Let yourself glide like an eagle over the ledge," a voice whispers to me.

"Who said that?" That freaked me out. I'm really freaking out here!

"Help! Somebody help me!"

But then, maybe I should just do it, step over the edge of this cliff, end it all, put me out of my own misery. I can barely stand myself anymore. It would be easier to do *that* than to forgive those pervs who bent me. They need to pay with every ounce of their lives!

But would it be enough? Will it ever be enough? If I killed them a thousand times over, would it take away my pain?

I remember Jesus saying to me: *"Unless you deal with your wounds, by forgiving and being forgiven, you will go through life with your heart filled with the filth of others, and your worms will feed on that filth until they explode, damaging your life and the lives around you!"* But what about all the backpacks I've filled with the wretchedness of my own sin?

The memory! *They're closing the door, locking me in with them....*

Those bastards stole so much from me!

I stop, catch my breath. I'm so high up. I could've found a safer place to stop, there's nothing keeping me from falling over the edge!

"*Just let go. Let yourself glide like an eagle over the edge,*" the voice whispers again.

Panic grips me. "Help me, Jesus please help!"

I see Jesus, high up, trudging the rock face as if he's carrying a heavy burden, like the rock he found at the bottom of the stream, a rock that represents my life.

He is carrying *me* up the side of this cliff.

The tears that streak down my face,
Trickle down the cliff face,
Join rivulets of pain from countless faces.

Tears of sorrow, humiliation and woe
Of fear and rage and abandonment,
Merge together to form rivers
That flood the nations
Filling the oceans.

I finally climb over the summit, soaked, weary, and exhausted. Every step felt like a battle.

There they are, Simon the trans, Émile the pedo, Renata the porn star and Anastazja the infanticidal maniac, lying in a heap like a pack of sewer-soaked rats. Who do they think they are, coming so close to the cross where Jesus kneels!

24

CROSSROAD

Storm clouds roil like a cauldron of darkness, the air thick with the acrid smell of burning. The cross looms, its wood splintered and soaked in blood.

Jesus turns, looks, and points to us.

"You! Each of you, justifying yourself while condemning everyone else around you! 'She deserves more judgment than I do!' you say! Glorying in your victimhood, basking in self-righteous judgment, you pick at every flaw in others while you avoid looking at your own! Do you think there is a classification system for sins? You're so worldly you think some sins are more *beautiful* than others! Look! Open your eyes and hearts and look!"

Beneath the cross: lurid snakes, shrieking phantoms, decrepit demons. Filth. Stench. Rot. A writhing pile of wretchedness. Blood. Excrement. Smoldering dreams. Crushed spirits. Broken identities. Devastated bodies. War-torn villages. Missing children. Trampled crops. Insulted beauty. Ravaged innocence. Aborted hopes.

The double-braided trail ends at the foot of the cross. I can go no further on my journey without first going through the cross.

A shimmering, a changing in the atmosphere: Jesus is taking on another dimension of himself.

Oh, God.

The Lamb of God who takes away the sins of the world, hangs now on his cross.

Jesus prays, "Father, forgive them, for they do not know what they do."

To see this so up close, the humiliations, the stab wounds, the blood. His flesh, torn. Thorns, pressed into his skull.

He tries to breathe, but when he does, he has to press up, which puts all his weight onto the nails in his feet!

"Oh, angels! Flutter your wings before my eyes and take this unbearable sight from me!"

No fluttering of angels' wings arrives to my rescue.

The dark presence hangs like a filthy stench in the air. The temperature has plunged.

Beyond the cross, hovering in the swirling storm, appear the faces of those who've lusted after us, forced us, tantalized us, touched us, grabbed us, used us, abused us for the fun of it, exposed us for the pleasure of it, taken advantage of us for the hell of it. We see the demeaning pictures we've posted of ourselves, the cuts we've made into our flesh to the accolades of unseen eyes so that we could eat from the crumbs of their flippant attentions. We have been consumed and have allowed ourselves to be so, in order to get one more "like," one more "follower," one more hug from one more brute.

This vile sight, this bile of the human condition spreads beyond the cross, endless pain, endless woe, the garbage dump of the universe, smoldering, writhing, groping.

We huddle together and watch in horror as our Savior suffers on the cross.

"If you want to be my disciple," he says, looking at us, "you must take up your cross daily, and follow me."

He hangs there, on that cross of shame, every breath a struggle, every heartbeat a testament to his unyielding love.

The faces in the clouds above the cross change: now appear images of public personalities, film stars, rappers, world idols, influencers who regurgitate the name of Jesus as a cuss word, spit it out as a vile expletive and then stomp on it, all at the behest of This Dark Presence.

Simon walks to the foot of the cross and bends his knee. He looks upon the passion of his master and takes a deep breath. His voice trembles as he speaks to the heart of Jesus.

"How they humiliate you, shame you, mock and scorn you on your cross! Yet daily you endure their scorn, in every song and tweet and speech and expletive in which they drag your name through the mud of their own sin. Forgive me for when I have spoken your name upon my own lips, in vain.

"Jesus, you understand the depths of my own humiliation, the shame I've endured, the pain I bear. You bear upon your body the shame and the humiliation I have known, as well as the shame I have placed on other people. Jesus, please have mercy on my soul. The day will come when the name you have been given by the Father will be spoken honorably on every lip and in every tongue, forever."

Simon bows his head. "By your grace, I surrender my name, my reputation, my profession, to uphold the honor of your name, the name that reveals who you are, both in this world, in my life, and in the heavens."

He hangs on that cross, powerless, controlled.

Émile joins his brother Simon before the cross. Horrific images of both human sacrifice and trafficking roar through the storm raging around us. Émile speaks tenderly to the precious heart of Jesus.

"Oh, Jesus, Master and Creator of the universe, pinned like a moth on the cross! You have been stripped of your rightful place in the world you created; you have been allocated a dusty place in the tomes of history books, disrobed of your divinity, reduced to being known merely as a good person.

"Jesus, you were with me when I was stripped, pinned and made powerless, offered as a sacrifice on the altar of my parents' cravings.

"And you were with every child I sacrificed on the altar of my own cravings. Jesus, please have mercy on my soul. To follow you I must receive your grace to take up my cross and surrender to your lordship in all areas of my life—I cannot do this in my own strength. I receive your power to obey you as an expression of my love for you, so that you are reinstated to your rightful place, both in my life and in a world that has rejected you."

Émile and Simon place their arms around each other and bow before their suffering King.

He hangs on the cross, Jesus, holy, unjustly accused and unjustly condemned to death.

Anastazja joins Simon and Émile before the cross. She looks upon Jesus, gazes at the horror of his crucifixion, then speaks to his heart of hearts.

"Oh, King of Kings, how unjustly you are treated, hanging there wearing a crown of thorns!"

I look up: Raging above the cross are visions of arrogant principalities and mocking powers and cunning kings who've placed the golden crown of Jesus upon their own hoary heads. They are pied pipers bewitching the unsuspecting throngs by their deceitful tunes, puppeteers who pull the strings of hapless marionettes for the advancement of their fiefdoms. They are the dummies of the Chief Ventriloquist, his hand thrust into their brains, massaging their messages, manipulating their mouths, so that they spew his lies and dictate his pompous, sacrilegious, vengeful declarations. All this is done to dethrone the rightful King and instate themselves on his throne.

Anastazja cries, "King Jesus, I also took your crown upon my own head, when I played God and took my own son's life. I was justly judged, and then imprisoned, for my crime. Yet Stefan also suffered the injustice of having his life snuffed from him, and by his own mother. Oh, Jesus, please have mercy on my soul!"

Anastazja continues, "Jesus, by your grace, I will not shrink back when the authority and identity you have given me is questioned because of my past, knowing that greater is he that is in me than he that is in the world!"

In the rain, Simon, Émile and Anastazja huddle together in sorrow and in repentance before the cross.

Jesus hangs on that cross, stripped, exposed. Wicked images appear in the swirling clouds above him, of the exposure of flesh and the raping of the innocents, sacrificed for the pleasure of both commoners and the elite.

Renata runs to join the others before the feet of Jesus.

"Jesus," she cries, "you see the wicked things I have done, that have been done to me. I hide nothing from you. My wounds, my scars, the piercings done to me by others, the cuts and abrasions I've done to myself. I have been defiled by those who've abused my body, and I have defiled my heart, your temple, by placing idols within it. I've tried to hide this from you behind a dirty blanket of shame. Please have mercy on my soul and forgive me. By your grace and power I will no longer hide from you; I will allow your winter storms to strip me of my dying leaves, to expose my wounds and my brokenness, so that you may cover me in your blanket of love, and heal me."

Simon, Émile, Anastazja, and Renata huddle together, shoulder-to-shoulder before Jesus on his cross, weeping their pain, expressing their repentance, and releasing their sin and unforgiveness into the miasma of woe flowing from the cross.

"We are all the same at the foot of the cross," I hear them speak; "We are all the same at the foot of the cross."

He hangs there still, Jesus.

I cannot move toward him. I cannot finish this race. It is time to admit this. It is time to go back to where I came from.

I turn from him, and walk away.

A blood-curdling scream rends the sky.

"*Eloi Eloi Lama Sabachthani?*"

I freeze.

At the moment when Jesus, holy, took upon himself the unholy sins of the world, his Father, holy, turned from him.

I quiver at the very core of my heart: my ache of abandonment is a pain that he, too has carried, in the depths of his own heart:

"My God, my God, why have you forsaken me?"

25

THE BASEBALL FIELDS OF ABANDONMENT

Flowing from the foot of the cross is the stream. Its waters shimmer with refracted sunset-light blazing through the retreating storm.

To our left is a low, sharp ridge of mountains, black and stark against the flaming sunset, beyond which flows the sins of the world laid at the foot of the cross.

Yet here flows this stream.

At the bank of the stream I see how the waters gather, clean and resplendent, beneath a dais covered in moss, soft and verdant.

Our motley crew, the worse for wear in our filthy Cardinals baseball uniforms, is sitting by a fire on a wooden bench. Not unlike a dugout bench.

Jesus is back to wearing his Cardinals' manager's uniform.

I feel like a chocolate souffle that is about to collapse.

I must look as strange as I feel, because everyone is looking at me, strangely.

"Jesus?" I'm falling into myself.

"I am going with you," shouts Jesus from above.

Back I fall, through shadows charged with tension.

Snippets of conversations swirl in my boyhood world…

"Dad had a heart attack, but he made it through the night."
"Dad's friend found him wandering on the side of the highway, barefoot."
"Dad's business deal fell through."
"Dad was found by the Great Lake trying to swim to Canada with his clothes on."
My little-boy mind tried to create wholeness out of pieces of chaos.

My father and me
searching for ways of connecting
Yet nearly always failing.

I wanted to share with him my thrill of the color crimson!
"Dad! Look at the trees, the leaves! Those grand oaks, they're painted in crimson and light!"
Crimson and light was not the language of my father.
So, I attempted to learn his language.
Dad was the baseball hero, so baseball must be his language!
I began to play baseball.
I didn't understand baseball. I didn't speak baseball.
This linguistic impasse remained between us for years.

Suddenly, out of the blue, my father learned to speak my language.
Over the course of a few weeks,
He took me with him on a business trip
(which he had never done before),
Attended my piano recital
(he made me nervous),
Made it a new habit of attending my baseball games
(that he had given up on).

One day he picked me up from school to take me fishing. He'd never once picked me up from school, much less to take me fishing. I found myself standing beside the river with pole in hand, next to my father in his brown business suit and wing-tip shoes.

I remember looking at him thinking, who is this man?

I think my head is in Jesus' lap.
Flames from the fire dance with fireflies swirling with the stars above.

With blankets around their shoulders, my travel companions are sipping steaming soup from tin cups. Their eyes are fixed on me.

"Jesus? You're here with me, right?"

"As I was with you when it happened, so I am with you now."

"Just checking. This isn't going to be easy."

"Go on!" urges Anastazja. "You can't stop now!"

It was during this time that my little league baseball team played its final game of the season, and we were one game short of winning the pennant.

It was a late-afternoon home game; the bleachers were filled with over-enthusiastic parents; my father was among them.

It was the bottom of the ninth and our team was up by three runs—the win was virtually ours!

I had more bench time than any boy on the team that season: to his credit, the coach was acutely aware of my utter lack of skill, and interest, in the game. That evening the coach was so sure of a win that he felt safe to put me in play. "To give the boy the feeling that he's part of the team."

The coach placed me in right field.

The ball is rarely hit to right field.

I rarely caught the ball.

Right field and I were a perfect match.

The coach was playing it safe, in other words.

THE BASEBALL FIELDS OF ABANDONMENT

I remember how wonderfully quiet it was out there that evening in right field, far from the screaming parents and the incessant "Hey, batta-batta!" chanting of my overexcited teammates.

I watched the setting sun cast long shadows upon the field, painting the grass in lovely hues of purple. The smell of my baseball mitt was comforting. Look how its leather conformed perfectly to my hand!

I followed the dealings of the game as best I could:

The first batter struck out.

One out.

The second batter hit a fly ball, caught by the pitcher.

Two outs.

One more out and the win was ours and I could finally get out of this place.

The third batter hit a single and made it safely to first base.

The fourth batter hit a single and made it to first base, forcing the runner on first to second base.

Two outs, two on base.

I could sense tension building in the air. The parents were working themselves up into a frenzy.

The fifth batter hit a single and made it to first, forcing the runner on first to proceed to second. Which meant that the runner on second was forced to third.

Two outs at the bottom of the ninth. Bases loaded.

But we were still up by three runs! I allowed myself to fall into ethereal consternations. Was there really such a thing as a tesseract like I read in *A Wrinkle In Time*?

Again, the crack of the bat.

A slight "thud" sound emanated from the dewy, dusky grass near my feet.

Glowing in the purple shadows was an alien, white orb.

It was The Ball.

I approached the ball, scooped it up in my nice leather mitt.

What to do with the ball I had no answer for. The question was framed in a context broader than the little league game disintegrating before my eyes. True, I was drawn toward discovery and exploration over perfecting the repetitive motions of sport. And I found no pleasure in a game consisting of knowing exactly what to do with a ball when nothing stayed in place. I detested every after-school baseball practice and feared every time at bat, not so much because I did not like playing the game, but because I knew I never could—at least not at a level that would make my father proud of me.

I hated every moment in the field, knowing instinctively that this one agonizing moment might indeed materialize, a moment when every disappointing thought I believed my father had about me would be proven correct. And I had endured all this to reach out to him, because it seemed he didn't quite know how to reach out to me.

While pondering all this, the baseball diamond had turned into a spectacle rarely witnessed at Busch Stadium. The crowds were wild, the coach was screaming and my teammates were about to pee themselves as the batter ran to first, the boy on first ran to second, the boy on second sprinted toward third, and the boy who had been on third was now prancing home for a run and a score to the high-fives of his teammates and the cheers of enemy parents.

What now? They just gained a run, though we were still up by two—but three more runners were scrambling around the diamond!

The crowd was chanting, "THROW THE BALL! THROW THE BALL!!! THROW THE BALL!!!!"

Realizing they were chanting to me, I threw the ball. So I threw that ball with every ounce of strength my skinny little arm could muster.

The ball flew directly over the heads of my stunned teammates.

The ball sailed past the baffled third baseman.

That ball flew so far that it landed in the bleachers among the frothing parents!

A collective Ohhhhhhhh exuded from the crowd as the second, then the third, then the fourth and final runner of the visiting team strutted smugly home, stealing the win and the pennant from my incredibly trounced-on team.

While my former teammates were heading home in abject confusion, my father found me out in right field cussing and cursing and pulling up clumps of grass with my fists.

"Come," he said kindly to me, "let's go get an ice cream."

This wasn't the first edition of my father; this was the second edition of my father that I'd been recently introduced to. I looked at him curiously while walking with him toward the car.

But what would I do with my bike? If I went with him, I didn't know how I'd get my bike home. I found the courage to admit this to him.

"We can put it in the trunk," he suggested and opened the trunk of his brand-new Chevy Impala.

But the trunk was already filled with something; there wasn't room for my bike. My father offered to lay my bike in the back seat of the new car.

The thought of messing up the gleaming interior of the new car with dirt and grime from my bike—I didn't know how I'd face my mother if that would happen. The situation quickly became too much for me.

I spat out in anger, "I wanted to ride home by myself, anyway!"

My father backed away, closed the trunk of the car, and became quiet.

He said, "Alright, then. I'll see you when you get home."

I watched my father drive away into the sunset.

I rode my bike to the river that ran behind the baseball field, where I threw a thousand rocks into the water to vent my thousand frustrations and shame.

I rode my bike home in the dark. Without saying good night to my family, I retreated to my room, defeated.

* * *

Tents have been raised just beyond the campfire. My friends are wearing matching plaid jammies and robes and bunny slippers. I must be feverish.

Simon hands me a cookie, passes me a tin mug of hot chocolate. "And then what happens? Kenny! What happens next?"

"What happens? What happens is that my father died from a massive heart attack, later that night."

* * *

Red lights swirl on the ceiling over my bed.

A heavy presence of unfamiliar men enter our house.

I pull my blanket up to my chin.

I listen to the sound of metal things clink through the front door, roll past my bedroom and stop at the end of the hallway.

I hear a man with a kind voice say, "I'm sorry, ma'am, there's nothing more that we can do."

I hear my mother howl.

I hear people in the hallway doing what they can to keep my mother from collapsing to the floor.

I watch as the swirling red lights recede from my ceiling and disappear.

I lay alone, waiting, contemplating, in the dark.

My bedroom door opens tentatively; a crack of light confirms my little-boy consternations.

I hear my big sister Suzy call to me, quietly, tenderly, "Kenny?"

I jump out of bed and into the waiting arms of my family in shock.

Blurry days.

Rarely-seen relatives gather from across the country,

THE BASEBALL FIELDS OF ABANDONMENT

Their voices a crescendo of chaotic love,
Muted by hushed condolences,
Stressed by primordial wails.

The cadence of the doorbell,
Alerting the arrival
Of yet another casserole
Or plate of ham
Or cake or pie.

I forced myself to believe that it was my fault.
It was easier to coat this emptiness with contrived guilt
Than to be butchered with the truth
That he had left me.

It was an anomaly to have a dead father—
None of my friends had one—
And the perk brought with it a certain prestige.
I rode my bike around the neighborhood
Telling anyone I knew that my father had died,
Generating the desired reaction
Of immediate shock
Followed by doting comfort.
This amused me.

I kissed his forehead
Because my mother forced me to,
Him lying there
In his brown business suit,
My siblings placing his favorite sweets in his casket,
Humor being our family's best remedy
For any sort of trauma.

A large American flag,
Draped over his casket

For his service to his country:
Playing baseball for the military.
He disappeared into that hole,
He disappeared from my life.

Or so I thought.

We moved to St. Louis,
Back to my parents' hometown,
Offering me a fresh start in a new school
Away from the man who'd left me.

The blur of days blurred into years,
The emotionally neglected boy deteriorated
Into an angry, directionless youth,
Hiding behind my good-boy intentions,
Exhausted from hiding my ever-growing worms.

And I played baseball—I became quite good at it, in the end;
I willed myself to perfect the repetitive motions of a sport I loathed,
Quenched my longing for discovery and exploration,
All to win the favor of a father
Who was no longer there.

My father's absence stayed with me,
Twisted me, plagued me,
The darkness whispered to me to give in,
How sweet it would be to *just give in*,
To drive the car into the River Des Peres,
To then float blissfully toward the awaiting arms of the Mississippi,
Forever entombed
In a Chevy Impala
With no bicycle marks on the back seat,

Finally ending
The tiresome, endless beating
Of my tired, troubled heart.

"And that's when you came to me, Jesus."
"That was when you opened your heart to me, yes, there in the high school basement."

26

STREAMS OF HEALING LOVE

The moon rises in the far western sky, its beams twinkling upon the surface of the great lake in the distance. The campfire has tempered to peaceful, glowing embers.

My fellow journeyers rest upon each other's shoulders like the teddy bears on Julia's bed. My head remains in Jesus' lap.

The gurgling of the stream, swollen from the day's torrents, blends with the croaks of frogs and the fiddlings of crickets.

"Does anyone sense the Spirit prompting them to share with Kenneth?" asks Jesus.

A hush descends upon the campsite.

I rest, trust, open my heart. I feel almost pregnant with anticipation.

No one speaks. Everyone is listening.

A single, subtle whimper exudes from Anastazja. Renata breathes a deep, melancholic sigh.

Again there is silence.

How come they're not getting any words or pictures for me? Have I done something wrong?

"It is just that, Kenneth's story, about his father. It touches something deep in me," says Émile, sadly.

"Simon, may I have you read John, chapter 1, verses 10 to 13 for us, please?"

"*Mais bien sûr, mon Seigneur.*"

Simon reads it silently to himself. He looks up from his Bible, looking lost.

Jesus' face is illuminated by the crackling fire.

I close my eyes. Something is touching me deeply. I feel the palm of a hand resting upon my heart. My body relaxes. I look up; it is Jesus.

"I will tell you what John wrote about me," he says. "He wrote that I was unrecognized and rejected by the very world I created. But you, you believed me, and you accepted me. And for your faith you are recognized and accepted by my Father in heaven."

Weeping breaks out among us.

"Oh, my children, my dear, precious, fatherless children. What pains would be released from the broken ones of the world, if they but knew the depth of my Father's love for them!"

"Jesus, I see the connection. I thought the attention I sought would give me the attention I longed for. I was left instead with this 'attention deficit', always longing, always searching for love in dirty wells."

"This is the very reason your fellow pilgrims needed you to journey with them, Kenneth."

I see, I see, I see: each of us carries this attention deficit. We all ache for the touch of a father.

He picks me up, walks with me along the edge of the stream, back to his cross.

It is now that I can do it.

I open my heart to release the unforgiveness, the dirt and filth of those who've wounded me. I watch it disappear into the cleansing flow of crimson red.

The blood.
The blood of the Lamb.
Flowing from the foot of the cross.

He carries me toward the others resting on the verdant dais, lays me in the cool, welcoming moss. I am next to Renata. I see the black, sinuous bonds that bind her. She speaks in German though my heart understands her:
"I speak to each person whom I have forgiven:
I cut off every bond you have placed on me,
Every soulish, ghoulish tie built between us,
In Jesus' name.
"Please, Jesus, fill my wounded heart,
Satiate the places where this person had taken control,
Where I allowed this person to control me.
And Jesus, please, dwell in me, fill me,
Make me yours,
Completely."

I watch as Jesus tenderly clips the bonds restricting Renata's heart, releasing her like a butterfly from a cocoon. She sucks in air as if it were her very first breath.

I am thankful for the bonds he's already cut from me. Yet I am aware of the bonds that remain, wrapped tightly like duct tape across my chest.

> They see me, the lonely boy,
> Me, the new boy on the block that knew no one,
> That no one knew.
> How open I am,
> Longing to be seen.
>
> I had rejected my body,
> But they've chosen my body.
> I thought I was someone unseen,
> But now they're exposing me.
> I saw myself as an untouchable,
> But they are touching me.
> They play with me.

But I am too young to do the things that they want me to do.

I am lying on this dais by the stream, on the dais in the chamber, and on the floor of the bathroom. Jesus holds me in this healing pool, covering me, sponging my brow, whispering to me—

> "I am here,
> Not to throw you a safety line
> From some lofty, delicate place
> But to rescue you with my own arms
> As I lift you up,
> Tenderly, gently
> Into myself."

> Jesus is my shield, my disappearing cloak.
> I'm looking at the boys through the veil of the Shimmering.
> The boys do to me what they do.
> Jesus kneels, looks directly into my eyes as they do it.

"I see you," he says, lifting my face.
"I know you," he says, looking into my heart.
"I want you to be mine," he says, speaking to my deepest longings.

> I am so little and Jesus so tall, his arms so big, mine so small.
> He helps to pull up my pants, finds my shirt and my little socks;
> He knocks down the locked door like a firefighter, looking into my face,
> attentive to my welfare;

> He takes me away from the groping and the titillating;
> He carries me out of the smokescreen of deceptive love,
> Where there is light,
> Where I can breathe.

He knocks down the doors of my heart,
And we are out, and we are here, and I am safe.

Another wormhole:
    There, here, then, now,
    The boy I was,
    The man I've become—
    Pain transferred
    From one to the other.

Who is this,
With arms I look for, the love I seek?
I give my all during my dark years (Not to Jesus):
Only to be left uncovered and shamed,
Twisted and unfilled,
As with the next one
And the next one
And the one after that.

I became hunted:
When I was caught by them
—or allowed myself to be so—
They chewed on my body
Then spat out the bones.

I became the hunter:
Ever hunting for twisted love,
Garbage love.
Poison love.

He was with me in my abuses
And by my father's grave
And on that wicked dais;
And now, he is with me by this pool,
    Upon this healing dais:

The altar of my surrender.

I say to a specific person who's wounded me:

> "I forgive you for what you stole from me.
> I know that Jesus will give back a million times over.
>
> "I forgive you for stealing my innocence.
> Jesus will restore me with his forever-love and purity.
>
> "And I forgive you for bruising me and abusing me.
> Because Jesus will heal me with the balm of his love for me."

I am the boy on the boat and the man I am now, shifting, shimmering back and forth, my pain transferred from one to the other, and now, finally, onto Jesus.

> "You robbed me of my innocence.
> You replaced it with this filthiness.
> But because Jesus will be restoring this,
> Through his perfect, lovely holiness,
> I forgive you for what you stole.
>
> "I speak to each person whom I have forgiven:
> I cut off every bond you have placed on me,
> Every soulish, ghoulish tie formed between us,
> In Jesus' name.
>
> "Please, Jesus, fill my wounded heart,
> Satiate the places where this person had taken control,
> Or where I allowed this person to take control.
> And Jesus, please, dwell in me, fill me,
> Make me yours,
> Completely."

I gasp for air:
> I am awaking from a dream
> In which I am being held under water.
> But I am not dreaming,
> And I am not under water.
> I am awakening
> To the realization
> Of the pain
> I have inflicted on others.
> "O God, what have I done?"
> Swirling in the clouds
> Above the cross
> Are the faces
> Of each person
> I have hurt.

For too long I have turned a blind eye to the pain I've caused others—specific others—my heart deceived by my rotting sin. I cannot go further on this journey without taking responsibility for my own painful actions. My wife, my children, those who've had no choice but to interact with me at work, at the store, at church, who've had to suffer my outbursts, my selfish tantrums, my futile tirades. And then there are those who've known what I've done to them that few others know about, who've suffered their own shame and pain at my expense, individuals whom I sacrificed on the altar of my selfish, broken need, greed, and pleasure.

I didn't know, while knowing.

And I pray:

> Lamb of God
> Who takes away the sins of the world,
> Have mercy on me.
> Please, have mercy on me.

And Jesus, please have mercy on them.
May your truth and justice kiss them,
Your love and mercy heal them.
And may you clip them
From every unhealthy bond
I created in iniquity
Between my soul, spirit and body,
And theirs,
In Jesus' name,
Amen.

"Renata?" I say, surprising myself.

"Yes?" She looks at me with open eyes and heart.

"Will you forgive me for using you?"

"Yes, I forgive you, Kenny." Her bottom lip begins to quiver. "And Kenny, will you forgive me for making it hard for you to remain holy?"

"It wasn't your fault—"

"No, not directly, but I did my part. And I need your forgiveness."

"Then Renata, I forgive you, too."

I sense an immediate change in the dynamic of our relationship. The attraction I've felt for her, the pulling toward sensuous thoughts about her, is gone. And I know, just *know* that the black bond between us has been severed.

"But Jesus, you're really going to have to help me with my, uh—it sounds so gross when I put into words, but I have to say it—with my porn addiction. I won't be able to do it without you."

"Nor did I ever expect you to do it without me, my dear Kenny," says Jesus, looking very pleased indeed.

✶ ✶ ✶

The moon hangs translucent, a pearly-pink disc in the early morning sky, studded with galaxies and laced with Aurora's emerald, flowing veil.

I've got my head on his shoulder, watching the valley awaken beneath the expanse of the eastern mountains. He adjusts the wool blanket he's pulled around us both. It is quiet over in the boys' tent apart from some snoring. In the girls' tent there is giggling then shushing then giggling some more. How he keeps up with all of our heart journeys at the same time, I'll never know.

The tiniest squint of dawn kisses the ridge of the snowy mountains.

He's humming a little tune. I think I recognize it...

Yes! It's *Easter Song*, by Keith Green!

My favorite Easter song. The words come back to me...

> *"Hear the bells ringing*
> *They're singing*
> *That you can be born again ..."*

Heads pop out of the tents.

Now he's dancing a jig! He waves the woolen blanket over his head while dancing the hora (his mop of hair bouncing up and down in syncopation, his eyes lost in a sea of smile) as Émile rushes to join Jesus in the dance. This is all very infectious, to say the least, though it does go against my Midwestern sensibilities.

> *"The angels up on the tombstone*
> *Say he is risen, up from the dead!*
> *Quickly now, go tell his disciples*
> *That Jesus Christ is no longer dead!"*

If Émile can cut loose, well, so can I, doggonit. And here come the girls, giggling, joining in on the hora by waving bath towels over their heads!

> *"Joy to the world!*
> *He is risen!*
> *Hallelujah!"*

Here we are, this band of fellow journeyers, celebrating Easter with the risen Christ before the empty cross.

With full lungs we belt out over the awakening world,

> *"He's risen,*
> *Halleluja-a!*
> *He's ri-sen!*
> *Hallelujah!*
> *Hallelujah!*
> *Hallelujaaaaaaaah!"*

We finish the final note in discordant though jubilant glee. And we laugh and hug and sing some more as the first rays of the new dawn burst forth in all its resurrection glory.

* * *

Jesus stands with his back toward the rising sun.

Behind him, a nearly imperceptible curtain, the thinnest of veils, flutters virtually translucent in a whisper of breeze.

I say, "My mother hung sheets to dry on the clothesline in bright summer sunshine when I was a boy."

The others look at me, baffled.

How embarrassing, why did I say that? Where did it come from? Oh! I know! My mother's freshly-washed sheets, their bleachy scent wafting on the breeze through my bedroom window, awakening within me the numinous, the longing for *more*.

Jesus is smiling that half-grin of his. With those perky eyes and his dark, curly hair speckled white with ash from last night's campfire, he says to us,

"There is someone I would like all of you to meet."

JOURNEY INTO THE SHIMMERING

Behind him the veil parts, oh so gently, revealing my deepest longings.

Glorious, brilliant light, Shimmering, singing Light.

It is him.

"Abba, Father," escapes from my lips.

We are wooed through the most delicate of dividers, toward this weighty, heavy Love.

Stopping in unison, we are unsure if we may enter. We look to Jesus for direction.

"I gave my life for this very moment," says Jesus, beaming.

"But Jesus, won't we be turned into pillars of salt?" I say, quivering with fear.

"Don't shrink back! Approach the Father with boldness, with your heads held high, in the full width and breadth of your identity as his adopted daughters and sons."

No, I will not shrink back. Not now, not after I see more clearly what Jesus went through to make me his own.

We take one, sure step beyond the veil.

I fall to my knees and bow my heart.

Émile falls prostrate, adoring.

Renata stands tall with open palms, countenance raised, shimmering in the Father's acceptance.

Anastazja, her tender heart open, lavishes in the glow of the Father's glow for her. Upon her lips she softly says, "*Święty, święty, święty.*"

Yes. My heart joins Anastazja's in giving the one true, proper response to the God of all Creation,

"*Holy, holy, holy.*"

I find myself shouting at the top of my lungs—

"Father! I see you now, though my eyes are closed, oh, how I see you! I will not shrink back, no! I will boldly approach your throne of grace! What a slap to the face of Jesus that would be, after all he did for me, to open the way for me, to take my sins, to prepare me to stand here holy and blameless in your presence, if I did not take this one step toward you."

We raise our voices together with those we met at the atelier, our tapestries playing like fine-tuned instruments in the most glorious of orchestras, singing, swooned by the Father's passion for each of us. Our heart galaxies swirl in joy, joy, joy, and now we see the heavens of saints and angels, and more than angels: beings with eyes all around proclaiming "Holy! Holy! Holy!" We see Him through Jesus, I fall before Jesus, oh, yes, my brother, my friend, and savior and redeemer yet he is the way to the Father, the truth of who we truly are and who we are meant be, and the life, eternal, holy, glorious, love-radiating life of knowing the Father, Abba, Daddy, I run up to Jesus and swing around his neck and almost plow him over and we dance in the utter joy of knowing that yes, this is what his cross is all about, his blood shed, cleansing us, so that we may stand holy and glory in Father's Daddy-Abba-love. I feel pure, and whole, and wholly accepted, wholly adopted and chosen, with my brothers and sisters swinging around with Jesus, "Jesus, Jesus! Thank you for what you did on the cross. Thank you. Thank you, thank you."

Will I see myself in the Father? Though I can't see him now, I just *know* I look like him; he's made me in his likeness! Will I see in him Simon's beautiful strength, Renata's unending depths, Anastazja's eternal gaiety, Émile's pools of wisdom and knowledge? Do I have his chin? What a funny thought! Maybe everybody has his chin! He's made so many Asians, maybe he's half-Asian! But in an African way, with a Caucasian twist and a Latin vibe. I bet there's something Himalayan about him, too, blended with Persian, and Apache and Cherokee and Sioux, topped with a big scoop of North African and sprinkled with Gaelic. And Incan! And Scandinavian! Tongan, maybe? Yes, that too. And Aboriginal. And Inuit. And French. His eyes probably have lovely Mongolian folds while being almond-shaped, in an intriguing blue-green-brown color with silver overtones. But he must be huge, with giant, safe arms. A giant of a presence. Yes, definitely Masai. And Dutch! Ha! With ginger hair like mine! Wouldn't that take the cake—we're all going to have red hair in heaven! Maybe he's a blend of everything! Or we're a blend of him! Yes! Wait—my quirky thoughts are drawn back to him, back to who he truly is—I see, I see—I see! I mean, I don't see, I don't see his face, though maybe someday—does the Bible tell us? Something Paul wrote, I think, in the section on love, something about us now seeing a poor reflection of him, like in one of those milky, old-fashioned mirrors hanging up in a second-hand store. But then we shall see him, face to face.

Oh! A new wave of worship is building around us! The air is thickening with music—with brass and stringed instruments, and bagpipes and sitars, accordions and didgeridoos—and with weighty crescendos of praise, with gathering angels joining us to fill the heavens with worship to the Glorious King. I can scarcely breathe; I can scarce take it in.

Again, I find myself shouting: "You are so much more than what I've ever imagined or contrived to imagine. You are beautiful in your holiness, holy in your loveliness, beautifully loving in your holiness!" I look around at the others, tears streaming down Renata's face, I hear her saying in German yet I understand her heart, "You hold us, move us, you are as near to us as our very breath. And you made us for you, for your heart alone, oh such wondrous, glorious joy. The joy of your presence. I love you, I love you, I love you, Father I love you, and I receive your love for me."

Jesus takes each of our hands into his, brings us closer to the Father, into his Shimmering light, the joy of my desiring.

"Oh, Abba, Father, I let go. I allow you to take hold of me, to carry me. I am so very, very tired of doing things on my own, doing things my way. I no longer have to do it all; I'm not meant to do it all. Oh, Father. Oh, Father." I can't stop weeping. I am his. I am his.

I'm blubbering on someone's shoulder. What a mess.

"I sense the Father say to you, 'It is I that you were made for, I am your rightful place, I am your home, and home you have arrived.'"

It is Émile. I see Émile, his eyes the purest of ocean blues, yet I also see the Father in Émile's eyes, his light, his care, his love for me.

I sense the Father folding me into himself. He is inviting me to nestle, to rest upon his heartbeat. I know it's Émile who is holding me, yet it's the Father holding me through Émile, and he holds me, holds me. My pent-up stresses, my layers of abandonment are flowing from me, they're flowing toward the stream, joining tributaries of tears, the tears of the nations, filling the oceans with peace. And now it is finished. And I am hugging Émile, thanking him for being there for me, for allowing the Father to love me through him, and we wipe away each other's tears, and laugh. I've never seen Émile look so comfortable in messiness, my slobber all over his shoulder.

But—where is Simon?

With Jesus' arms around him, Simon sobs bitterly, there, outside the veil.

"I cannot do it. Jesus, I cannot open myself up to him, no, not just yet. I am so sorry, so very, very sorry, but I just cannot do it."

"You have come so far, Simon. I am proud of you. I will never leave you, no, not ever. Someday you will meet your Father. But now, rest in my arms."

PART SEVEN

Coming Home

27

THE PLACE OF PRAISE

The weight in the air lifts as the Shimmering presence recedes. Angelic song yields to the twitter of bluebirds resting in pink-blossomed dogwoods. I am both filled and emptied; Émile reaches out a hand to help me to my feet. Anastazja, out like a light, awakens to Renata's gentle voice.

Simon rests with his face buried in Jesus's chest. We gather around him, laying our hands on him as we speak blessings over his life. We understand without Simon having to explain. No more judgment, no more name-calling, no more finger-pointing. We are all the same at the foot of the cross—and beyond.

"The time has come for the five of you to part ways," says Jesus, kissing Simon gently on his forehead.

We put our arms around each other, and wail.

I've got to say something.

I pull myself from Anastazja's tear-soaked embrace and rise, trembling slightly. I glance at Anastazja, Émile, Simon, and Renata before turning to Jesus. A new sensation rises within me: I no longer feel the need to defend, belittle, or shame myself. Or belittle or shame the others. What is this new feeling?

"It is humility," says Jesus, pleased.

"Jesus, I know. Yes, I see. I have done unspeakable things. Dark things." I look at the others. "Things that I can't talk about at the Wednesday evening Bible study group." They nod in understanding. "Jesus, you know what I've done." I walk up to him, standing before him.

"Yet I am yours, and you are mine. You're my Master, my Savior." He looks at me with such tenderness I can scarce continue. So Anastazja continues for me. There is something stately in her countenance, royal in her presence, giddy in her exuberance. She speaks to him with voice and dance.

"I want to sing for you! Shout to the nations of your goodness and loving-kindness and your mercy toward me!"

She stops, her gaze dropping as shadows of her old self cloud her face. "And yet, my neighbors know what I have done. I can't go to my mailbox without someone peeking through the blinds, checking to see if I'll do it again.." There is a forlornness to her words.

"But I won't! I can't! I cannot, could not, tarnish your name, my King." Her voice breaks as she begins to weep. Simon picks up where Anastazja leaves off.

"My heart is scared, scarred." He stands, approaches Jesus, and bows his head. "Because the temptations, the weaknesses—they're waiting around the corner to trip me up, to bind me, to drag me down again into the depths of the dark world." Simon's humility shows his strength.

"Jesus, have mercy on us!" It is Émile. "Day after day, I live for you. Yet day after day I live in this fear of falling."

Renata stands beside Émile, placing her arm around him. "Jesus, my heart, though mending, still hurts. It is so broken. I am ashamed of what I have done. I've felt so alone. There has been no one I could share these things with, no one who could understand. Until you brought the five of us together." Jesus gathers all of us into himself like a mother hen.

"Hush, my children. Shhhhhhh.

Rest in me.
Now look into my eyes.
See? You find no shame,
No scorn in my eyes, for you."

Jesus is also in tears.

"Remember my children, practice remembering:
That I have called you
I have chosen you
I have redeemed you
And that
You
Are
Mine.

"I know you; I know all about you.
Yet I cover you with my mercy
Smother you with my grace
Knowing full well that
Those who have been forgiven much,
Love me much.
And your love for me
Makes my heart
Shine.

"I still have a plan
Even for you!
Layer upon layer, line upon line, day after day
I am building, healing, redeeming
You.

"It takes time to rebuild something as precious as a heart.
Give me time. Give me years. I know what I am doing.

"In the meantime—no, in the moment:
Serve me with your worship
Honor me with your purity
Remain faithful in my Word.
Find ways of blessing me
By blessing others.

"I know about the neighbors.
But I have hidden you within myself.
When you walk out your door
You walk truly
As the daughter
Or as the son
Of the King.

"One warning:
Do not push yourself into ministry.
Do not proclaim that you have a gift, a story, a flashy history.
Keep yourself hidden in me.

"When I deem it is time,
I will open the shell
And let my pearl shine,
In my way, in my time, for my glory.

"Do not open doors for yourself.
Serve in little ways,
Make hearts shimmer with my love.
And when doors do open to you
Make sure they are *my* doors for you.

"And when doors open for you:
That is when you must walk
Carefully,
Staying small,

Resting your head upon my heart
Allowing me to remove the dross that surfaces
In the crucible of opportunity.

"And when you fall (or dishonor my Name):
Pick yourself up, let me clean you up, rinse you off
With the blood that I shed for you
(And for your neighbor staring at you through the blinds).

"After you fall, repent.
Repent from believing that I love you less now.
You are still my pearl
That I have given my all to find.

"Falling, sinning, messing up
Means that there is work still to do,
That I'm not yet finished with you
(I never will be, this side of heaven).

"Falling means that you cannot do it alone, go on your own.
This is what my brothers and sisters are for.
We are family.

"No, you may not be able to share everything
At the Wednesday night Bible study group.
But I will give you someone,
Or a handful of faithful, lifelong friends,
Who will love you
With your past,
Your struggles,
Your story.
And, because you dare
To share your story with them,
They will love you all the more.

"One more thing:
There is a price to pay
For living long in darkness's world.
You may walk with a limp
Even after I've made you whole.
Fewer doors, fewer opportunities
May open to you than for others.
But so what!
It only takes the door I choose for you,
To turn your world
Upside down with my love.

"The scars from your life may still be seen
And misunderstood by misunderstanding eyes.
Wear your scars with pride:
'This is what Jesus delivered me from!'
My scars, gouged for you,
Are still visible,
And I wear *them* with pride,
As I wear *you* with pride,
Like a jewel on a strand near my heart."

Jesus moves closer and whispers, "You lacked the insight to realize that your temptations stem from your wounded heart. You've carried immense pain and brokenness, unknown to you, until now on this journey."

"I don't want to leave all of you," I say, bowing my head. "Though you're probably glad I'm leaving." I can't believe the things I've called them, said to them. "I'm really sorry for the pain I've caused you."

"The pain in the butt you've been to us?" Simon says, lifting my chin. "Ha! You're one kind of pain we don't want to live without!" The others burst into laughter.

I look at each of them, think of the shared experiences I have with each of them, and remember Renata.

"But Jesus! What will happen to Renata when she goes back? Can't she just stay in The Shimmering so she'll be spared from the life she's lived? What will she do?" I'm genuinely freaking out on Renata's behalf.

Renata blushes at my concern. She is leaning against Anastazja, who has an arm around her. They look at each other, and smile.

"I have a plan for her," Anastazja beams. "—or Jesus and Renata and I have a plan for Renata: she will leave Berlin and her life there entirely, and move into my home in Krakow, where I will love her and care for her and fatten her up with good Polish sausages!" Renata tickles Anastazja in the ribs with that newfound giggle of hers, and then leans in Anastazja's arms. What a relief!

I panic: "But Émile! What will become of you? Must you go back to France and turn yourself in? There must surely be another way. Jesus there must—"

"Kenny, you said yourself that justice must be served," Jesus reminds me.

"But the things they will do to him in prison—"

Jesus speaks softly, "I will be with him, every moment of every day—"

"Until I see you face to face—" says Émile to Jesus.

"When I welcome you into Paradise," says Jesus to Émile.

Simon speaks up, taking Émile by the shoulders, "*Mon frère*, you know I want to be with you, defend you, take you by the hand when you face your trial and your victims—"

"But the personal and professional cost to you would be too great, I understand, *mon cher Simon*," says Émile, lovingly.

"Maybe Renata and I can come visit you, in prison. Poland is not *so* far from France!"

Émile brings them toward him, pauses, and says, "I may not be long on this earth. They are not kind to people like me in prison, who have done the things that I have done, you see."

His sisters look at him, confused, then understanding dawns. The three of them weep bitterly in each other's arms.

It is Simon. "And what about you, my little 'pain in the butt'? What are you going home to?" The four of them look at me, eagerly desiring to know. I have never experienced this depth of fellowship, ever in my life. We no longer hide anything, no longer need to, so nothing in our past matters to us anymore. But I have no idea what awaits for me at home, so I don't know what to say to them.

Jesus places his arm around my shoulder and says, "When you lose everything, you still have me, and when you have me, you still have everything."

With that, he gathers the five of us into his embrace. He holds us so tight and so secure that we can let go of all of our questions, and rest in the One who has all the answers.

28

JOY IN THE JOURNEY

Standing at the edge of the face of the cliff, we embark on the trail leading me home. The sun shines brightly, and the view is magnificent. I recall climbing this trail in the wind and rain, my rebellion slowly ebbing. Much has happened, and much has been forgiven.

The valley below hums with color and delight. I take in the vast landscape, noticing a tiny speck at the foot of the snow-capped mountains: my home, or rather the dingy bubble that envelops it. Longing imbued with undertones of consternation fills my soul.

"Yes, tomorrow you will return home," Jesus says. "Today, however, is for rest, for joy in the journey, and reflection, so that you'll be refreshed for your family."

I think about what is awaiting me at home and sigh deeply. But tomorrow's tomorrow; today's today.

He leads me down the cliffside, an endeavor more adventurous than treacherous, for my heart is light. Instead of taking the way we came, we take a trail that veers toward the west. I love taking new trails!

Down, down, down we descend the rockface, hugging the granite wall where the trail is narrow (peering queasily over the edge at the valley far below), descending with bravado where the trail is wide.

It hits me: Here there is but one trail, carved finely into the granite as if sculpted by Michelangelo—and not that blasted, braided trail we slipped and slid and almost broke our necks on all the way up here! Descending from the cross, where truth and mercy meet, the way is single and sure. And the confounded rain has stopped!

Turning a corner, we are hit by a deep rumbling emanating from further down the trail. The air is laden with anticipation.

We stop: Out from the side of the granite rockface gushes an immense waterfall, and the trail leads us directly under the water's flow!

We enter the chamber behind the waters. Light becomes muted; sounds reverberate off the smooth marble walls like vespers in an ancient chapel. I stand in silent awe.

I think, I ponder, I wonder: Could it be that these waters flow directly from beneath the cross above?

My theological conjectures are interrupted by an irreverent splash from this baptismal font, perpetrated by theology's Master Thesis himself.

We make it to the valley floor by early afternoon. We cross a lovely wooden footbridge traversing the stream. With the stream now to our right, we follow the trail south through piney woods.

I'm beginning to grasp what it means to be 'in Jesus'. It's like he's my disappearing cloak: that when God looks at me, he does so by looking through Jesus and his sacrifice for me. I don't have to prove anything to anyone (especially him), and I don't have to live up to anyone's expectations (I'm going to disappoint people no matter what I do). Besides, Jesus will be helping me along the way. I have a feeling that this humility-thing is starting to suit me.

In the peace of these lovely woods, I again hear the quiet gurgling of the stream. I slow down, turn my ear, listen:

"Joy in the journey—joy in the journey—joy in the journey—joy in the journey!"

I get all teary-eyed. Jesus, obviously understanding what's going on in me, turns and runs and embraces and twirls me around in his huge safe arms. I just know that I'm on the right track, that the whole point of this journey is to come nearer to him, deeper into the Shimmering, into the sacred heart of Jesus. How much more is awaiting me? Will I ever know his depths?

The stream is becoming exuberant in its frolic descent from the foot of the Cross. I'm picking up all these messages, one after the other—or plaited between each other— much of what I'm hearing seems to be for my heart only, wordless words implanted in me that will grow, mature, flourish, and create new life. My spirit swells with anticipation and joy. I've stepped into a world of hope and I'm caught off-guard.

We are approaching the rapids, nearing the giant tree trunk. Seeing it provokes him to call me a wimp over his shoulder. I duly remind him that I'd crossed back over quite nicely without his help. He throws a pinecone at me, and I throw one back.

I have an idea.

"Hey Jesus. Of all your creations, which is your least favorite?"

He slows down, ponders. "As Creator, or as the Son of Man?"

Thinking quickly on my feet, I answer, "As the Son of Man."

"Snakes, no doubt. They give me the heebie-jeebies. Why?"

"No reason. Just wondering."

We continue walking.

Quietly, I sneak up behind him, pinch the back of his ankle and scream, "SNAKE!!!"

The Son of Man probably has never jumped so high in his life.

I dissolve into a fit of hysterics. He's lying on his back, trying to gain some sense of composure.

"Now we're even," I say slyly, "for you calling me a wimp."

He jumps up, charges after me, tackles me, throws me over a shoulder.

"Heh! What're you doing! Put me down!"

He's carrying me toward the Bridge of Doom!

"It is time to teach you the lesson of your life," he huffs, and scurries toward the giant log.

"What lesson? I'm sure I've learned everything there is to know!"

"Do you trust me?"

"It depends!" I squeal.

"Am I your King?" he asks while removing me from his shoulder and putting me on the ground. "Are you willing to surrender your life to me, completely?"

"I—I—" I'm stuttering from fear or from shock or from I don't know what.

"Kenny, do you trust me?" Those eyes of his, comforting, imploring. I keep my eyes fixed on his eyes. My heart beats rapidly in my chest. I catch a vision of what it would be like to let myself go into the care of the One who holds all things together. Anticipation, expectancy, the thrill of the unknown race through my veins. I am stirred with a thirst for more—for more of him, more of what he has for me.

"Okay, Master, whatever you think is best, I will trust you."

"Good! In that case, take off your shoes and socks and place them inside your backpack."

"Wait—what?" He's already pulling off his shoes and socks and placing them inside his backpack. I find myself following suit.

"Are you ready?" he yells over the roar of the rapids.

"Ready for what?" I scream as he again picks me up, throws me over a shoulder like a sack of potatoes, carries me onto the log and stops just above the center of the rapids. He plops me down next to him on the bridge.

"Good! Now, on the count of three—"

"Wait—what?"

"One—" He grabs my hand, positions himself to jump.

"Two—" I grab his hand for dear life.

"And THREE!"

We jump off the bridge and into the rapids below! We're airborne, sailing over the stream! My stomach hits my throat as Jesus breaks into whoops and hollers and childlike glee. Sunbeams transform into a billion tiny rainbows upon the spray of the rapids, covering us in a refreshing robe of a billion faithful promises. I brace for the imminent impact of our feet hitting the water's surface, which doesn't come, because we don't sink but slide upon the waters. I've got a surfing Jesus in front of me, gliding with reckless abandon, laughing and maneuvering around giant boulders like a pro. I can't quite get my head around what's happening, it feels like we've been doing this forever and I don't want it to stop, I want to do this with Jesus forever but we've probably been gliding only for a handful of nanoseconds and it's about to end because we're quickly approaching pools of water gathering below the rapids. We remove our backpacks and cast them onto the dry bank as we submerge into the cool waters of the pool.

I bob my head above the surface. I'm amazed at what just took place and look at him in disbelief. The joy found in recklessly abandoning myself to his sovereignty and goodness —it's got to be one of the best things in the entire universe.

He bobs up next to me. "And that, my dear Kenny, is just for starters!" he says with a snap.

We wade in calm waters warmed by sunshine; every bone and muscle and sinew in my body lets go and relaxes. Birds chirp from summer-clad branches hanging over the pool. Fish swim lazily under the glass-green waters, the braver ones nibbling at our toes, as June bugs skitter and buzz across the mirrored surface—not unlike our glide over the stream. I still can't believe what we just did, Jesus and me.

It is so lovely here, so refreshingly quiet, the buzz of my life buzzes far beyond the boundaries of my trysting Place.

But I miss the buzz of my life. I miss my family.

I hoist myself out of the water, squeegee myself as best as I can with my hands, and retrieve our backpacks—they're quite dry, under the circumstances. My remaining worms are looking more like fishing tackle than leviathans. One flimsy worm looks up at me with his eyeless face and whimpers, craving attention. I will not give it the time of day.

A sunny spot on a large, flat slab of granite beckons to me. I spot Jesus under a large oak tree in animated conversation with a family of squirrels.

I open my backpack, smear sunscreen all over me then clean my hands on a dirty T-shirt in my backpack. I put on my baseball cap and adjust it just so. I retrieve my blue Naugahyde pencil case, open it and place it by my side, then find my notebook and turn to the next virgin page. Next to my pencil case, Jesus sets a small tray holding a club sandwich and a tall, sweating glass of iced tea. I smile my appreciation. When he returns to his discussion with the squirrels I quickly place the tray with its hazardous liquid and crumbs far from my notebook and pencil case—I'm surprised he didn't take the potentiality of spillage into consideration.

I ponder, choose a pen from my pencil case, and begin.

I wanted to give up, throw in the towel. Family, bills, working for my father-in-law. I'd felt emasculated for years. The energy I had to nurture my relationship with Jane, I squandered on that woman at work. And on porn. I nearly sacrificed my wife and our marriage for a fling, a tempting option. How stupid could I be?

I glance over at Jesus. There are a half-dozen monarch butterflies line-dancing on his arm. I shake my head and return to my writing.

What did Jesus do for me? He endured for me. He hung on that Cross, for me. The one who sacrificed everything to restore my relationship with the Heavenly Father now asks me to give my all for my family. How weak I've become! "It no longer feels good," as they say. Will I walk out, say "good riddance," slam the door behind me? Leave shattered hearts in my wake?

I had abandoned the primal quest to defend, to sacrifice my rights and comforts to protect those dearest to me, surrendering my wife and children into another's care because I lacked the will to fight for them.

I know now that there is hope. He's shown me that there is always hope. When I can't hold on or hold out, my desperate plea to the Creator brings his divine intervention. He moves heaven and earth to come to my aid. When the dark forest of temptation offers tantalizing paths of escape from my difficulties, I must look up and see the mighty hand of God reach down and grab me up and out of the forest so I can see again, breathe again, discover new options for my life and move forward.

In faith in God's good character and the promises of his Word, I will not relinquish my family to a fate without me. I will hold on, keep on, move on. I will look for the simple joys of daily life, look for signs of health in our relationships, fan the dying embers, give a little more to someone who can't give much to me right now. I will find help when needed. I will lean in and not away from the holy mess, because my family is worth it, for crying out loud, my family is worth it.

And when I've given my last drop of blood for them and have little more to give, I will receive Jesus' invitation to our trysting place, where he will fill me, love me, refresh me, reward me.

29

THE HEARTBEAT OF GOD

A bug flitters by my nose, stirring me from sleep. Too tired to lift my head, I lie still, listening to birds, bugs, and the gurgling waters around me. I hear something else too—a low, rumbling din, a sound likely masked by the roar of the rapids. Where is it coming from? I put away my notebook and blue Naugahyde pencil case, stand up, take my backpack, and go to look for him.

I find him downstream, his back toward me. He is standing at the edge of an overlook where the stream tumbles down.

Below is a broad expanse, a vast valley. In the bowl of the valley is a city teeming with humanity. This is the source of the din that has captured his attention. I stand next to him.

He has closed his eyes, so I do the same.

A wind streams over us, rising from the valley.

The wind carries to us the sounds of the city.

I hear what he hears—what his heart hears.

I hear the collective loneliness of a billion souls, their cries reaching my heart—desperate, sorrowful, woeful.

I find myself weeping.

My heart has never felt this soft, this in tune with the Master's heartbeat. The overwhelming compassion is almost too much for me to bear, and I step back. He holds my arm, calms me. I breathe, listen, until my heart again is in rhythm with his.

"Now that your pain is healing, you will be more attuned to what pains my heart. And I say—

Go to the nations and neighbors,
Go to the addict, the strong.
Go to the haughty, the lowly,
Go to the maiden, who's wronged.
Spread hope to the aged and to children,
Bring my healing to the hopeless throngs—
Until my enemies are placed at my footstool
And my Kingdom is established through song."

* * *

We sit on a boulder, shoulder to shoulder, deep in thought in the deep of night. Our heads move in unison as we trace the trajectory of a shooting star across the expanse of an indigo sky.

"That was—" he says excitedly, articulating the impossible-to-articulate name of the star. He was certainly creative naming that one.

"*You* try naming all of them and see how well you do!" he rebuffs, reading my thoughts, again.

We fall into silence, lost in our own conjectures. My heart wanders toward Kevin. I'm beginning to think that my worst fears for him have happened. That what had happened to me as a boy has happened to him.

I know what I must do. I must leave Kairos, and return to Chronos.

I turn to him. His face is powdered in fluorescent starlight.
"Jesus?"
"Yes, Kenny?"
"I'm ready to go home."

He pulls me closer, guides my head to rest upon his chest. It's as though my very being was made to rest upon this chest.

"Well," he says, looking at me, his curls framing his shimmering face, "you *are* home—you've never left, really. The Shimmering is just another layer of reality, as real as—"

"As real as my tattered marriage and family life?" I finish his sentence, for once.

"That would be one way to describe it, yes."

I reach my hand through this purple cloak of sky and stroke the sleeping brow of Kevin. I move to Kyle and speak over him words of purpose and destiny. I linger upon Keenan, out walking deserted streets, feel his frozen heart, and envelop him in prayer. I see my daughters, in their beds at Matt's house, underneath the covers gazing at their smartphones, and embrace them with my daddy-love. Over Julia I speak health, a future and a hope; over Jessica, my divergent one, freedom to be whom the Father has made her to be, for his purpose and glory.

My children. My wounded, brittle children, fragile, cherished, priceless.

And then I pray for Jane.

A drop of water falls upon my cheek from above. I look up and see the tears of my Master merging with the stream of my own sorrow.

I sit up, wipe my face on a sleeve, look at him earnestly, and ask, "There is hope for them, too, isn't there, Jesus? Is there hope for my family, too?"

"You have no idea what I have in store for them, as you apply the healing balm of my love, poured from your earthen vessel, upon the tender hearts of your family."

Sliding down the boulder to the ground, we walk to our original campsite and its welcoming fire. We eat a simple meal over simple conversation.

I nestle into my bedding. He brushes my forehead with a goodnight peck. He stretches and yawns, tames that unruly curl of his, whispers a prayer to the Father, and snuggles into sleep.

I dream.

In my dream, I see my heart tapestry, each strand detailed in stark contrast, illuminated by the deep angle of the final rays of daylight. I gently sweep my fingers over the strands and hear the unique tones of my weave. The dark and dank strands of my tapestry have been turned into liquid strands of gold, feeding purple pools of wisdom. And in these pools the wounded ones find rest and healing for their weary, tattered souls.

30

ABIDING IN THE SHIMMERING

"Are you ready?" he asks. We take one final look around the trysting place, then gaze nostalgically across the vibrant meadow before us, toward the massive granite cliff now shaded in mist. I shield my eyes and scan the vast snowy eastern mountains, now brimming with morning light, a place we have yet to visit. I give a silent nod as we set our sights on those mountains and step onto the trail toward home. I *am* ready, and yet. And yet I'm not sure if I want this journey with Jesus to end.

We'd awoken early to the chatter of chipmunks pulling at Jesus' bedding and winsome rainbow-tinged butterflies fluttering by his nose, their contribution in getting him up for the day; they couldn't wait for Jesus to lead them in praise to their Creator in the light of the glorious dawn. As Jesus and I worshipped with creation on top of the granite rock, my heart reverberated with his heart, chords of joy and thanksgiving to the Father who chose me, adopted me and who calls me his own. We then enjoyed a luxurious breakfast in what has to be the most beautiful place I've ever been to, my trysting place, oatmeal cooked over the open fire and topped with butter, cinnamon and maple syrup. As a symbol of where our journey ends today, Jesus is back in his tunic and

I'm back in my green Cardinals polo shirt and khaki pants, the clothing we wore when we first entered the Shimmering. And now we're on the trail home.

There isn't a silent moment between us as we walk—he probably wants to utilize every second he has with me while he still has my attention. I'll probably be pulled in a thousand directions by a million commitments and a zillion distractions once I go through that fuchsia-colored front door of mine. Not to mention that unfinished level awaiting me in *The Quest of Articand*.

We walk through golden aspens. The sun immerses us, first in morning's creamy calmness, then in noonday's yellow gayety, now in early evening's glowy mellowness.

He stops in front of me so suddenly and unexpectedly that I careen right into him!

With hands on hips, he walks nonchalantly around me as if he's inspecting cans of beans in a grocery store. He strolls around me in a broad circle, whistling. Now he's picking up speed! Round and round and tighter and tighter and faster and faster he goes until he's standing smack-dab in front of me, eyeball to eyeball!

I've got to get to the bottom of this. He tells me to shush even before I open my mouth.

"Close your eyes," he says. What else can I do but close my eyes?

I hear him walking in circles around me, casually humming, directing me to "Keeeeep your eyes closed," until he narrows in on me like a hawk on a rabbit. We'd be standing eyeball-to-eyeball if my eyes weren't closed. Yet I sense him there—his presence, his breath, his nearness, his warmth. I even get a slight whiff of whatever cologne he's wearing, imbued with Christmas spice.

He says, "Now, open your eyes on the count of three. One, two, and…" When he gets to "THREE!" I open my eyes and find him huddled on the ground, looking up at me with a sheepish grin. He doesn't know how to hide very well, is all I have to say.

He stands up, brushes off his tunic, and stands directly in front of me. He tells me to close my eyes, then open them, then close them, then open them. Each time I open my eyes, he's looking at me; when my eyes are closed, I sense his warmth and presence. He is just as real to me whether my eyes are closed, or not.

"Soon after we get back to you house," he starts, "you won't see me as you do now—at least not very, very often. But you will sense my nearness, my breath, my eyes upon you, just as I've been teaching you on this journey."

A light goes on in my heart.

"And, when you sense my presence like you do now," he continues, "I want you to stop, listen, and be with me. What I want you to do for me will come from our times together in our trysting place."

I know what he is asking of me: to lay down my right to be with him in the way I've had on this journey, my Brother, my King, my Savior, Redeemer, even the Lover of my—

"Yes," he says to me, "you are the lover of my soul."

I feel myself blushing, from head to toe.

We turn a bend and I see it—my house!

I dart in front of Jesus, dash across the grassy field vibrant in every Crayola green, where my neighborhood once was but still isn't—and stop.

Before me is my home, bubble-wrapped in the everyday atmosphere of normal St. Louis life.

"Jesus?"

"Yes?" He's caught up with me.

"Will you be going with me?"

He looks at me in disbelief. "Of course I'm going with you, you silly goose!" I get the feeling he wants to pinch my cheek like one of my old aunts would.

I look down and pout. I say quietly, "But I'm not sure if I want to leave this Shimmering place." I scuff at the kaleidoscopic, shimmering grass with a foot.

He takes me by the hand and has me turn toward him. With his cinnamon-translucent eyes, he gazes wondrously into mine. I gasp. For in his eyes I see the Father's eyes, pools of love, expanding galaxies of love, love ever joyous, ever searching, ever embracing, me—

Oh my gosh, here we go again—he just flung me into the air and we're back in the *The Sound of Music* and I'm swirling around him, he's singing and serenading me and speaking while we twirl, "Kenny, through my Spirit you are always but a heart-turn away from our trysting place, here in the Shimmering…"

An isolated downpour drenches us like the final rinse cycle of a washing machine.

"See! What did I tell you!" he laughs as he slows down the spin. I land with a face full of wet tunic as he enfolds me in his arms.

We catch our breath. My head is swirling. I regain my orientation and locate my home. The front door is open.

"Jesus, one more thing. I'm not going to smash my face into that bubble like slamming against a window in a cartoon, am I?

"Go! Shoo!" he says to me, and I sprint the rest of the way home. I puncture the bubble, run across my front lawn, dash through my fuchsia-colored front door and enter my house, breathing hard.

"Jane! I'm home! I'm back! I'm sorry!"

The house has an empty echo to it. I walk into my living room. My ransacked living room. My life, my marriage, my family are all in tatters. I'm the one who tattered them.

Jesus is silhouetted by sunshine shining through the open, fuchsia-colored door to my home. He closes the door behind him and the house is suddenly, eerily dreary. He steps into the living room from the darkened entryway.

"You could have at least warned me," I say to him with more venom than he probably deserves. Besides, who am I kidding? I knew what would be waiting for me. My grandmother's cherished porcelain vase, taken with her from Ireland when she was a lass and given to us on our wedding day, lies cracked on the floor. The family picture, having fallen off the wall when I threw the vase, is also broken. I attempt to pick up the pieces to the vase and the picture frame.

Ouch—my finger! Stupid sliver of glass. Man, it stings. My blood drips red from the cut.

I look at my wrist, that I'd hurt back at the atelier; I remember how he healed it with a touch. Healing my family, putting it back together again—just like with my own pain, it won't happen without his healing touch.

Even with him, what will my new normal look like?

I suck on my finger and hang the picture back on the wall, even as it is.

We make our way upstairs to the second floor.

What's that scrap of paper lying there in the hallway? It's Kevin's homework, decorated with thinking doodles and a series of complex mathematical gobbledygook.

The bathroom is cluttered with a thousand indications that a real family lives in this house. Look at all those toothbrushes, and as many half-empty toothpaste tubes! Twenty different shampoo and conditioner bottles cling for dear life to the rim of the bathtub. The children's growth marks are engraved on the doorframe.

In the girls' room, Jessie's diary is peeking out from beneath her pillow. She always takes it with her wherever she goes. She must have left it here for a reason, maybe to let me know that she's hoping they'll be home soon—I don't know. I'll put it back clumsily enough to let her know that I know she left it there for me to see.

Jewel's book—*A Wrinkle in Time, Limited edition*—she's thrown it to the floor, the binding is split. She rarely shows anger. She must hate all the tension in the family. I hold the book near my heart. If Kevin is my Charles Wallace, then Julia is my Meg. As if I'm as smart as Mr. Murry.

Who knows? Maybe I am?

I peak into Kevin and Kyle's room. Kevin always keeps the items on his desk in perfect 90 degree alignment. Kyle's bed looks un-slept in. No wonder, since he ends up in our bed almost every night.

Keenan's room, devoid of non-essentials, feels barren and lonely—the way I feel when I am with him. I will do everything I can to make him feel loved, seen, accepted by his father.

Back in the hallway: the crayon drawings on the wall. Too precious to paint over, Jane nailed picture frames around them, willy-nilly down the hallway.

The air in our bedroom is scented with her blend of running clothes and Chanel No. 5. And there I am, in the mirror, looking back at me. My dad is looking at me from that snapshot. I see him with new eyes. It's like he's seeing me with new eyes, too.

My baseball mitt is on my nightstand; I place *A Wrinkle in Time* next to my baseball.

I set myself on my lonely bed.

"Jesus, is that you?"

He sets himself beside me. "Yes, Kenneth?"

His face—a face that can be viewed objectively: the eyes, the lips, the nose, the cheeks. Yet this only captures a blurred snapshot of him. For as he looks at me now, I see the kindest, most patient, enduring, endearing, penetrating, worn, childlike, rambunctious face I have ever encountered. And that's just the beginning. It would take tomes of adjectives to fully describe his face. Back to my tattered life. I could probably fill several books describing that, too. There are so many things I need to talk to him about. But all I can find to say is,

"Let's go downstairs. I'm getting a bit hungry."

We pull ourselves up from my bed and plod down the steps to my ransacked kitchen. We rustle up some instant coffee for him, a Diet Coke for me, and half a pack of Oreos for the both of us.

✶ ✶ ✶

It is one of those strangely warm early-spring days in St. Louis, laden with the threat of an approaching storm. The temperature might plummet, bringing ice and sleet that downs power lines and snarls traffic in the morning—or it could summon ominous, yellow-tinted clouds, tornado warnings, and sirens that drive us into the basement for safety. But right now we're sitting on the steps of my back deck in our shirtsleeves, or tunic sleeves as the case may be, each slurping his refreshment of choice. Or lack of choice: Jesus is probably longing for one of Simon's perfectly drawn espressos.

Simon. The thought of him detesting every second he spent in his Cardinals uniform. He'd be a will-o'-the-wisp in these more common, vanilla-flavored, middle-class surroundings.

Yet Simon, even Émile, and of course Anastazja and not the least Renata, have become special to me.

Are they real, these relationships flung from the outer reaches of my galaxy, helping me to become a better version of myself? I feel uncertain, blue.

I look over at Jesus with watery eyes. He hugs me, absorbing my blues into himself, and he gets teary-eyed, too. I brush his tears away, very real tears. Someday there will be no more tears, even for Jesus.

Our view is of my ramshackle back yard. Jane's running clothes hang limply over the clothesline. The haggard lawn is dotted with forgotten toys and outgrown sports equipment and the telltale sign of Jessie's "secret" use of snuff. Kyle's blowup pool lilts to one side, filled with water collected since last summer, covered in a layer of green algae. Julia's chair, set carefully under the shady oak tree early last fall so that she could get some fresh air while reading, is occupied by a layer of damp, matted leaves. There's the garden shed, and the damage done to it by Kevin's failed rocket experiment. The basketball hoop, bought years ago with the hope of bringing Keenan and me closer, leans against the back of the garage, faded and frayed, unused. I've got some work ahead of me to do.

But it's my real back yard, with real traffic noise floating up from good 'ol Route 66—Watson Road in these parts. Which means that Webster Groves, the St. Louis metropolitan area, the entire state of Missouri and probably even Illinois are all back in their original places. As is my retired neighbor with his irritating, immaculately pruned yard.

Are the eastern mountains still there, just beyond my view? Maybe I'll see them if I look for them from the corners of my eyes.

I'm sitting next to Jesus. A very real Jesus. He's turning a nice shade of lavender in the gathering twilight. We're finished with our Oreos and drinks. Very real drinks. He's looking at me strangely as I look for the eastern mountains from the corners of my eyes.

"What you're looking for is found in the One with whom you now speak."

I stop my ridiculous doings and listen to him.

"Finding the balance between truth and justice, between love and mercy, is found only by keeping your eyes on me, by listening to my Spirit, and by resting your heart upon the heart of my Father. Otherwise, you will follow a path toward truth devoid of mercy, falling into militant judgmentalism, or a path toward love devoid of holiness, leading to ruinous relativism.

"Only in me does graciousness meet truth. Only in me does righteousness kiss the peace of my Spirit to become holy love. These cannot be achieved through human striving or cunning."

"That's really good, Master! Wait a sec, let me write that down." Where's my notebook? Where'd I put my backpack? Next to the chair in the living room? No, I think I might've dropped it in the front yard when I ran into the house.

Jesus pulls something out of his tunic pocket, presents it to me like a magician: It's my Dad's baseball!

"Hey, thanks! Where did you find it?"

He lightly tosses it to me; I fumble the play but jump up like a pro and run after it. It thumps down the wooden steps into the dewy grass. I swoop it up for the save.

I roll the ball between my hands. The baseball, glowing like a white orb in the purple-dark, is a very real baseball. The memory attached to it is a very real memory, though no longer deep and sorrowful.

Hmmm. I just might know why I've been so obsessed with baseball all my life. Do I really like baseball as much as I've convinced myself I do? Probably not. Absolutely not, if truth be told. That's a very good broad truth.

Which reminds me. My compass, in my pants pocket.

It's not there!

I suppose the heart truths have been imbedded in my heart, or at least I hope they've been. How much healing he's done in me! He's taken my heart of stone, in that deep dark chamber, and turned it into a heart of flesh—or less stony, at least. One thing's for certain, I'll never be able to look at a compass the same way, ever again.

I want to ask him if he knows what's happened to my compass, but I'm feeling suddenly, strangely, extremely tired. I can't do anything else but lay myself down on my back deck that is in definite need of some maintenance.

Jesus, lounging next to me, places his hand on my heart. He says softly, "Remember, my precious one, that when you lose everything, you still have me, and when you have me, you still have everything." He's looking at me so kindly, so lovingly. But I can't keep my eyes open anymore. I have to give in to sleep.

* * *

I stretch and yawn myself out of my nap. Gosh, my back aches, from sleeping on this deck. What?! Oh my gosh—I'm back in my rumpled business suit and blood-stained shirt and penny loafers?

"Heh Jesus, what's going on—"

His coffee mug is on the wooden step. A torn piece of paper sits underneath the coffee mug. Let's see here. I wouldn't say he has the neatest handwriting in the world. Or the universe, for that matter. What does it say here... 'The final verse of the Song of Songs.'

"Jesus? Where are you?"

The lawn is streaked in black and orange, dark shadows contrasting with sunset's intense light shining horizontally between neighboring homes..

What is it I see, there toward the east, shimmering in the last rays of light? A long band of thick, black clouds descends like a window shade across the horizon, extinguishing the sunset, taking the vision with it. I shiver in the sudden drop in temperature. I jump up off the wood deck and frantically look around me.

"JESUS! WHERE ARE YOU?" My shout echoes through the neighborhood as I panic in fear. He can't leave me, not now—not when I need him most, not when everything's turned inside out and upside down and I've finally, *finally* given my whole heart to him!

I bolt into the house, tear through the family room and kitchen, throw open the garage door before dashing upstairs to look for him in every room on the second floor, then fly downstairs through the kitchen and open the door to the creaky basement steps. I stop at the top of the steps, remember Bernie the turtle living alone in the basement, race through the sliding glass door, pull up tufts of grass from the back lawn, fly down the creaky basement steps and into the laundry room, zigzag between piles of laundry and find Bernie where he pretty much always is, near the water heater. I throw the grass at the end of the shell where I *think* Bernie's head is located, patting him kindly on the shell. How he survives down here with so little attention is a wonder.

I dart up the steps, race through the kitchen and into the entryway, and Jane is standing there, backlit from the open front door.

The air is sucked out of me. Unspoken words weigh on my chest, making it hard to draw a breath.

"Jane! Hi! Gosh, you about gave me a heart attack! What? You're back, right? Where are the kids?"

She turns her face from me and folds her arms across her chest.

She might feel threatened if I move toward her, so I remain where I'm standing.

It is uncomfortably quiet between us. She sets herself on the bottom step of the stairs leading to the second floor. She says,

"Kenny, the way you've treated us… you should've gotten help years ago."

This is the moment I've dreaded but have also longed for. All I can find to say is,

"You're right."

She looks at me curiously, then says, "I didn't want to leave you, you idiot! But after what happened this morning, and then with Mitt—Kenny, you put your best friend in the ER—I had to get the kids out."

"Jesus has shown me things, about my heart, about why I've gotten so angry—" My words fall to the floor.

She brushes back dark bangs with slender fingers. She looks distraught. I envision the wounds I've wrought upon her heart. I say a silent prayer for her.

She's holding a bag, probably with things she'd forgotten to take with her. She asks if I'd seen her running clothes, which I have, and tell her that they're hanging on the line out back.

She moves toward the back of the house. She stops, turns, and says, "I'm not a saint, either."

"You are, just battered and bruised like the rest of us."

Wiping away tears, she quickly walks into the family room and through the sliding glass door. She returns stuffing her running clothes in the bag she's carrying.

She walks past me as she moves toward the front of the house. She brushes up against me as she passes by me. Was the gesture inadvertent, or intentional? I don't know, but I still sense her body heat. I miss her sorely.

"Jane?"

She stops before going through our open front door.

"Are you, are you having an affair with Mitt?"

She tenses up. She looks over her shoulder toward me, though she does not look at me. She begins to quiver.

"Mitt has been a perfect gentleman," she says, fighting back tears.

"Jane—"

She's already reached our minivan. I step out of our doorway and onto our porch. I watch her as she kicks the back tire to check if it has enough air before climbing behind the steering wheel. She starts the minivan on the second try, pulls out of our driveway, drives down our street and out of my view.

My wife is gone. My children are gone. I put my best friend in the hospital.

I step into the stillness of my front yard. My neighborhood is settling down for the night, homes twinkling with various forms of family life. My home remains empty and dark.

The streetlight directly in front of the house pops on. I step toward the lamp's radiating light and stumble over the garden hose still waiting to be put away for the winter. Ah, it might as well stay out for spring.

Look at the damage I did to my poor neighbor's flower bed! That's just the tip of the iceberg—I've hurt so many people in my life—my wife, my children, those that I cherish the most. How can I live with myself? I want to crawl out of my body to get away from me.

"Jesus, wherever you are, how do I live with this guilt?" I almost can't breathe from the weight of it.

I'm reminded of Anastazja. I remember the miasma of black snake-like strings that swirled atop her head—until she forgave herself for taking the life of her son. Will I allow myself to be crushed by a guilt Jesus has already died for? Or like Anastazja, will I allow him to help me to forgive myself?

My neighbor over there, maybe I can knock on her door tomorrow, apologize, get the garden hoe out, fix my mess.

Maybe I can buy a gooey butter cake at Federhofer's Bakery, bring it to the older couple, tell them I'm sorry and that I appreciate their concern for my family.

I better buy some flowers and go visit Mitt in the hospital. Will he want to see me? Will he ever be able to forgive me? Will we ever be reconciled? Whatever he chooses, I cannot force friendship on him.

What about Jane? What about Keenan and Jessica and Julia and Kevin and Kyle? How can I fix what I've broken in them? I could never be perfect enough never to hurt them and I never will be. I don't like this broad truth, but it is true, nonetheless. Each of them must embark on their own journey with Jesus, allow him to heal them of their wounds, even the ones I caused them, and reveal his high truth to each of them. I trust that he will show me how to do my part.

What's that there, propped up against the lamppost? Is it my backpack? No—it's the part of Julia's respirator that cracked-off when she fell to the ground that morning. I almost ran over her. Lord, have mercy on my soul.

I suppose my backpack and my compass and my notebook had to remain in the Shimmering. At least I was able to get my memories out of my heart and into the open, understand them, and allow him to bring healing. I can always buy myself a new notebook—maybe even a blue Naugahyde pencil case!—and write them down again. The worms, I suppose, are out of the backpack and back into the darker waters in my heart, at least the ones that have yet to be dealt with. I know the Master has a plan for them, too. I just have to remain open and not get all defensive when he starts harping on me about some hidden sin or something. As the Good Book says somewhere, he makes all things beautiful in his time.

The note! That Jesus left under his coffee mug. I put it in my pocket and forgot all about it. But wait—it's gone! Of course it is. But what did it say? Yes, I remember, the final verse of the Song of Songs. I memorized that verse for my wedding speech to Jane. It made the entire wedding party blush, from head to toe.

> "Come away, my beloved,
> And be like a gazelle
> Or like a young stag
> On the spice-laden mountains."

There is a tingling in the air. It's probably just the first iodized air molecules of the approaching storm. Or is it—

The faintest scent of Christmas potpourri wafts through the air.

I close my eyes, hold my breath…

Yes! A breeze of joy!

I just *know* that Jesus is standing here, eyeball-to-eyeball with me, with his crooked grin and dimpled cheeks and corkscrew hair—

Will I see him if I open my eyes? Or will it suffice for me to simply see him with the eyes of my heart?

The gentlest of mists falls from heaven upon me.

A peck of a kiss brushes my forehead.

No, it couldn't have been him—or was it?

In the midst of my mess, Jesus calls me his beloved.

Beloved. The mountains of spices…

I close my eyes and listen.

Wait, Kenny. Kenny, wait.

Yes. His still, small voice speaks to my heart of hearts…

> *"Here!*
> *Sample the spices*
> *Of my love for you!*
>
> *"And here!*
> *In the cleft of this rock,*
> *Rest, and allow me to tend to you,*
> *My garden, my Bride.*
>
> *"And here!*
> *On these mountains of my passion,*
> *Let me reveal to you*
> *The height,*
> *And the depth,*
> *And the breadth*
> *Of my tender loving kindnesses for you.*
>
> *"For I am always bounding,*
> *Always leaping,*
> *Always singing*
> *Over my mountains,*
> *To greet you."*

I allow him to love me in all my precious, broken humanity.
I open my eyes.
Turning, I enter my empty, aching home, but not alone.

ACKNOWLEDGEMENTS

This book began as a collaborative effort with Gro Rykkelid, Ann Elisabeth Skjekkeland, and me. Although the original project has evolved, the foundational inspiration remains a tribute to this partnership. Gro Rykkelid, this book would not exist without the inspiration I received through your life, illustrations and writing. Thank you for painting the book's cover illustration. Ann Elisabeth Skjekkeland, thank you for the encouragement you've given me from the moment the idea for this book was birthed at your home on Flekkerøy. It has been an honor to work with both of you.

Lesley Barker, thank you for being my writing mentor, idea spawner, encourager, and friend.

Tommy Vestøl, thank you for helping me hash through various theological themes presented in the book, and for being one of the few in the world who understands the way I think, dream, and pray.

Jud and Julie Bliss, thank you for your friendship and faithful prayer support.

Thomas Maldonado, thank you for starting on the journey with me, envisioning with me a higher way.

Thor and Magrete Stensby, Jill Cartledge Dew, Ramona Kennedy, Scott and Anji Smith, Linda and Peter Harre, Lori Galaske, Romaine Mauldin Bosma, Hanna and Tormod Undheim, and (last but certainly not least) my wife, Lene Kleiven Freitag: thank you for your time and dedication in reading through the book, giving me needed critique, correction, input, and encouragement.

Lin Sexton, for your whimsy, Wendy Marmon, for your joy, and Mary Arunski, for making me laugh.

Jahn and Agneta Barje Westerlund: Jahn, for your illustration of a musical tree that inspired me, and Agneta, for your faithful friendship.

Janine Frackowiak, thank you for allowing me to weave your picture into the story.

Elizabeth Woning, your simple sharing with me over coffee altered my walk with Jesus and brought depth to this book. Thank you.

Tim and Maureen Deves, for your lifelong friendship, for opening your hearts and home to my family throughout the years, and for our heaven-scented sharing-times beneath the stars.

Bob and Cathleen Westwood, for 'Brother Sun, Sister Moon' and all that followed after.

Mike and Kristin Troxel-Stokke, for being family.

Sigrun Lauvland Ek, Lill-Kari and Per Valebrokk, Karsten and Gunbjørg Bakke, Asbjørn and Ingunn Berntsen, Frode Høyland and others who have been part of our home group in Hånes through the years—and for everyone at Hånes Free Church in Kristiansand, Norway, who have prayed for me and encouraged me and walked with me as I've written this book. I particularly want to thank Andreas Magnus and Øyvind Akselsen for encouraging me at my lowest point, when all I wanted to do was throw this book in the bin.

Eric Reid, my editor at Skinny Brown Dog Media, for seeing what I see, and helping me see what I couldn't.

All my darling sisters, Nancy, Mary, Joan, Jean, and Janet: for growing up with me, loving me, putting up with me, and for caring for my family and me—remembering together our parents and our brother, Jim.

ACKNOWLEDGEMENTS

To all of you who have shared unique experiences with me in different seasons of life, in different cities, schools, nations, teams, churches, ministries, organizations, and friendship circles: thank you for journeying with me, deeper into the Shimmering.

Lene, Benjamin, Katrine, and Elisabeth, for being my family and loving me, for going through life together with me, and for giving me the space and time to write this book—and for your patience in hearing one too many times, "it's almost finished!"

Made in the USA
Columbia, SC
04 May 2025

07863729-518e-4897-805d-08bf7564fca5R01